The Cowboy Guardian

FOSTER RANCH
BOOK TWO

BA TORTUGA

The Cowboy Guardian

Copyright © 2023 BA Tortuga

Cover Art Illustration by Alexandria Corza. Used with permission.

Editing by Sue Meadows

This is a work of fiction. Any resemblance to any person, living or dead, is purely coincidental.

All rights reserved. No part of this eBook may be used or reproduced in any manner whatsoever without written permission except in case of brief quotations embodied in critical articles or reviews. For information electronic address Turtlehat Creatives help@turtlehatcreatives.com

1st Edition Turtlehat Creatives 2023

BA's Cozy Cowboys

If y'all are interested in warm, joyous novels where the cowboys have kids and love saves the day, please check these BA Tortuga books out:

Back in the Saddle

Cowboy Haven

Cowboy in the Crosshairs

Cowboy Logic

Cowboy's Law

In the Morning Light

Ranch Manny

Security Detail: an AusTex novel

Silver Buckle Linings

The Cowboy Contract

The Cowboy Guardian

The Cowboy's Texan

The Meaning of Life

Trial by Fire: an AusTex novel

Two Cowboys and a Baby

Two of a Kind

For those people who stand up for what is right, even when it hurts. For my found family.

Chapter One

Okay, Wat. You can do this.

Watson Torres needed someone to give him a fresh start. He had his graduate degree. He had background checks and ideas, enthusiasm and huge love for children and education.

Now he needed a job that paid enough that he could move out of his in-laws', a place for little Naomi to continue to heal and thrive, and a chance to reinvent himself after the damn tragic movie his life had become.

Was that too much to ask?

He chuckled to himself. God, he sounded like a whiny kid. Times were tough all over, and...

And he was sitting in front of a giant-assed adobe that was the heart of the Broken C Ranch and Rodeo Company in northern New Mexico to interview for what amounted to the lead childcare coordinator. There were a lot of kids at this ranch from what he understood.

That sounded like a position Michelle would be proud of, didn't it? She'd expected him to become a professor, an academic.

Now he just had to get up and get this job as a glorified babysitter.

A giant St Bernard rose off the porch as soon as he opened the door to his Jeep Renegade. It woofed, tail lifting to wag in a lazy kind of way, and he nodded. "Hey, buddy. I have an appointment."

As if that prompted someone inside, the front door opened, and a compact middle-aged lady smiled at him from the entrance. "Hola, señor. I'm Nanette. Come on in. You're Señor Torres, no?"

"Si, señora. ¿Buenas dias? ¿Como esta?" He was a New Mexico boy, after all, and Spanish was his second language.

"Bien, bien. Come in. Aren't you polite? Kase will be interviewing you. Ryder is out helping round up cattle." She rolled her eyes and grinned. "Playing cowboy."

The words were teasing, but Wat didn't hear an ounce of meanness in them. In fact, they were filled with a fondness that had him grinning and nodding like he knew what she was saying, when really he had no idea what that entailed beyond what he'd seen in the movies. "Yes, ma'am."

"Nanette, is the— Oh, hey." A slight man with blond hair and bright blue eyes limped out of a room off the main entry, smiling. "I'm Kase Chiara. You must be Watson Torres?" He held out a hand to shake, square and tanned and scarred up.

Not as scarred as his kid's arm, but not a smooth executive's hand for sure. "Yes, sir. Pleased to meet you."

Chiara, huh? The guy didn't seem Italian, but Watson didn't look as if his name ought to be Torres, so...

"Good to meet you. Do you want some coffee? There's doughnuts, too. Or, uh, conchas?" Kase glanced around like he was a touch dazed.

"No. No, I'm fine, thank you." The last thing he needed was to spill hot coffee on his shirt or smear sugar everywhere. He wasn't as steady as it had been, once upon a time.

"Well, if you change your mind, let me know and I'll tell Nanette. Come on to the office." Kase led the way past a family room that looked as if a bomb had gone off, where two more dogs lay on the couches, almost raising their heads as they passed.

"Excuse the mess. It was blanket fort night last night, and everyone's scrambled to school and lessons and the barn."

"Oh?" He was surprised. He wasn't sure how big a class he'd have, but he'd expected a varying number.

"Yeah. Charlie and Leanne were in last night. They're in community college right now. We have our other three, and then we have a six and an eight-year-old right now on short-term foster while their dad waits on a custody decision." They made it to the office, where Kase waved him to a chair. "Have a sit."

"Of course. Thank you. So, I know you're foster parents. You're brave men. I think I told you in our email correspondence, but I am registered with the foster system. I tutored foster kids when I was in college." He started to feel a hint of excitement.

"Yeah?" Kase leaned forward, expression intent. "That would be really helpful."

"Yes. That was my master's focus—at-risk children, including kids in the system, underserved populations, homeless children, and LGBTQIA plus communities." He nodded, warming to the idea of helping. He hadn't thought he could really help outside of the city, and maybe he was better used there, but he wanted to try something unusual.

"Now, that's near and dear to my heart. My hubs and I are all about a safe space, and Charlie is genderqueer. Our oldest. So, we foster a lot of kids no one else is willing to take on, short or long-term. I'm glad to know you'd be a help with that and not just okay with it." Kase was grinning at him now. "Are you family?"

God, he didn't quite know what to say, but it wasn't like he could hide things forever. "I'm bi. I haven't been interested in a man since high school, and I just lost my wife in a house fire, so I'm not..." He would not fall apart like he was burned to ash himself. "I'm not looking. I need a safe place to work and raise my little girl."

"Right, your daughter is...eight?"

"Almost nine. She was in the fire, and..." Wat swallowed hard and lifted his chin, refusing to be cowed. "She had some injuries and some reconstructive surgeries."

His beautiful girl had lost a hand and had some skin grafts, but worst of all, she'd lost her mother.

"Well, this is a good place to recover and heal." Kase's gaze seemed empathetic and dear.

He clung to the sight. "I appreciate it, very much, and—"

"Am I late?" A tall, steel-gray-haired woman with a stern face rapped on the doorframe, a cup of coffee in her other hand.

"Come on in, Granny. This is Watson Torres. Watson, Antonia Chiara."

"Ma'am." He stood, holding out his hand.

"Mr. Torres. Pleased." She shook, and her touch was firm. Clearly, this was the matriarch of the clan. She sat, sipping her coffee. "Don't let me interrupt."

"Wat was just telling me he's foster certified."

"Are you now? Oh, well, that's wonderful." She smiled at him, which warmed her face a bunch.

"I am. It's important to me. I have references from Santa Fe, Espanola, Las Cruces, and Albuquerque in tutoring, both virtually and in person. I'm qualified to teach, but my focus is early childhood intervention."

"I like that. And you have a child?"

"Yes, ma'am. She's got a few special needs, so I want a place she can thrive."

"Huh." Wat wasn't sure if that wasn't disapproval or not, at least not until Mrs. Chiara glanced at Kase. "Do we have anyone else? I like this one."

Kase's lips curved in a smile. "I would like Ryder to meet him."

"Picky picky." She winked at him. "Ryder is my grandson. He'll love you."

"Thank you." He sure hoped so. It couldn't be that easy, right?

"He'll be in for lunch. Would you like a tour?" Kase rose.

He stood too, almost going ass over teakettle as his whole body tried to give out on him.

"Careful, son." Mrs. Chiara caught him, her grip surprisingly strong.

His cheeks heated. "Sorry. I'm great with kids. Little bit of a klutz."

"Nonsense. I'm not stupid, son. I did your background check myself. I'm sorry about your wife, by the way. That's an awful business." She dusted off Wat's shoulder with a gentle touch. "Now, I need to get back to my own office. I have a Zoom meeting with the mayor. Ryder will like you. Don't you worry." She strode off, and he glanced at Kase, who grinned.

"Yeah, she's a force of nature."

"She seems like it." And of course, he had to almost fall all over his truth in front of her.

"She made me nervous as hell when I first came here." Kase chuckled. "Sorry, I got a hitch in my getalong today. So if I'm moving too slow, just let me know."

"Man, I understand. You're fine." He knew that Kase McDaniels-now-Chiara had been in a wreck on the rodeo arena. He'd done his research, as best he'd been able to. That accident had been a career-ender, they said, and Kase had been laid up a long time. He guessed it was like being in a bad car accident.,,

"Cool. Well, come on. I'll show you around the house, and you can see what we have set up for homeschooling and child-care right now."

"Sure. Do you have full-time permanent homeschoolers?"

"Dani is ten, and she's not ever going to be a public school candidate. Nell is four and needs a little support, so she's in pre-K half day and then comes home, has lunch, a nap, and then a little more practice." Kase chuckled and shook his head. "We have built space for an additional thirteen children at max capacity. We have four bedrooms that sleep two, a nursery that can hold four, and there's a single room if someone needs privacy."

"So anywhere from two to fifteen?" Flexibility was going to be key on this job. "Is there an assistant?"

"There are a number of them—there are two tutors available, along with our office manager, Nanette, and both Antonia and Alba can be there if needed in short bursts."

"Okay, that sounds fair." He mulled over his plans. "Can you tell me about Dani?"

Would she vibe with Naomi?

"She's one of our three daughters—we have one in community college, Charlie. Our son Elijah is an eighth-grader and is thriving in public school. Their mother died when Nell was an infant, and they lived on the street. Nell is catching up, but Dani is not only behind, she remembers the street, and she's sensitive." Kase smiled, so gentle, and Wat could see the love. "She loves animals more than anything on earth. She wants to be a vet."

"Oh, that's a great thing for kids with a tender temperament. Animal welfare. And helpful here too." Okay. Okay, Naomi could handle gentle.

"Very. And that motivates her, but she is very shy around new people, and we have a revolving door of children and cowboys and staff."

"Sure. It takes a lot to run an operation this size." Then Wat laughed. "I sound like I know what I'm talking about, but really, my folks took me to the Rodeo de Santa Fe every year. That's it."

"That's more than some. We've had an animal rights activist, a lady who was allergic to dogs and goats, and a seventy-five-year-old woman with a paddle around her waist that have applied."

"A paddle? What on earth was that for?" He blinked at Kase, not sure he was following.

"Like a spanking paddle."

His lips popped open. "You're not serious."

"Yep. She was something else." Kase winked. "So, here we are in Nanette's realm in the kitchen. We have an outdoor one too, but this is the heart of the house."

"Hola," Nanette said again. "You sure you don't want coffee?"

"Actually, I'd love that, thank you."

"Of course. How do you take it?"

"Cream and sugar, please." He'd passed the point of his stomach tolerating black coffee. But heck, he'd already had his almost-falling spell and no one had freaked. If he spilled the coffee, he would clean it up.

"Supuesto." She poured him a cup of delicious-smelling coffee, then added cream and sugar before handing it to him. "If you want a cookie or a doughnut, they're there." She waved at a platter, and Kase nipped a chocolate-covered doughnut. "Ay! Did I say you, Mr. Kase?"

"Nanette! You wound m—"

"NONUTS!" The cry was loud, and three sandy, filthy young children came running in.

"Hey! We have company, y'all. You be good." Kase didn't exactly raise his voice, but it was clear he expected to be heard. And to their credit, the kids all skidded to a halt, staring at him. "This is Mr. Torres. Watson, this is Nell, Christiana, and Raul."

"Hello." He gave a little wave. "Nice to meet all of you. I was about to have a doughnut too."

"Everyone needs to wash their hands in the mudroom, please, and then y'all can have doughnuts."

"Yessir!"

"Okay, Daddy." Nell grinned, looking utterly unrepentant.

But the kids trooped back out, and he heard the familiar sounds of water running, soap squirting, children giggling—normal washing up noises.

"Oh, they are something."

"There's a play area in the back that is fenced. They were obviously in the sandbox." Kase rolled his eyes, oh so dramatic.

"Oh, that's nice." Play was important. Possibly more important than study at an early age.

"We're all clean now, Daddy." Nell trotted back in.

"Hands, please." Kase studied all the hands. "One per, if you will, and let Mr. Torres pick first."

"Oh, I like an apple fritter." There were enough of those that no one would go without in case it was a favorite.

"Me too." That was Christiana. "Me and brother is here 'cause Daddy is trying to find a house and works."

"Is he? That sounds hard and exciting." He hated that life was so hard, but he was thankful the children had a safe place.

"It is! We're going to have a bedroom." Christiana beamed. "Like here. Only not like here, 'cause here is *huge*."

"Here is a good place, but we want Daddy," Raul explained.

"Of course. I'm glad you got to meet Nell while you're waiting." Hopefully that was the right thing to say.

"She's so cool! We're gonna be pen pills."

"Pals," Kase corrected. "One of the tutors explained the concept to them, and they already bought stationery and stamps and crayons." Kase winked.

"Oh, that's a great idea. I love writing letters."

"You do? Are you going to be our teacher?" Nell asked.

"Well, I'm talking to your daddy about it, but that's up to him and your other dad." He was pretty good at the minefields.

Sometimes he still put his foot in his mouth, but Wat knew kids were way more forgiving of that than adults.

"Okay. Can I have a blueberry, Daddy?"

"Yep." Kase got a paper towel and a doughnut. "What do you two want?"

"Jelly!" Raul danced.

"Chocolate like you, Mr. Kase."

There was a little low table with colorful seats for the kids, and they settled in easily, munching away.

"Very yummy. Thank you."

"We like our food here." Kase winked at him. "Nanette? You got this?"

"I do." She chuckled. "Vaya."

"Come on, Watson. We'll look at some other spaces. You said you were interested in the on-site living quarters?"

"I am, yes. My—" Former in-laws. Dead wife's parents where I'm living until I get my shit together? "—current situation is about three hours away."

"Then let's have a look at that. And the school area, huh?" Kase munched his doughnut on the way.

"Absolutely. I love that there's a separate educational area." That made for a nice visual break between relaxation and work.

"Yeah? We thought it was important. I mean, we have the space to make it so, and I remember doing homework at the kitchen table and always being distracted." Kase shook his head. "'Course I wasn't the best student."

"No? What did you like best in school?"

"Math, like my eldest daughter. She's thinking about accounting for her major."

"Would she come back and work for the ranch?"

"I think so. I know Granny is talking hard about it. But she might want to go to a city? We're not sure." Kase grinned at him. "It's up to her. She's amazing and strong."

"That's awesome." This place was looking too good to be true. He hoped it wasn't.

"This is the school room. It's set up with this weird partition because we wanted to separate the little ones and the teens if we had to. We have three computers and six iPads for the kids to use. The computers are hard-wired in. There's satellite internet, so it can be frustrating."

"You get solid cell service?" That would be important if the internet was iffy.

"We do. There's a tower not too far, so we hit on that." Kase showed him where the computers were set up. There was even a little nap area, which was nice. Sure, this was the kids' house, but it would be better to treat the school day as a whole and have littler ones nap with him in the school area.

"We have a series of bunk houses, and they head out past the property. We start with the foreman's house, and you'll be the third back. It's not fancy—two bedrooms, one bath—but it's clean and solid, and there's furniture."

"That's amazing." He chuckled drily. "I feel like I should ask what the catch is."

Kase turned to face him, expression serious. "We're out in the middle of nowhere. It can be isolated, and the hours can be long. We sometimes ask for all-hands-on-deck for stuff not in their job description. And the kids can be rough. Some of our fosters have had crazy lives for such youngsters. And they take patience."

"I understand, and I admit, I've never lived on a ranch, but I'm not frightened. Is… I mean, are people generally friendly?" He did have a daughter who needed friendly, warm.

"Very much. We cultivate that in the rodeo company and on the ranch. And most of the town relies on us for their business."

"Good deal. I'm just… I'm a people person. I love to hear stories and talk, so I hope there's a community here." And Naomi needed to learn to grow, to thrive again. To recover.

"I think you'll find there is. And if you sign on, we'll have a cookout for y'all to get to meet everyone socially right off. That helps." Kase winked. "And you know my little girls will be over the moon to meet your daughter."

Well, that was fair. He liked that.

The little house was adorable, simple and weirdly masculine, but blank enough that Naomi could make her room her own. There was a tiny kitchenette, a bathroom, a sitting room-dining room together. A man could live here for a while.

"Of course if you came on, there would be fresh bedding and towels, but all the kitchen stuff is here. And the plumbing is good." Kase's grin told him how important that was.

"That's the important part, right?" Because this ranch thing was outside his comfort zone right now.

"Yep. And we have people on staff for all that kind of stuff as well. What else would you like to see? Do you ride?"

"Horses, yes. My uncle taught me when I was a kid. Bulls? Nope." He wasn't interested in that at all.

"Oh, lord. No. No civilians on the bulls. That includes me." Kase led him outside and toward the barns.

"But you do have a big rodeo company, right?"

"Yeppers. We run rodeos in five states, and provide stock for a host more."

He didn't even know what that meant, not really, so he went with impressed. "Wow."

Kase snorted. "You'll figure it if you stick around."

"I will. I'm nothing if not into learning. *Nothing*." He would make this work. He didn't have to be a cowboy; he just had to teach them.

"Well, how about you stay for lunch? Or come back if you want to run into town and check things out. Ryder will be here for that."

"Do you mind if I stay? I'd love to hang around a little while."

"That would be great, man. Come on back to the house. We can hang with the littles and Nanette."

Yes. Get to know the kids. They would be in his corner then, right? Get Granny Chiara and the wee ones on his side and he might make it even if the other dad didn't like him.

Wat wanted this job, bad.

Chapter Two

Tygh Korden stomped into the kitchen of the main house, hunting one of the bosses. There was some asshole out there in a tiny SUV who was blocking the whole damn world, parked back in front of the staff housing. Problem was, that blocked the lane to the barn, which he was trying to get through on the tractor. With a trailer of feed.

"Nanette," he said with a nod. "Bosses around?"

"They're playing video games with the hooligans, last I heard." She was stirring a huge pot of spaghetti sauce.

"You got any idea who belongs to the baby SUV?"

"The new teacher. He's moving in to Derrick's house with his little girl."

"Huh." No wonder. Guy had probably never even seen a tractor. "Well, I'll just go ask him to move, then."

"You want an oatmeal scotchie? Make you sweeter."

"Listen to you." He took two.

He just needed the guy, whoever he was, to get the hell out of his way. He wasn't sure why they put the teacher out with the cowboys anyway. Shouldn't they be sleeping closer to the kids? He guessed he was a teacher, not a babysitter, but still...

He munched his cookies on the way back out, and while it didn't improve his mood, it did taste damn good. It was probably better to talk to the teacher anyway. Tell the man to keep the kids out of his damn barns.

He saw a slight redhead carrying a box from the car to the house, the freckled cheeks bright red with the effort. The guy was really laboring, and damn if Tygh didn't automatically offer.

"You need a hand?"

"Could you open the door, please? This is my last box." He got a warm, crooked smile, and Tygh felt the need to snarl crawl right up his spine.

Instead, he opened the door. This meant that car could move now. Boom. "There you go."

"Thank you! Do you know where I need to park, by any chance? I'm Watson, by the way. Watson Torres. I start on Monday."

"Tygh Korden. And there's spots behind the houses. If you go around the back of the last house..."

"Oh, cool. Thanks. I appreciate it. I can't wait to make this little house our own!"

"Sure. Can you move your car now? I need to get the tractor through."

Oh, damn. "I'll totally move it now. So sorry!"

"Thanks." He just stared, and the guy ran to move his car. Excellent. Now he could get back to work. He wasn't trying to be rude. Just— he didn't play well with others.

"You scaring the newbie, buddy?" Anna was head of the road crew with the rodeo, and she was spending more time at home as the season wound down.

"Nah. I just need to get my work done. At least he saved me bitching at the bosses. And I got cookies."

"Ooh, what kind? Snickerdoodles? I love those." Anna

winked at him. "You want to have a beer after work with us, man? There's a group of us having a bonfire."

"Uh—" He glanced at her wicked grin and sighed. If he said no, she would tease the fuck out of him. "Yeah, okay."

"Poor cowboy, having friends and stuff that want to hang..."

"Shut up, you old bitch."

A soft gasp sounded, and the teacher rounded the corner, expression pure shock.

Anna laughed. "Oh, now. Don't you worry, honey. He's just being friendly. You'll see. I'm Anna. You must be the new teacher."

"I am. Watson Torres. Pleased." The guy held his hand out to shake, and Tygh would bet that it was smooth and soft.

"Anna Naton. Nice to meet you. You get settled in all right and we have a bonfire tonight. You're welcome to come."

Really? Did she have to tell the new guy?

"Oh yeah? I'm spending the night here, so I'd love to. Should I bring something?" Like it was a damn dinner party. You brought your own beer. And the son of a bitch was moving in, wasn't he?

"Whatever you want to drink. The bosses are sending out munchies. Well, Nanette is on their dime."

"There's cookies," Tygh said grudgingly. "Oatmeal scotchies in the kitchen right now."

"Ah." That earned him a smile. "Thanks for the help."

"No problem." He nodded once before heading off, Anna's laughter floating behind him. God knew what she would tell the guy, but he had work to do.

He drove the feed back between the two big barns. They housed their main stores closer to the rodeo folks, and he only needed enough for the rehabbing guys, but it was still too much to carry.

All he'd do was carry bags all day. And he had two horses, a mule, and a mini horse in the vet barn right now, as well as two new riding horse rescues in quarantine, waiting to join the herd.

That didn't count the two sheep that had tied it up with some barbed wire or the pot-bellied pig that was somehow not a cute pig, but closer to a pissed-off wild boar. And always hungry. Always. Damn thing would eat him if he wasn't careful.

He wanted the bosses to get rid of it, but Dani started crying every time someone mentioned it. No one could deny that little girl anything.

Not even him.

Speaking of which... "Dani? What are you doing in the barn alone?"

Dani looked up from where she was sitting in front of the miniature horse's pen. "I was worried about Minnie. She seems sad."

"Does she?" He blinked at the gremlin with the not mini-sized teeth. "I know she likes you a lot."

"She does. Can I help you out here, Mister Tygh?"

He would not roll his eyes. This child loved the animals as much as he did. "I reckon so. Let's get everyone some grain."

"Yes, sir!" She beamed at him. "Where should I start?"

"With the cup here. See how everyone has a bucket hanging off the rail? Just one cup each." And he would give them all a flake of hay.

She started singing. "One cup each. Yes, sir. One cup for the horses. One cup for the donkey. One cup for the—does Minnie get the same cup as the big horses or does she have another one cup?"

"She can have about half of that one. Do you need help?" He wasn't going to smile.

"No, sir. I know about halves. I learned. Two halves make

one whole apple." She began to feed, singing like a little bird, and it was impossible to be growly.

She loved this life, and Tygh had never heard her fuss about an animal.

He did text Kase to let him know where Dani was, though. Just in case.

<Oh ffs! I'll send Ryder out. Sorry, man.>

<Nah. I'll bring her in when we're done feeding. I want more cookies> He grinned then, because that was an ingenious plan.

<Thanks, man. I'll remind her to ask. She's our cowgirl>

"No no, Strawberry. No biting. You have to try to be nice, even if you don't feel so good. I know it's so hard, but it's super 'portant."

Words to live by.

Maybe not for him, but for horses? Sure.

Dani was super careful not to spill, to feed each animal. She spoke to them, petting every one if they let her. Then they refilled water before he held out a hand to her.

"You ready to go in?"

She beamed at him and took his hand. "Yes, sir! Thank you so much for letting me help. Do you think everyone is going to be okay?"

"I do. Mostly we got simple injuries, you know? Like Strawberry cut herself on the side of the shed. I fixed that board right off."

"You are a good cowboy." She squeezed his fingers tight.

His heart warmed at that. "Well, thank you, Miss Dani. I appreciate it." He let her swing his hand as she danced along, because she was in such a damn good mood.

He got her in the house, where Ryder was waiting at the table, a plate of cookies and three glasses of milk there.

"One of those for me, Boss? Or is this a family time?" He could take his cookies to go

"Milk and cookies, man. Please. Have a seat." Ryder winked at him. "And you, my little cowgirl? What did I say about the barns?"

"Not to go, but Minnie called my name, Daddy. Minnie needed me."

It didn't even sound like bullshit.

"She was pretty lonely, Boss. And Dani cheered her up."

Ryder gave him an amused look. "Uh-huh. Since when do you stand up for her?"

"I ain't a snitch." He winked before washing up. "Come on, Dani. Up you go to wash your hands."

"Thank you, Mister Tygh! I was super good, Daddy. I fed them all one cup except for Minnie who got one half cup, which is less than one!" That little gal was so proud of herself.

"It is at that. Well, good for you. Did you give them water too?"

"Uh-huh. Mister Tygh helped me with the hose. He's a good hand."

"He is." Ryder's grin was so proud. "And so are you. You've always got the animals' best interests at heart."

"I do, Daddy. I love them all, *so* much."

"I know. I'm happy you love them, but you gotta ask before you go to the barn, okay? If you got hurt out there, think how lonely they would all be."

Dani chewed her cookie slowly, then nodded. "Okay, Daddy. I promise. I'll ask."

"Good deal. Thank you."

"I love you." She pushed up and kissed him on the cheek. "Can I go play with Snuffy?"

"Yep. No cookies for the dogs, though. Not unless it's their cookies."

"Yessir!" She pelted off.

Tygh grinned, enjoying his last cookie. "She's a good kid, Boss."

"She is. Stubborn, though. The critters call to her." Ryder shook his head and sighed. "She just can't resist."

"I get her. I would rather be with them." Animals could be a mess, but they were rarely ugly just to be that way, and they didn't talk too much.

"Well, I hear that, and I'm awful sorry she bothered you, but I appreciate that you cared for her."

"She didn't bother me a bit. That new teacher of yours now..." He chuckled. "He blocked the lane."

"Que horror, man." Ryder laughed out loud, taking the joke as he meant it.

"I had to talk to someone new, you know." Tygh opened his eyes very wide.

"Oh, and he's a little ball of energy, too. He's very... enthusiastic." Ryder winked at him, then leaned forward as if he was sharing a secret. "He just got out of a shit situation. Lost his wife in a fire. Him and their little girl got burned pretty good. He's needing a place to heal."

"Oh, damn." That made him swallow hard. "That energy's good for the kids, though, right?" He could get behind that. He loved that Ryder and Kase gave kids like he'd been a chance.

"Yeah, he's smart, eager, full of ideas, and his thesis was on helping foster at-need kids. He's perfect for the job, if he stays." Ryder rolled his eyes. "He's a townie."

"Yeah, I can tell. He has one of those little SUVs." Not that he could really judge the guy by that. Seriously, as much as he would tease someone for it, gas mileage was a thing.

"Yes. If he stays, it'll be a truck in a year, I bet you."

"I bet. Or a Suburban." If the guy had to take kids all over, he would get a boat with a wide wheelbase.

"There you go. Something solid, cushy, and able to take some damage." Ryder chuckled and shook his head. "I'm going to go get my ass kicked at *Mario Kart* again. Have a good evening."

"You too." He figured he wouldn't mention the bonfire. Anna had said snacks were coming from the big house, so the bosses had to know. He headed out, knowing he had a ton of work to do before he got that beer.

At least he had cookies to fuel him.

Chapter Three

W at wasn't sure where the bonfire was that the cowboys were having, or if he could see it, so he went on the tiny front porch with a beer and sat to watch.

He only had tonight without Naomi. Bill and Dana were bringing her down from Denver tomorrow.

This place was a city, all by itself, but with its own rules, and where everybody knew everyone else.

Except him.

But that was okay. He had time to get to know people, he thought. Or, if not, he would make some friends in town. Surely the library did events. He wasn't a church guy, but he could go wherever the other hot spots were.

He'd picked up a rocking chair and a bug zapper at the feed store, and he was happy out here, wide-eyed and watching. He'd never seen anywhere so dark.

He heard laughter, and groups of folks walked by, but no one even saw him, he didn't think. They were all pretty intent on where they were going.

Should he say something? Should he not? He didn't want to be somewhere he didn't belong, but he didn't want to be rude either.

"Hey. Did you want to come to the bonfire?"

That gruff voice he knew. He'd met... uh. Tygh. He'd met Tygh when he was moving in.

"Oh, yeah. I wasn't sure where." He stood and grabbed the six-pack from the tub of ice. "Thanks."

"Come on." Tygh didn't really wait for him, but that was fine too. He was kind enough to show the way.

He didn't jabber or anything. He just followed. Although he wanted to. He wanted to say hey and how are you and did you have a nice day...

That was only polite, right?

When Tygh stopped, he damn near ran up the guy's ass. "You seeing okay?"

Fuck. Friendly. Smile, even if no one could see it. "Yeah. Sorry. It's crazy dark out here, huh?"

"It is. I don't think about it too much, but you could break an ankle."

Jesus. "Well, that would be awkward. I wouldn't want to do that..."

"Nope." But Tygh hung back a little to walk with him, so that was fine.

"Have you worked here long?" That was a safe question, right?

"Five years or so. Came up from southern New Mexico."

"Cool. I grew up in Santa Fe and went to college in Denver and stayed." It had been boring and normal and simple. He'd loved it. Michelle had loved it.

"Yeah. I'm a vet, so I get it." That came his way with a glimmer of a smile in the dark. Then the glow of the bonfire and of a ton of string lights came into view, and they were surrounded by people in no time.

He avoided being in direct eyeline of the fire, occupying himself with wondering if Tygh meant vet—veteran—or vet—veterinarian?

"Hey, you must be Watson," someone said. "Come put your stuff in the ice."

"I am. Thank you." He put his beer in the cooler and glanced around, seeing a sea of cowboy hats and gimme caps outlined by the light of the bonfire.

Man, that would be an amazing picture. At least it would if he could breathe, if he could see anything in his mind's eye but his wife's hair creating a fiery halo as she tried to drag their daughter out of a collapsing second-story window to safety.

God, Mich. You were the bravest woman I ever knew. He turned to leave, his heart clenched so tight it hurt.

"Hey, man." A couple of young guys came up to him. "You're the new teacher?"

"Yeah." *Please don't haze me. I'm not into initiations.*

"Cool. I'm Hugh. I'm with the rodeo company. Mostly bookkeeping." The pocket cowboy wore wire-rimmed glasses, a T-shirt with a Death Star on it, and a gimme cap. He got a big grin, and he had to laugh. Geeks unite.

"And I'm Linden. Sports medicine. Pleased." His T-shirt read, *SuperWhoLockians Unite!* and Wat almost forgot about his imminent panic attack.

"Watson. My full name is Watson Holmes Torres."

"You're a hedgehog!" Linden cheered, clapping him on the shoulder.

"I am." Watson loved it. Fanbois. Out here. Lord. They were everywhere. It was a happy-making thought.

"Excellent. You'll have to come hang with us sometime. We're home together a lot in the winter." Hugh grinned at him. "So, you have to tell us all about yourself. Seriously."

"I'd love that." He glanced around, looking to see where

Tygh had gone. The cowboy had gone to the far side of the fire and was sitting out of range of the flames.

Alone.

Watson kind of felt bad for him.

Hugh followed his line of sight, chuckled a little. "Don't worry over Tygh. He's an island."

"Yeah? I met him earlier. He seemed unhappy."

"Oh, he's a grumpy puss, but he's a good guy."

"Y'all leave Tygh alone." That was the cowgirl from earlier. Anna? She whacked Hugh. "He's just the silent type."

"I hear some boys like that!" Linden's laugh filled the air.

"Mmm." He just—had no idea what to say to that. It seemed tacky, honestly. So he simply sipped his beer and avoided staring at the fire.

Anna winked at him before steering Hugh and Linden away, and soon, he had another lady wrangler sitting by him, handing him another beer. "I'm Mina. Nice to meet you, Watson."

"Pleased. Thank you." He smiled and nodded, hoping that he could... figure this out.

"Don't let those guys get to you. They forget this isn't the *Big Brother* house or something."

"Oh, they were friendly. Seriously. They weren't being cruel." And he was thankful for it, too. It was weird enough being the new guy on the ranch-block, but here he was the new guy with the dead wife and the devastated child who'd lost her home and her mom and her dog and her right hand.

"No, but they can be gossipy. You just keep on keeping on." She toasted him.

He clinked bottles with her. "Yes, ma'am." Like everywhere else, the politics here were... stunning. He wasn't playing though. He didn't have the spoons for that shit. He had a little girl to keep it together for.

She patted his arm, then got up to go talk to someone else, and Wat just— well, he rose to go sit with Tygh. The guy didn't seem to have an agenda.

"That went fast," Tygh said, but that was it. He didn't even crack a grin.

What went fast? He just smiled, because it was the only thing he could think to do.

"You can hang with me." Tygh's voice reminded him of Sam Elliott's.

"Thanks." That was a relief, and they sat and didn't watch the fire crackle while the crowd of cow folk ebbed and flowed around them.

There wasn't a lot of talking, but it was okay, because he was listening. Listening about—everything. Singing and riding, dancing and cooking, movies and flirting—this wasn't what he'd expected.

This wasn't... crass and mean.

And Tygh was this solid presence at his side. Not chatty, by any means. But secure. And every so often someone would give them a quizzical smile, so he got the idea Tygh didn't hang out much.

See him. See him be...

God, see him be whatever this new part of life was. Was it always this hard? To move from one thing to another? He had been scared leaving home to go to college. He'd been terrified when Michelle caught pregnant while he was still in class. He had been worried about committing to grad school. He was fairly sure he was still brokenhearted.

Now he was here, on a ranch, with cowboys, on his first real teaching job without his main moral support.

And he was going to be successful here, dammit. If it killed him.

It might, when it got right down to it. Between bulls and

horses and cowboys and children, it might just tear him up, but he'd take it.

He was on his own, living his post-Michelle life, raising their baby without her.

Fuck, he was scared.

Chapter Four

"And this is the barn with all the sick ones and the sad ones."

Tygh bit back a sigh. He knew that voice too well. There was Dani. In his barn. Again.

In fact, when he rounded the corner from dosing Lil' Foot with wormer, he found two little girls and one slightly larger redheaded teacher in his barn.

"Howdy."

"Hello, Mister Tygh!" Dani beamed at him. "This is my new friend, Naomi. Her hand is gone, and she is sad, so I told her we could come meet you!"

Naomi seemed to sink into the floor, her face hidden in her father's arm. Presumably her father.

"Well, you know I'm always ready to meet new folks." He wasn't going to scare that child for love or money.

Dani's merry laughter rang out. "Mr. Tygh is like me. He likes animals more than anyone else."

He had to smile. "Well, that's true. But I also went to school to help animals."

"You did?" Watson's eyebrows went up.

"Yessir. I have a bachelor's in animal husbandry and a DVM from Colorado State."

"Ah. So not army vet. Got it. Still, thank you for your service."

"Oh!" Tygh laughed, surprising himself. "Well, I did both, actually. I did four years before I came back to go to school."

"Come see the horses, Namomi." Dani tugged the other girl over to the stall. "This is Mama Cass. She's nice, and she loves apples best."

She lit up as soon as she saw that big old critter, her smile almost blinding.

"That one is yours, huh?" he asked Watson.

"Naomi. She's eight." Watson's smile spread wide, and his love was evident.

"She's got an amazing smile." He went to pull out an apple so he could cut it up. That way the girls would have something to feed the horses.

"Thank you." Watson watched the girls with an eagle eye.

"Cass is a lover. The last one of the horses you need to worry on," Tygh said, keeping his voice low.

"Yeah. She's just... she's so excited."

"Ah. Gotcha. No running into stalls, right?" Tygh cut the apple with his belt knife. "Okay, ladies. Back up for a few seconds while I come get Mama Cass ready for a treat."

"You have to stand away from the door, Namomi. Horses are good, but they're big and heavy and they need space." Dani spoke like a true horseman.

"Okay." Naomi held Dani's hand, and even he thought that was cute, and he was a grumpy old bastard.

"All right, let me bring Cass out, huh?" He opened her stall and hooked a lead on her halter. "Come on, lady. Kids are your jam."

Cass bobbed her head, and she went right to Dani, nibbling her shirt.

Dani giggled. "Hello, lady. Are you hunting a treat?"

"Will she bite?" Naomi reached out her bandaged arm, then jerked it away.

Oh, poor sweetheart.

"No, ma'am. She's very polite. Now, of course we set her up for success. Dani, can you show her how to give Cass a treat?" He handed Dani an apple slice.

"Yes, sir!" She put the apple on her palm and stretched her fingers out wide. "This way she won't accidentally bite."

"Okay." Naomi looked at her daddy, who nodded. She used her less bandaged arm to stretch out, and Tygh put an apple on her hand.

"Now, feel how soft her lips are."

"Oh." Naomi stared at Cass as she nibbled the apple out of her palm. "Oh, she's so pretty."

"She's a gentle old granny horse."

"I have two grannies," Naomi whispered.

Dani beamed at her. "Me too! Mimi and Granny!"

"I have MeMaw and Nana."

Watson grinned at him. "God, they're cute."

"They are. You mind if she meets a few more animals?"

"Of course not."

The little one was healing, and he hated to see that one arm—hand gone, scars up to the shoulder. She seemed fairly unscathed otherwise, at least on the outside.

Tygh reckoned she had some healing to do on the inside.

Watson watched her, his smile wide but his eyes sad.

"Come on, you two. Let's give Minnie her treat. We'll avoid the pig today, but I have a goat in who would love a bite too."

"Oh, Franny is a good goat. She's pregnant, and no one wants to chase the baby goats," Dani explained, and Tygh corrected her.

"Kids."

She shook her head. "No, Daddy wouldn't let me go hunt for the baby goats alone again. I promised to *God*."

He grinned. "Well, that's a good thing. No one needs to get lost or run down."

Dani nodded, even as she rolled her eyes. "I telled him I was careful, but daddies are weird."

Naomi gave her dad the side-eye. "A little."

Watson sighed, the sound exaggerated. "We worry."

"And little girls who chase goats can be a bit unaware of where they're putting their feet." Tygh led them to Minnie the mini's stall. "Okay, now, she's a little more ornery. She won't bite, but she'll play games. So be sure to keep your hand flat."

"I only got one hand. I don't want her to hurt it."

God, that was brutal. Like a kick to his gut.

"She won't. I'll be right here with you." He moved closer, peeking in on Minnie to check her mood. "Gentle, now, missy. Naomi wants to say hi."

"It's a donkey!"

"Uh-huh." Dani put some apple in Naomi's hand. "I'll help."

"Okay." Naomi looked nervous but determined.

"I am a cowgirl. I will 'tect you. I swear."

His heart hurt when Dani said that. She was so fierce in her own little way. "That's a girl. Cowgirl up."

Dani nodded and smiled at Minnie. "Come say hi to Namomi. She's nice, and she loves aminals like me!"

They fed Minnie, then a few more of the bigger animals before Watson was finally getting antsy, shifting from foot to foot.

"Okay, y'all. I need to get some doctoring done, and I need to be able to focus," Tygh said. "Let me walk you out."

"Naomi, what do we say?" Watson encouraged.

"Thank you, Mr. Cowboy."

"You're welcome, Miss Naomi. I like cookies. If you were

on your way by someday from seeing Nanette in the kitchen. But only if your dad is with you, okay?"

"Cookies. Okay. I like cookies too. Chocolate chip ones."

"Mr. Tygh likes oatmeal scotchies," Watson said, holding out his arms for Naomi. "You remember when gran made those."

"Uh-huh. Yummy."

An SUV pulled up in the yard as they started to part ways, and Tygh squinted. That was Jennifer, the social worker. That always meant upheaval.

Dani wrinkled her nose. "Can I stay with you, Mister Tygh? Please? I'll be still."

"Sure. Let me just text your dads and let them know where you are. Unless she's here for Chris and Raul. Then you got to go say goodbye."

"I think you might want to come say goodbye to Chris and Raul, honey," Watson murmured. "Their daddy found an apartment and a job. They get to go home."

"Oh." Her nose wrinkled and her lip quivered. "Can you come, Mr. Tygh?"

"Of course I can." Shit, he would do anything that baby girl asked to keep her from crying.

Watson gave him a grateful look, mouthing, "Thanks."

He shrugged and shook his head. It was okay. Dani was sort of... special. Sometimes, she needed a little extra support. He took her offered hand, and the four of them headed down to the house.

Jennifer and Kase were on the front porch, and she waved at them, offering a warm smile. "Hey, guys!"

"Hello, Miss Jennifer!" Dani swung his hand. "Are you here to take Christiana and Raul to their daddy?"

"Not today, actually. I'll come get them Saturday, so your dad was just saying you all would have their favorite dinner tomorrow." She beamed. "I wanted to talk to your dads about a couple of kids who need help."

"Oh? I will make up the beds. Namomi! Come and help. We'll make up the beds!"

"Daddy?"

"Go on, baby girl." Watson watched them run off. "Is that okay, Kase? She's just so happy to have a friend."

"Hey, she needs a boost—and I mean Dani, not *Namomi*."

Tygh rolled his eyes. "So what's with the new kids?" He might as well hang out and hope for a cookie. Sooner or later, Nanette would make them all come inside and sit and have a drink and a snack...

He really did love this gig. He'd spent a lot of time traveling miles every day to get to patients, but this ranch had enough to keep several full-time vets busy.

"These two were dumped at a hospital in Española. We don't have ages, names, nothing. A toddler and a newborn. You're set up to take them both, and you have an at-needs specialist at hand."

"Wow." Kase nodded slowly. "Okay. When do they come in?"

"Saturday or Sunday, they think. They're both dehydrated and undernourished. The doc wants to keep them until their numbers improve, and I figured that way the other two would be out their way home before they came."

"Come on in and let's find Ryder. You two might as well come or Nanette will fuss," Kase said.

"Of course. Poor babies. There's no one reporting missing children? Nothing about the parents?"

"Not yet, but if they did, they'd be arrested for child abuse and endangerment, so..."

Watson winced and shook his head.

"Damn. Come on." They all trooped in, and Nanette already had the coffee pot going. He could smell it.

"Señora Jennifer. You look serious."

"New babies, Nanette. It's so sad, and they need help."

"Oh, no." Nanette shook her head. "So sad. Come and sit."

"Thanks." Jennifer pulled out a chair and flopped down. "What a week."

"Busy?" Watson asked, handing her the plate of cookies first.

"Crazy. In and out. I've been all over the state." She shook her head. "I swear, the beginning of the school year is nuts."

Tygh was proud of the Chiaras, proud to work with them, but he couldn't imagine how they did it—all these kids, all this stress and worry. It hurt his heart too much. It was awfully like his own upbringing...

Watson made a sympathetic sound. "Is there anything I can do to help?"

"I imagine you'll be spending extra time with Dani and even Nell and Elijah as the babies settle in," Kase said. "Let me go get Ryder."

"Of course." Watson grabbed coffee cups out of the cabinet so they could all have some. Tygh was gonna sit, because he'd been asked to stay. He had time.

"Are you settling in okay, Watson?" Jennifer asked.

Watson chuckled. "I am. It's a huge learning curve, but I love the kids, and they're doing well with their lessons."

"Fantastic. I hope you'll be happy and hang out here awhile. The kids who come through can really use your skills."

Watson's whole face lit up. "I hope so. I mean, I think this will be a great place for Naomi, but I want to do some good for the ranch too."

"You will." Nanette nodded like that was that, and she was rarely wrong. "Just like Señor Tygh is so good with animals."

"He's amazing with the girls too. Dani told me she wants to be just like him." The teacher nodded to him, smiled, and he tried not to scowl.

He wasn't a hero. He was a vet. And a cowboy. But he wasn't—special. He just did his job.

"Stop that frowning, Tygh. You're a good man." Nanette put a plate of cookies on the table with scotchies.

"You're a queen among women."

"Mmm. And you want milk, not coffee."

"Yes, ma'am."

"Do you not like coffee?" Watson asked. "I don't think I could survive without my daily bean juice."

"I love it. But I can have about two cups in the morning." Tygh chuckled. "It doesn't love me. Like I can have one beer like I did at the bonfire." He'd had ulcers on and off for years. These days he was doing good, so he liked to keep it that way.

It kept him happier, so he did it. Milk was pretty good with cookies.

"That makes total sense. I'm that way with cucumbers." Watson pulled out a glass for milk. "I love them, but the gas. Blech."

"Ah. No cucumber salad for you, hmm?" Nanette laughed, the sound merry. "I will remember."

"Well, just warn me. I'll buy Tums." Coffee and milk settled on the table, and then Watson sat as well. "Nell's going to be so sad when Raul goes. I'm so excited for them, though. They're so ready to be home with their dad."

"Yeah. He seems like a good guy." Jennifer nodded at Nanette for the coffee, giving her a grateful smile.

"Hey, sorry." Ryder bustled in with Kase. "I was deep in feed orders. So, tell me all."

"Christiana and Raul are heading home Saturday. Jaime has a job cooking at Wecks and an apartment that isn't a palace, but it's clean. He's excited."

Ryder clapped. "Good deal, so, what's the news that needs me here, then?"

"Babies," Kase answered. "Abandoned. No names. No ages."

"Madre de Dios…"

Tygh could see the wild fury in Ryder's eyes, and it would be echoed in Antonia Chiara's eyes as well. These people believed in the calling to take care of the kids who came their way.

"Yeah." Jennifer shook her head. "I knew you'd be willing to take them on."

"Of course. They can come. We have Wat here, and he's a specialist in helping little ones reach their potential. Where are they? When can we get them? We haven't had a long-term infant. Wat, we need a list. Supplies. What about names?"

Tygh almost hid his smile. There was the boss that he knew.

"We're not sure about their names. We're trying to find records, but it's a needle in a haystack at this point." Jennifer made a face. "It's a cluster."

"That ain't right," Tygh rumbled.

"No. No, it's not. I'm not calling them baby one and baby two." Ryder rumbled.

"We could let Nell name them…" Kase drawled, and Ryder fastened him with a glare.

"If we can't find out what their names were, you guys will have the honor. Right now, they're Does."

"Aww… Poor babies." Watson actually looked devastated. "How are they, medically?"

"I'll be sending you reports as they come in from the hospital. Like I said. They're dehydrated and hungry. That's made them lethargic, but we're doing a ton of tests."

Tygh munched his cookies, his gut starting to churn a

little. So he drank some milk, too. Nanette put a hand on his shoulder, and he smiled at her, but he had to go.

"Well, if you need anything from me to help, you let me know, Boss. Bosses. I need to get back and doctor that mare's hock now that Dani doesn't need me for moral support." He stood, then clapped his hat on his head.

"Thanks, Tygh. I appreciate your help with her." Ryder nodded to him. "I'll be out in a bit to have you talk me through who needs what."

"No problem, Boss." He nodded all around, then fled, because he couldn't listen to how someone had abandoned those kids anymore.

The memories hurt too much.

Animals were safe.

That was why he did what he did.

Chapter Five

"Are you okay, Daddy?" Naomi asked as he rebandaged her poor baby arm. It was healing well, and even though he hated to see that missing hand, it was just a hand.

Once she was healed and ready, they'd get her a prosthetic, and she was already learning to work around it.

"Daddy? Did you hear me?"

"Sorry, baby. Yes. I was woolgathering. We're going to say goodbye to Christiana and Raul tomorrow, and Miss Jennifer says the babies are ready to leave the hospital, so we get to meet two new little ones. Are you ready?"

"Uh-huh. They're nice, but they need their daddy." She gave him a very serious look. "Like when I stayed with Nana."

"Yes. Yes, exactly." He was not going to cry. "I needed my baby girl, too. More than anything."

"Loves you, Daddy." She leaned against him when he was done, sighing dramatically. "I like it here."

"Do you?"

"Uh-huh. I like horses and Dani and Nell..."

"What's the best part?" he asked.

"That no one asks me about my hand all the time." She'd been through so much, trying to save that hand, that it had almost been a relief to get to a total amputation. Twelve surgeries and two years, and she was finally healing.

"I bet." Poor kiddo. Cowboys had all kinds of injuries. More than one here at the Broken C was missing a finger or thumb. Naomi wasn't an oddity at all.

"Do you miss Mommy?"

"I do. Every day."

"Dani and Nell's mommy is dead too. Did you know that? And Raul and Christiana's mommy."

He nodded. "I know. Your friends know how it feels."

And as sad as that was, it was validating as well.

"Uh-huh. But Dani and Nell have two daddies now. That's cool?" She chewed her lower lip, thinking hard about that.

"They do. Neat, huh? They really love each other. You can tell."

"And some people have two mommies?"

"Oh, baby. Family is about love. It's not about anything else. Family is loving and taking care of each other." It was the hardest concept and the easiest one, all at the same time.

"Okay." She took that pretty well, he figured.

"Are you ready for a scoop of ice cream?"

"Yay!" She smacked a kiss on his cheek. "Ouch cream."

"We have chocolate and strawberry. What do you want?" He knew she wanted some of each, but he always asked anyway.

"Some of both, Daddy." She went to get bowls, which he kept in the cabinet next to the dishwasher on the bottom so she could reach them. They both had a plastic ice cream bowl. His was green. Hers was purple. They had rubber grippy rings on the bottom so they didn't slide when Naomi dug in with her spoon.

"Are you excited to meet the new babies tomorrow?"

"Uh-huh. Dani says they got no names. How could they not have names?"

"I'm sure they do, but no one can find their families to ask. Someone just left them, baby. We don't know why. So maybe it would be better for them to start with new names. Like a new life, right?" He didn't know if she would understand it all, but he did, and it was heartbreaking.

"Left them? Like all alone?" Her eyes were huge. "Why?"

"No one knows. But they left them at a hospital, somewhere they could get care." That's what he wanted her to remember.

"Oh." She scowled. "Hospitals are not fun."

"No, but they are safe." God, she'd been through so many surgeries and treatments. No wonder she thought that was awful.

"Well, I will be nice. So will everyone else. I know it. We will love them."

"I know, baby. You are the greatest. Do you think we should have music day tomorrow?" Nell and Dani didn't care what they did, but Naomi would.

She gave him one of those raised eyebrow, oh so disapproving expressions. "Daddy, tomorrow is Saturday. Tomorrow is games and playing outside!"

"It is." He laughed, pulling ice cream out of the freezer. "I forgot. Everyone gets to play, huh?" He knew from the weeks he'd been here the ranch hands sometimes had cookouts, and that Ryder and Kase often had stuff with their kids to do. Maybe he would take Naomi into town for lunch.

It depended on the two new babies. Maybe breakfast, that way he could be home in time to help if he was needed.

"Uh-huh. Mimi is making pancakes for everybody. Like anyone that wants some." Her eyes sparkled and she grinned. "And bacons."

Well, that settled that. He laughed. "I bet we see lots of people at breakfast. I'll totally go for that."

"Me too!" She took her bowl with careful fingers. "And I get to see Snuffy and Mookie and Birdie!"

"Oh wow. You're going to hang with the dogs? I love that. Mookie makes me laugh." The ranch dogs were goofy, sweet beasts.

"I like them. Do you think Mr. Tygh will be at breakfast?" She didn't look at him when she asked, so he wondered what was up there. Did she want to see Tygh, or did she worry about him.

"Maybe. Is that bad?"

"Do you think he would let me see Mama Cass?"

"Well, honey, I don't know. I bet we can ask. You like her, huh?"

"I do. She's big, but she's so gentle. Minnie has soft ears though. I like the barn. It smells neat, and it's got all the animals. And Tygh helps them feel better."

"He does. He went to school a long time to learn how to be an animal doctor."

"Like you?"

"Longer than me, even."

"Wow." She made wide eyes. "You were in school forever."

"I know, right?" He scooped his own ice cream, then put the rest away. "Dani wants to be a vet when she grows up, just like Tygh."

"I want to be a teacher like you, and I want to ride horses and go to the moon."

"I bet you do all that." Maybe not the moon, but hey, more people were shooting into space these days than he'd ever thought possible as a kid. So who was he to harsh that dream?

"Do you think I could ride horses on the moon, Daddy?"

He had to smile. "Well, I think that it will be a challenge, but I think if anyone can, it would be you."

"Even with one hand?"

"Even with one hand." He held her gaze and said it like he meant it. The doctors had insisted that she would be able to function and have a basically normal life without the hand. That was why he'd agreed to the amputation.

He would worry about whether he'd made the right decision for the rest of his life. But he had to soldier on and believe so she could. He'd read endless articles, watched dozens of YouTube videos, talked with doctors and the prosthetic company they would be working with...

He took a deep breath, then let it out. No letting the anxiety creep up on him.

"Will you read the wild horses girl book to me, Daddy?"

"Of course I will." He loved that she knew when she was ready to settle in for the night and get comfy.

"Good. I'm going to ride horses on the moon one day. I promise."

"I believe you." With his whole heart. God, he loved her.

"I believe you too, Daddy. I believe you all the way."

"Thanks, baby girl. Okay, book time!" They had a parade to her room after they put the bowls in the sink, and he sent up a thank-you to the universe for bringing him this job.

Naomi was smiling more than he'd seen in forever, and her dreams were getting pretty big if the moon was involved.

That was damn cool.

Chapter Six

"Dammit." Tygh stomped into the coffee shop in town, pissed as fuck that he had to go back to the feed store in an hour to pick up his order of wormer and other meds. He didn't know who had their head up their ass, but who the hell needed an hour to get that shit together when he'd ordered it a week ago...

"Hey, Dr. Tygh, how goes it?" The teenager behind the counter couldn't have been six years old. Maybe five. It was ridiculous.

"I'm grumpy." He tried not to growl. Or at least not to bare his teeth. "What do you have for that?"

"Mint and white chocolate latte with an extra shot and a croissant?"

He tilted his head. "What kind of croissant?"

"Chocolate or almond."

"Mmm. One of each." He was starving.

"I'm on it!" She grinned and winked. "Have a seat, and I'll bring it out to you."

"Thanks." He paid for it, then headed to a table to nurse his wounds.

"Korden! How goes?" Anna Landry came galumphing in, heading right over to him. "Hey, Tina. Cherry turnover and an iced latte, please."

"On it!" Tina called.

"Well," Tygh rolled his eyes. "They didn't have my order ready. Bouncy House pulled that same damn muscle at the bull-riding futurity. I had to run over to the Jansen place to deliver a litter of puppies. It's been a morning."

"How many puppies?" She grinned at him, winking.

"Eight." He shook his head. "Heelers."

"Oh man. They'll be busy, won't they?" Anna leaned back in her chair. "So, do you know what happened to the new teacher's little girl?"

"Huh?" He looked at Anna, trying to parse what she'd just asked. "You mean Naomi?"

"I guess? I haven't met her yet. Just seen her at a distance."

"She was in a house fire. Her momma passed on from it." Poor baby girl. He'd just come out and asked Wat, because as a medical guy, even if it was a vet, he was too damn curious for his own good. "She's been through a lot."

"Damn! That's scary. She doesn't look all that burned."

"It was a couple years ago. Apparently they tried to save her hand, but it just didn't happen."

Anna winced. "Oh, that's a shame."

"Sometimes it's better to lose it and have a clean start." He saw it over and over again. The nerve damage and pain could be debilitating, but after amputation, the subject could flourish again, as clinical as that sounded.

This way Naomi could heal up, move on, and get a prosthesis. It wouldn't be easy, but it wouldn't be impossible, either. She was a heck of a strong little girl.

"How long ago was this?"

"Um, maybe two years?" He had a vague idea, but Wat

had been pretty sparse on details. "You hear Christiana and Raul are headed to their daddy?"

"I did. Good for them. I know that's the best case, right? When the parents just need a little hand up?"

"Yep. As long as the kids want to go back, it's usually a good deal." Not always. False loyalty could be a real thing. Sometimes what a kid told themselves was happening and what was were two different things. But their dad had come to see them every single weekend. Had gotten a job. Had found an apartment. All the Chiaras liked the man, too, so...

"Well, I'm glad. Since there are two new kids coming in."

Tygh winced. "There are. Just babies." God, what a mess that was, and he hated it for those little ones. But Wat had a degree in that stuff. Babies who had problems. So he should be able to really help.

"Everyone will be home for the winter in a few weeks. I'm looking forward to that."

"I bet." Anna was one of those hands who worked the ranch and the rodeo, and had a lot of friends and family on the road.

Tygh only went out if he had to, and usually just to go doctor a specific animal. He was way better suited to the ranch and his little place.

His spread was across the highway from the Chiaras' main gate. In fact, that was how he'd gotten the best job of his career. The Chiaras gave him total freedom with the ranch animals, and he worked a lot with the animal medicine team via Zoom while they were on the road. He was able to walk home for lunch, welcome to stay at the ranch to eat, and he could even bring his dogs to work.

Their drinks and food came, and they fell silent to munch. He liked that about Anna. She got that silence wasn't a bad thing.

"Well, that was yummy. You want me to pick up your

order? I need to run about three more errands here in town," Anna said.

"Would you? That would save me a ton of time, and it's paid for."

"I'll drop it by the barn on my way back."

"Thanks, lady." He took his plate up to the counter. His cup was a to-go deal. Then he paused. "Tina, can I get one of those little bitty caramel shake thingees and an iced coffee with one cream?" He'd heard Wat tell someone his order the other day. It might be nice to take something to him and Naomi.

"I can, totally." She nodded and bebopped around, producing two more cups. "Here you go, Dr. Tygh. Have a great day."

"Thanks." He was in a much better mood when he left than he had been on the way in, and he headed back to the ranch, humming along with the Eagles on the radio. That was always a good sign too.

Watson and Naomi were sitting on their front porch, Watson rocking and watching his baby girl color in her coloring book.

"Hey, y'all." He stepped out of his truck, smiling at Naomi when she gave him a bright grin. "I brought you fuzzy coffees."

"Oooh! Cowboy Tygh! Thank you! Daddy, look! Fuzzy coffees!" She stood and did this adorable dance, complete with butt wiggle.

Watson stared at her a second, then began to chuckle. "Well, thank you, sir. Very much."

"You're welcome." He handed them out. "I was having a rough morning, and coffee made it better, so I thought I would share." Naomi was making him grin like a fool. She was so cute it hurt.

"Oh, I'm sorry you had a crap morning. Come have a seat? It's nice out here today." Wat motioned to the rocking chair.

"Thanks." He could sit a minute. He couldn't dose anyone until Anna got back. And since he lived across the road, if he was working at nine at night because he didn't start until noon, well, no one cared. "No school today?"

"Dani and Nell are at the dentististstes, so me and Daddy are having a relax day, since the babies might need extra times."

"They might at that. The dentist doesn't sound fun, huh?"

"Nope. I brushes my teeth really good. I don't like to go."

"Yeah, me either." At Wat's look, Tygh grinned. "But I go twice a year for cleanings."

"We do too. And our dentist is super gentle, huh?"

She wrinkled her nose. "I guess. Still. Dani cried."

"Oh, no." Not his baby cowgirl. He would have to do something nice for her too, when she got home. Fuck, he was such a damn softy. He really was.

"She was pretty upset," Wat said, in a low voice. "That sort of thing is really sensory overload for her, and that's on top of going into town."

"She seems so steady here that it's easy to forget that she gets..."

"Worried. Yeah, I know. She has a great support network here for herself."

"She does." He sipped his own coffee, rocking some. "This is nice."

"It is. I'm super grateful to Kase and Ryder for the housing. It's been tough, getting back to any kind of normal."

"I get that." Buying his own place had been the proudest moment he could remember.

"Yeah. We'll buy a house again someday, but this is perfect for now."

Naomi sipped her milkshake. "We lived at Nana's house after the fire and while I was at the doctor all the time. Daddy couldn't work, 'cause I needed him so bad."

"That's tough, huh? But sometimes that's how it works." He couldn't even imagine. "Your dad's a good guy, huh?"

"The best. This is a good fuzzy coffee. Thank you, Mr. Tygh."

"You are very welcome." He ought to get back to work, but his butt just wanted to stay in that chair.

"Yes, thank you. I love the way the light is in the fall. So soft and almost filtered."

"It's amazing up here. When it gets all crisp... I'm from Las Cruces, and it never really gets like that down there."

"Ah, close to the giant pistachio!" Wat grinned like a monkey. "Do you remember that, baby? We did that and White Sands?"

Naomi shrugged, crossing her eyes and shaking her head. "We did? Was I just a baby?"

"No, silly. You were five? Four?" Wat's cheeks pinked. "I was very busy working and going to school."

"Yeah. Alamogordo. They have a zoo, too." When he was a kid, that had been his jam. They'd had this raven named Edgar who talked...

"Oh, I love a zoo! Daddy, can we go to that zoo?"

"Oh, baby. Maybe we can all plan a field trip to the Biopark in Albuquerque this fall? That would be fun."

"That would be cool. There's all sorts of neat animals there." He'd thought about being a zoo vet once upon a time, but his passion was horses and cattle and other ranch animals.

"Yeah? Can you come too? You love animals. Daddy can drive."

"If we can all get together on a time, sure." He loved tigers...

"Okay! I will ask Mimi and Granny. They will do it."

Watson rolled his eyes. "They're superwomen, aren't they?"

"They are at that." She was already calling them Mimi and

Granny... Miz Alba and Mrs. Antonia would adore that. "They raised the boss, after all. Homeschooled him, even."

"Ryder? Honestly? Wow. That is admirable. That man has a will."

"He does. His daddy was a famous bullrider from Brazil. But I think he gets his temper from Mrs. Antonia."

"Do I have a temper, Daddy?"

"A little bit, yeah. You get that from your momma."

Naomi grinned a little. "Daddy is always calm."

"Uh-huh." Still waters ran deep. He would bet Wat had a goodly bit going on in there.

"He mediates every day."

Watson's chuckle was soft. "Meditates, baby."

"Right." Naomi closed her eyes. "Ooooohm."

Tygh raised an eyebrow, but Watson didn't flinch. It was a touch hippie-dippy, but he guessed if it worked...

"You should try it sometime, Tygh." Watson did wink at him then, sharing the joke.

"Next time I get kicked, huh?"

"Oh, no kicking. God, that sounds distressing. No kicking."

Laughing, Tygh held up his hands. "Can't promise that. Animals can be unpredictable. But I do my best to be safe."

"I've never even had a dog. I mean, I think animals are great, but I wasn't raised with them. My baby girl, though, she's an animal person."

"She is." He glanced at Naomi who was back to coloring, ignoring them in the way only a kid her age could. "She's great with them."

"It doesn't make sense, but a lot of things in life don't." There was a wealth of meaning in that sentence, and Tygh had to agree.

"You know it." He rose, knowing he'd spent enough time jawing. "I need to get back to it. Y'all enjoy your downtime."

"Do you need help, Cowboy Tygh? I can help you?" That baby must have her momma's eyes, because they were blue as the sky.

"I thought we were going to spend the day together. Maybe go to the library and lunch?"

"Well, if you want to come for a little bit and help me with the feeding, then I'm game. But if you and your daddy have plans, little bit, you can help me another day."

"Can I help just for half an hour, Daddy? Just for that?"

"If Mr. Tygh doesn't mind, and you promise to be very good."

"I promise."

"We'll set a timer on my phone." Tygh gave Watson a wink over Naomi's head. She was dancing again.

"All right. I'll be right here, should you need me."

"We'll be back." He held out his hand so Naomi could take it with her good one, and he checked her shoes before they went too. She would need some mucking boots soon.

She was wearing little tennis shoes, but they didn't look fancy. Still, they would do well enough for now.

"I love the barn," she said.

"But your dad talked to you about not coming in there by yourself, right?"

"Yes, sir! He said that this is your working place, and I have to respect that."

"That's a good way to put it. But you also need to remember that animals can be unpredictable. And they're way bigger than us. So even if they're trying to be nice, sometimes they can hurt us." He didn't want to scare her, but all ranch kids had to learn this fact.

"Yeah. Like fire. Fire isn't bad, but it can do bad things. Did you know about my hand?"

"I did. I hope it's okay, but I asked your daddy. I didn't

want to say something that might give you bad memories." He knew it was important to let her know that.

"Yeah. It's sad that it's gone, but it feels better, and... can I tell you a secret?"

"Sure, kiddo." Lord help him, why did kids talk to him like this?

"The burned-up hand was ugly. This is just an arm. I hated that hand."

"Well, then, it's good to start over, right?" He was going to tread so careful there, but he was totally about encouraging her.

"Yeah. Daddy says when it's healed all the way, if I want, I can get a fake hand."

"I think that's too cool." It wasn't really time to feed, but he would let her give everyone some sweet feed and some pets. And since he didn't have to watch Dani too, he'd let her meet the goat, pig, and the new resident, a sheep from the mutton bustin' crew that had a bum knee from a fall.

Once Tygh got her healed up, she would come live at his place with the other retired animals.

"Oh, is she hurting bad? Can I help? Does she need a hug?" God save him from little girls.

"She's not much of a hugger, but she likes when you scratch her chin. It's a little crusty under there."

"Oh. Okay." She reached under, the touch gentle as anything. "Is this a momma sheeps?"

"She is. She's a good girl." All of the mutton bustin' sheep would run like the wind when the gate opened, but they were chosen to be gentle enough with little kids. "Her name is Wanda."

"Wanda. Is she a mommy?" The quiet questions kept on, but they were reasonable, curious, and when Watson came for her, Tygh was shocked at how fast the time had gone.

"Time to go, baby girl. Let's go wash up, hmm?"

"Okay, Daddy. Thank you, Mr. Tygh."

"Thank you for all your help." He nodded at Wat, and Anna pulled up just about the time Naomi came back to give him a hug.

Dammit, he was going to get no end of shit about this.

Still, he'd made that little girl's day better, hadn't he?

Chapter Seven

Watson was in the family room with all the little ones. It was a huge day for them.

Christiana and Raul were leaving, and the two new babies were coming. Talk about a switch.

Christiana and Raul were happy, healthy children, secure in the knowledge their father was coming back for them, that this was only a short-term situation.

These two new little ones didn't even have names yet. They didn't have official birthdays. Birth certificates. Medical histories.

And they would need a ton of care. They had been neglected. Who knew if they had any bonding skills? Or if they had any disabilities? The whole lot of them were flying blind on all this.

And all of the other children would need equal support as well, because they were losing contact with two very good friends.

Nell was already ignoring Christiana and Raul, demanding that her Mimi hold her. Dani was more quiet than anything, sitting on the couch and watching everything with sad eyes. Elijah had pretty much said his goodbyes and gone to his room.

Charlie was there, though, helping buck everyone up, and Wat really liked that kid. Mature, level-headed, and willing to throw in and help with everything.

She even talked to Naomi about her hand as if it was the most normal situation on earth. It amazed him, more than a little bit. Naomi seemed to like the straightforward approach, so it worked.

"Daddy's here!" Christiana bounced away from the window, twirling. "I get to go see my new room!"

Jennifer pulled up, the kids' dad in the passenger seat. He was all grins as he got out of the car.

Dani crossed her arms, her lower lip quivering.

"Dad!" Raul waved out of the window, then ran to the kitchen to meet his dad at the door. Wat got it. They had to be so excited to be with family again, to know that their dad had meant it when he said he would come for them.

"Dani? Did you need a hug?" Naomi whispered, and Dani shook her head.

"No. I want to be left alone."

Naomi blinked, and then turned her back on Dani, beelining for him. "Can we go home now?"

"Not yet. We need to see if the new babies need us."

"Oh."

"Come here." He picked up his girl to take her to the other side of the room. "You remember how it was in the hospital when you said if one more person was nice to you that you were going to cry?" That had just been after her last surgery, so she should. At her nod, he kissed her hair. "That's how Dani feels right now."

"Oh. But I'm going to stay here, so that's good, right?"

"It is. But you know how Sara Lynn at the hospital said 'you feel how you feel'? It's the same thing." They had both done a lot of therapy, and it had helped, had made them both able to begin to heal.

She nodded again, more slowly. "So I should wait for her to tell me she needs a hug?"

"Or you can wait a while and ask again, but let her sit with how she's hurting for a bit, okay?" He patted her back. He was asking a lot of someone her age, and he knew it, but she could handle it. He had faith.

She'd had to sit with her own pain for months.

She was better at it than he was, when he got right down to it. He was still wandering—vacillating between guilt and loss and this hope that life wasn't over.

She had a lot less on her mind, he guessed. Which might not be fair, but how did he know?

"Okay, I have to go," Christiana said. "Dani... Will you tell me goodbye? I'll miss you so bad."

"Will you come spend the night sometimes? For a slumber party?" Dani offered over the olive branch, even as he went to help welcome the new fosters in. Naomi stayed close, peeking at Jennifer as she started to unload car seats.

"Uh-huh. I will." Christiana managed a smile.

"Stay up here, love," he told Naomi. "How can I help, Jennifer?" He ran down the stairs to assist.

"Oh, here, can you take this little one?" She handed him the smallest baby in the carrier as Ryder and Kase walked out to join them.

"Totally. Come on, sweetheart. Let's get you inside so that the other two can say their goodbyes." He headed into the nursery, Naomi at his heels.

"Is she sleeping?" Naomi peered into the carrier, so curious.

"Uh-huh. She's so little, isn't she?" The doctors assumed she was three months old, but Jesus... she was the size of a newborn.

"Was I ever that little, Daddy?"

He smiled, easing the little one out of the carrier. He was fairly sure Jennifer would need to take it back. "Oh, yes. You were tiny and cute. I was so scared I would hurt you, but I didn't."

"No. You're the best daddy ever." She gave him a quick glance, her admiration real. It made him feel ten feet tall and bulletproof, that his kid trusted him so much. His strongest hope in all the world was that he could live up to her belief.

"I sure try. Can you get me a little blanket to cover her up, please," he whispered, settling the little one down. Her lips pursed, and she sucked, brow drawing down in a frown. "Let me see if you have a pacifier. Oh, here we go."

It was a Nuk with a ladybug on it, and she started working it, right away. He needed to see what the feeding schedule was.

"Here's the blanket. There's another baby. She's crying, Daddy."

"Okay, let's go help."

"Will she be okay here?"

"I'll keep an eye on her." Charlie walked in, smiling.

"Thanks, Charlie. We'll be right back."

Ryder had Dani, Kase was talking to the kids' dad, and Jennifer seemed panicked, so he just traded out car seats and scooped the older of the two up, holding her real careful. "Hey, baby girl. You're okay. You're fine. This is an amazing place with all sorts of kids and grannies and cowboys and dogs. You'll be okay now. Life is going to be good."

He put all of his faith into the words, because he had to believe that things were good, down at the core.

She hiccupped, her baby body shaking with sobs, but the storm was ending. He could tell.

Kase shook hands with Raul and Christiana's dad, then knelt to hug both kids. He joined Ryder, and they all walked over to Watson as Jennifer loaded the others into the car. Whew.

"How's it going?"

"I think it might be feeding time."

Ryder nodded. "They didn't eat on the way up in case they got sick."

"Poor babies." His heart was breaking for them. So tiny and stressed.

"Yes." Ryder sighed and rubbed the back of his neck. "Can you feed the one you have, Wat? Kase can get the baby, but I need to deal with Dani."

"Sure. That's why I'm here."

"Can I go read a book with Granny, Daddy?" Naomi's eyes pleaded with him, and he had to laugh, because Antonia Chiara and Naomi were forming a bond.

"Sure, baby. If she doesn't mind."

"She asked *me*, Daddy."

"Okay, sweetie. You sit with her and Nell, huh?" He glanced at Kase. "Do we know what they're eating?"

"They're both still bottle-fed, and the docs said it's more important to get nutrition into the one you're holding than to wean her." Kase rolled his eyes. "Children need names, dammit."

"So we'll name them." Watson didn't believe for a second anyone would care. "How about Emma and Maggie? Those were my grandmothers' names."

"I like that." Ryder grinned, Dani leaning on his shoulder. "Littlest bit can be Emma, and the one you have can be Maggie."

Kase nodded. "Sounds good. Okay, bottles ahoy... Oh, Nanette, you are a queen among women."

Nanette handed them bottles. "Those poor niñas. They need some food, eh?"

"They do." Kase grabbed a bottle and headed off to get the baby.

"C'mon, Maggie, you hungry?" He held out the bottle, and she looked at him, so distrustful. "You want to sit down?"

This little one should be jabbering, should be walking around and getting into trouble.

Naomi disappeared with Nell, Alba, and Antonia, so he focused on wee Maggie, tempting her by rubbing the bottle nipple across her lips.

She grabbed the bottle with both hands and dragged it in, sucking good and hard, so hungry.

"Good girl. That's it. You've got this." They needed to see what she felt about mashed potatoes.

In fact, they could try a bunch of different soft foods over the next week or so and see what she liked. He would talk to Nanette about purees and such.

He could see that she had a full mouth of teeth. They needed to start brushing them too. Lord have mercy, this baby girl was hungry.

"Nanette, do we have any Cheerios?"

"Si, Señor Wat. I will get some, huh?" She bustled off, and Kase, who had brought Emma back in, grinned at him.

"She needs more, huh?"

"I think she might need to crunch a little. Right, Maggie? Would you like to eat some cereal? Work on some Os?"

She stared at him, her near-black gaze distrustful.

"I know, honey. I do. It's been a crazy few weeks, huh? Are you so worried? I got you, though. I promise." Nanette came back out with the cereal, and he pulled out a couple of Os.

She knew what those were, her eyes sparkling. She took one from his palm, and held it in two fingers.

"There you go. See, they're yummy." He took one from the bowl and ate it. "Nom nom nom."

She blinked, then looked at her O before popping it into

her mouth and glomming it. Score! He felt like he'd run a marathon.

"You want another one?" He offered it over, and she took it, with much less hesitation, munching like a fiend. That was it. She just needed food. He'd have to make sure she didn't get sick, but heavens, she was so ready to get back to the business of growing.

Growing, learning, experiencing the world, being loved—this was their job, all they needed to do. He was going to help.

Kase burped Emma, and she was asleep in seconds, worn out from trying so hard to suck down her meal. "Let me change her and put her down," Kase said.

"I'll see if I can get this one to eat a few more Cheerios and interact just a minute."

"You got it. Charlie said she'll stay with Emma here and read a book out loud, just to get her used to the noises around here."

"Oh, that's a great idea."

"Thanks. I'm going to pick up Leanne around six, and I thought, if it was cool, I'd take everyone to get ice cream. Even Naomi."

"Yeah?" Elijah bounced. "Can Rick and Sam come too?"

"Why don't we come as well?" Miz Alba came bustling through. "That way we don't have to try to stuff everyone in one vehicle and we can buy, huh? Me and your granny."

Charlie shot Alba a smile. "Thanks, Mimi. I don't want to leave anyone out."

"Can I go, Daddy?" Naomi asked, tugging at his jeans, and he nodded and turned, Maggie catching sight of her, the expression curious.

"Yes, but it's three o'clock. Ice cream is at six o'clock. Okay?"

"Okay!" Naomi did her goofy dance, which had Maggie smiling, a bubbly laugh breaking out. "Daddy! She liked it!"

"She did, baby. Do it again?"

Naomi wiggled and danced, shaking her booty, and Maggie clapped her hands.

"Look at that." Kase chuckled. "You go, Naomi. You have a great little dance."

"Thank you, sir," Naomi said, bowing, which made Maggie clap again.

"Someone likes you," Ryder told her. "Good job!"

"Maggie and I are going to be friends," Naomi said. "I bet she will be with Nell and Dani, too. They're just sad."

"They are," Kase said. "We all are some, huh? But Raul and Christiana are so happy that I have to be glad for them."

"They liked it here, but they love their daddy more," Naomi said with wisdom beyond her years.

"As it should be." Ryder handed off Emma to Charlie, sighing as his back pocket seemed to buzz. "Be right back. That's bound to be the guys at the rodeo company. I need to take it."

"Can I sit up there with you and her, Daddy?" Naomi waited for his nod, and she snuggled in and handed Maggie another Cheerio. "She's so pretty."

"She is, and I bet she's so smart."

"Uh-huh. She has to be. She made it through all the yuck to get here."

"She did at that. You're so smart too. Have I told you lately?" He glanced up to see Kase with "aw" face, grinning at them. He got it. He did that with parents and their kids all over the place, so he got it.

"Uh-huh, because I made it through the yuck too."

Charlie nodded to Naomi, sitting with little Emma against her chest. "All of us have gone through the yuck. We have to stick together. Did you know that my dad lost his parents too?"

"No." Naomi shook her head. "I don't know lots of things."

"Oh, you could fill a whole library with things I don't know," Charlie said, laughing.

"Sh—oot," Kase agreed. "We're all that way."

"Not Daddy. Daddy went to school forever, and he is so, *so* smart."

Watson's cheeks heated. "Thanks, baby, but there's a ton I don't know."

"Well, I did go to school a lot, but I have a lot to learn. We always want to keep learning."

"Yes!" Charlie lowered her voice when Maggie jumped.

Wat rocked her, letting her know she was safe.

"Sorry, Maggie Mae," Charlie said. "I get excited. But I love to learn. Some of school was really hard, but I've always loved books and like, documentaries."

"What are docdentaries?" Naomi asked.

"TV shows and movies about real things. Not actors, you know?"

Naomi glanced at him. "Daddy?"

"So real shows—about Egypt or music or dogs—not make-believe."

"Oh! Like the one about if they peel the ocean back and see what's underneath?"

"Exactly like that, kiddo."

Charlie tilted her head. "What's that one?"

So Wat told her about *Drain the Oceans* while Maggie fell asleep. He loved sharing things with kids like Charlie, who was still a kid, even if she was in college, and even if she'd been through a lot.

"Dude. We should have an a-thon! I would love that." Charlie grinned at Naomi. "You could tell me which ones were the best."

"Is an a-thon like a binge-watch?" Naomi was so in love with Charlie just like she was Mrs. Antonia and Tygh. It warmed his heart to see her open up. She loved her grandparents, but they remembered her from before the fire, and that always made it hard. They would look at Naomi with sadness in their eyes, and Naomi knew it on one level or another.

"It is! Good job."

Naomi's cheeks went bright red, and she ducked her head. "Thank you. I will watch with you."

"Cool." Charlie winked at Watson, expression warm and friendly.

Wat laughed. "Naomi knows the ones we like, so I say we go for it. Maybe tomorrow, if you're around?"

"I am. I won't go back down until late so I can be in class Monday. I told the dads I'd hang out and help with the new arrivals."

"Sounds good to me too," Kase said. "I could use a day to rest this hip."

"You'll end up watching through your eyelids," Ryder teased as he came back in. "Everyone asleep?"

"These two are, and I haven't seen Nell and Dani since they arrived."

"I'll go check with the moms." Ryder hardly ever sat still. Kase was more the one who everyone seemed to revolve around, the one who stayed put. It was a fascinating dynamic.

He grinned, watching as Naomi's eyelids started to droop. She was so ready for a nap, even if she didn't want to miss anything.

"Well, we're all here. Let's put on a movie or something until it's time to go for ice cream," Kase said, grabbing the remote. He winked at Wat.

"Fair enough." He kept holding Maggie. He figured it was important to hear someone's heartbeat. To learn how to be safe. So he could sit with his baby girl sleeping against his side and make this new little one feel warm and happy.

It was a good place to be.

Chapter Eight

"You know, Miss Moe, I have to go home at some point." Tygh kept his tone gentle, his hands gentler as he wrapped a bandage around a leg on the second sheep this week to get an injury. What was that road crew doing wrong, dammit? At least Miss Moe's was a cut. She'd be carrying lambs again in no time. "There's a chill in the air this morning, isn't there?"

His phone buzzed, and the text tone was a klaxon, so that was the boss, sending a ranch-wide alert.

<Main house has COVID. Quarantining for 5 days. Doc is here for testing.>

His eyes widened. Shit. That was a mess waiting to happen. He would stay well away from the big house, and he would self-test this morning.

Well, fuck.

<You need anything?>

<For y'all to stay safe. Charlie brought it. She and Leanne are quarantining at the college.>

<Got it, Boss. The babies?> He would help with any of the kids he needed to.

<With Wat. Wat and Naomi and babies negative.>

In fact, he saw Wat loaded down with supplies and babies and a stroller, struggling over the uneven ground.

<I'll do what I can to help> He headed out, pretty sure he was okay. "You need a hand?"

Watson damn near jumped out of his skin. "Oh, please? They're all positive. I need to get these three somewhere safe."

"Sure. We'll take them to your place. I'll need to test, but I've been out of the loop more than most."

"Thanks. I appreciate it."

Naomi had a mask on, and she was skipping beside them, singing, and Watson nudged her gently.

"Can you open the door for me, baby girl? We have to make room for the girls to sleep and play."

"Uh-huh. We're having a sleepsover, Tygh. Can you come?"

"Well, we'll see. But I like those." Lord help him, that conjured up inappropriate images about Wat all of a sudden.

"Me too! Maggie and Emma can sleep in my bed with me!" She opened the door into a tiny home with a kitchenette.

"Oh, wow. This is—" Small. "Cute."

"It's perfect for a little girl and her skinny dad." Watson winked at him, eyebrows waggling dramatically. "Just perfect."

He chuckled. "It does make me feel... wide."

"I have tests in the bathroom. Did you want one?"

"Yeah. That's a good idea." That way if he came up positive he wasn't all up in Wat's business for long.

Wat pointed to the single bathroom between the two bedrooms. It was clean, but there wasn't a bathtub. Didn't little girls need bathtubs?

He ducked in, finding the tests in the medicine cabinet. "You need one too?" he called.

"I just took one. That's why I got the babies."

"Ah. Okay. Well. Gimme fifteen then." If he had to he

could clean the bathroom and make a run for it, not breathing on anyone.

He stuck the cotton swab up his nose and scraped his brain, then sat to wait. The bathroom was scrubbed and shiny, and there were books on the back of the toilet—a novel and a book on early childhood education.

Huh. He wanted to grab the novel, but he was conscious of contaminating as little as he could. He'd not seen Charlie but in passing, but he'd been around the rest of the family on and off. So he got on his phone and played games and answered emails. See him. See him be all functional.

Fifteen minutes later, his alarm went off, and the test was negative. Good deal.

"I should be good." He left the bathroom. "What can I do?"

"Good deal. I'm trying to figure out where to put them to sleep for five to ten days..."

"Huh." He glanced around. "Yeah, not much space. I mean, you won't have to be here teaching the kids."

"True. We'll have a little mini-homeschooling here with diaper changes."

"No, I just mean—" He took a deep breath. "I have a sh— A ton of space."

"Do you? Are you close?" Watson blushed and chuckled. "How don't I know?"

"Just across the road from the main gate. That place with the big blue mailbox."

"Oh, the adobe with the pretty roses!"

"Yep. That's me." His gran had loved roses, so they'd been the first thing he'd planted. "You can come stay there, seriously. I have way more room, and a big kitchen, and two bathrooms."

"Oh, that would be... That would be so much easier than

trying to keep the kids separated here..." Oh, right. Dani could slip out of anywhere.

"Yeah. She knows she's not allowed to cross the road. D-girl, I mean."

"What do you think, Naomi? Should we go see Mr. Tygh's house?" Wat seemed a touch desperate, and Tygh couldn't blame him. This place was too tiny for two babies.

"A slumber party with Mr. Tygh? Yes! Let me pack some toys and my pillow and a nightie." The happy squeal made the smallest baby cry.

"Whoops." Wat grabbed her up, bouncing her. "Okay, you go pack. Tygh, can you hold her while I get some things together."

"Uh, sure." Couldn't be that different than a puppy or a goat, right?

"Thanks." Wat plopped her into his arms, and she was tiny—absolutely defenseless.

Her tears dried up when she stared at him, and he knew it was because he was a whole new face. Her little lips worked hard as she tried to decide whether to snuggle in or scream, and he would bet she was hungry. He had no idea when they'd last ate, but they should probably wait until they got to his house.

"Does she have a binky?" Tygh called. "She's sucking hard."

"It should be in the stroller. It has a ladybug on it."

"Gotcha." He dug through until he found the pacifier, and then he moved to the sink to wash the damn thing, wanting to sanitize it in case. Someone as tiny and as malnourished as she was could really be in trouble with something like Covid, so it was better to be safe than sorry. He was all about creating as sterile a field as possible when there were those kinds of germs lurking about.

His place was much better suited for these little ones and Naomi.

He supposed he should call his boss and let him know what was up. He dialed Ryder, and got a growled, "'lo."

"Hey, Boss. How you feeling?"

"I feel fine. I imagine I'll feel like shit soon, since I tested positive."

"Lots of fluids and rest. Hey, look, this place of Wat's is a tiny house."

"That's kind of exactly what it is. It's based on a mother-in-law outbuilding."

"Well, that's fine for him and Naomi, but it's cramped for the rest. So I'll take them to my place for the quarantine."

"Oh, that would be a blessing. You've tested? You're negative?"

"Just now, yeah. And it was one of the new tests. I mean, I'll test again tomorrow, but I think I'll be all right."

"Sounds great. I'll get Gareth to do your rounds, so all you have to do is dose anyone that needs it badly, or tell him what to do. That way you can hang out at your place in case Wat needs a hand. That work for you?"

"Yeah. He's got his hands full, and I don't want to leave him in the lurch."

"Sounds great. Nanette is quarantining with us. I'm calling in a food order. Just text me a list for all of you. I'll hook you up. Diapers, formula, whatever. Even a couple of Pack 'n Plays."

"I'll get Wat on it." Groceries he knew how to ask for, but he would let Wat make a list of baby stuff. That way they would have what they required without him having to run into town and risk picking up the bug on the back end.

"Thanks, Tygh. This is above and beyond, and I know it. I'm grateful."

His cheeks heated. "Bah. We've talked about this, Boss. The foster program is one of the reasons I signed on."

"Yeah, but still, I appreciate you. I have three unhappy kids, three grumpy ladies, and a sick husband. You're helping a ton."

"You're welcome. We'll send that list, and if you need me to go into town instead, just text."

"Will do."

Tygh hung up, laughing as little Emma sucked her binky as if it were a lifeline. "Soon, sweet little girl. Let's get across the road, first."

"I don't have the car seats for them," Wat said, coming out of the bedroom.

"I can get them out of the SUV." No one locked their cars on the ranch. "I'll wipe them down with some alcohol and put them in... your car?"

"Yeah, I have room unless you gave a full back seat in your truck?"

"I do, actually." He would get it figured. "Be back."

By the time he got done, Wat was loading his car with perishable groceries, pillows and blankets, and two suitcases. The man knew how to move and move fast.

"Okay, let's get in the cars and head over to my place. Boss says to send him a list of all we need and he'll have it delivered."

"Like pizzas and ice cream?" Naomi asked.

"Mmm. That too, kiddo. I like it, in fact. But he meant cribs for the kids, blankets, clothes, formula, diapers." Tygh grinned. "And maybe a book or something for an amazing big girl who's helping so good."

"Okay! We're going to have the most bestest slumber party together! Jammies and laughing and being together!"

Wat gave him a grateful smile. "Possibly a b-e-e-r too, later. Thank you for this."

"You're welcome. You made this place really comfy, but it's just tiny. I can't imagine two Pack 'n Plays in it."

"No. I was going to have to put one in the bathroom." Wat laughed, getting Naomi into his car before coming to help him settle the kids. They bumped hips, making him grunt.

"Sorry. Sorry, I didn't mean to."

"No worries." He grinned. "Caravan ready."

"I'll follow you." Wat chugged to his car, and they drove down the lane and across the road, repeating the whole process as unloading. It occurred to him as he opened the door to wonder what Wat would think of his place. It was... pretty spare, but it was clean. Not bachelor-y at all.

It was a good place, not particularly homey, when you got right down to it. It was as if he was always ready to move on, even though he'd bought the house.

"Oh, wow, look at all this space." Wat turned in a circle after he set down the baby carrier holding Emma. "Wow."

"You might want to put her up." He grabbed the carrier right in time. The doggie door in the kitchen flapped open and two monstrous mutts came racing in. Biscuit and Tater both screeched to a halt, heads tilting as they stared at the babies and Wat and Naomi.

"Puppies!" Naomi clapped her hands, and the boys went to her, sniffing.

"Not in the face, guys. Gentle."

Two butts plopped on the floor, his dogs behaving well, panting as Naomi petted them each in turn.

"Puppies. You are good puppies, aren't you?" Naomi was over the moon. He could tell.

"This is Biscuit." The big yellow lab-Great Pyrenees mix wagged like crazy at the sound of his name. "And this is Tater." Tater lifted a paw to shake. The big old boy was a crazy mix of border collie and Anatolian shepherd.

"Oh...Daddy, he shakes." She took his paw, so careful while her father tried not to panic.

He grinned at Wat. "They're pretty good with kids, I promise. I take them into town a lot. Tater is trained to be a library dog, in fact." Not that he'd had time to go do that, but he'd had all the good intentions in the damn world. That just —well, it required peopling.

Watson's face relaxed. "Oh, that's cool. Did you hear, baby? You can read to them."

"I will read to them, and they will be my best friends, okay, Daddy? I will tell them about my hand, and they won't be worried."

Wat nodded, offering over a gentle smile. "No one's worried, baby."

"Nope. Look here. Biscuit, paw."

Biscuit offered up his paw too, and he showed it to Naomi. "See how's he's missing a toe?"

"Oh, Biscuit. Me too!" She showed her arm. "It got burned off in a fire, but it's okay. My daddy was there the whole time to help me. I'll help you."

When he glanced at Wat, the man was watching his little girl with misty eyes. He got it. She was something so special.

"So, we need to get that list to Ryder." He put Emma's carrier on a chair at the dining table so he could grab a dog biscuit for each of the boys. He handed them to Naomi. "Always make them sit."

"Okay. Sit down, please."

Both butts hit the ground again, the dogs losing interest in the babies in favor of cookies. He watched to make sure they were good boys, then sent them back outside with a flick of his hand.

"Prime hooligan hours," he told Wat. "Come on, and I'll show you the guest room and the spare room for the kids." He had several rooms he wasn't even using.

"I can't thank you enough. Seriously. I was going for calm and studly, but inside I was panicky idiot number three."

"Hey. No problem. I can't guarantee that the dogs won't want to sleep with Naomi. She's their new best friend."

"That's okay with her, I'm sure."

Maggie started to fuss, struggling to get out of the stroller.

"Hey, Maggie! You want to get up. You want a drink?"

She waved her little arms, and Wat came to get her. "I know, huh? So much excitement."

She gurgled and vocalized, smiling huge as Wat picked her up.

"She's got such a pretty smile," Tygh said, peering at her, making her giggle.

"She does, huh?" Wat bounced her a bit. "And she's turning out to be very sunshine."

"Not like me at all." Tygh made faces at her.

"Oh, now..."

Watson stopped as she giggled, focused on Tygh's face.

Tygh made another face, this one with his tongue out. What was she seeing there?

She tried to stick her tongue out too.

"Dude..." Watson breathed out.

"That's a smart girl." Tygh bent to nuzzle noses with her. "Okay, Miss M. You come too. We'll all see the rooms."

She reached for him, her little face so focused. Damn, he couldn't refuse that.

"She likes you, Mr. Tygh!" Naomi applauded for him, and his cheeks heated.

"I'm easy to like." He winked in an exaggerated way for Naomi, who also laughed.

"You got dogs! Of course you are."

"Clever girl."

Watson grabbed Emma and followed him as they made a conga line down the hall.

"Okay, here's the guest room. It has a nice double bed, and there's room for all your stuff." He figured Wat would want to stay in there, possibly with Naomi. He had no idea if she slept in her own room most nights or still did the parent bed crawl.

"This is amazing. Thank you." Wat put his suitcase down. "You rock."

"You're welcome. I'll go get some towels and stuff out if you want to settle in and let Ryder know what you want for the babies." And he would send the request for pizza and ice cream and something special for Naomi. And a pair of mini mudding boots. "Naomi, after a bit, you can come help me feed all my beasts."

"Am I sleeping in bed with Daddy and the babies?" She bounced over and hugged him tight. "Thank you!"

"You're welcome, kiddo." He hugged her back, and then he had to escape before he broke down and asked them to stay with him forever. It would pass, that urge. He was feeling the wonderful family vibe Wat and Naomi had from the outside and wishing he was in on it, that was all. "There's another bedroom, if you want to sleep there."

"Oh, can I see? Is it pretty? Do you like it?"

"It's kind of plain, but we can make it nice for you."

"I'll see." She chewed her lip, looking at Wat.

"We'll look at the room, huh?" Wat gave Naomi an encouraging glance. "Come sit with me and tell me what we need for Maggie and Emma."

Tygh escaped, texting Ryder. *<Pizza and ice cream has been requested.>*

<I'll call Frank.>

Frank was Ryder's cousin, and he lived in town. He had an in with the pizza place.

<Wat is sending in the list for things for the babies. Can I get 2 portable beds?>

<You got it. And I'll send a bill of groceries.>

<You're the best. Tell Gareth it's just Miss M who needs the meds today>
<Sure man. They're okay?>
<They're fine. Maggie stuck out her tongue at me>
<Whoa!>

He had to grin. He had to. She'd actually focused on him, seen him. It made him feel like a stud.

Tater came padding in to nudge his hand, and he reached down to stroke the big guy's ears. "You are gross. I need to wipe you down before bed tonight, huh?" Sleeping in his bed with all that dirt was one thing. Kids? Not so much.

Tater wagged, and then padded off, sniffing, searching for his new very best friend on earth.

"Be good," he called. He would bet Biscuit was on the porch, still soaking up the fresh air. He came in at night, but spent most of the day out guarding the other animals.

"Okay, so, we like the room, very much. I'm not sure where the other room is..." Wat and Naomi came out of the bedroom hand in hand. "The other two are ready for a bottle, so I brought the diaper bag too."

"So how long will Maggie take a bottle?" He wasn't sure how all that worked in humans. Animals? Totally.

"Right now we're working on trust and nutrition. Then we'll focus on catching up with where she needs to be."

"Sure. Is there anything else she likes though?"

"Applesauce. Cheerios. Carrot puree." Wat grinned. "She doesn't love peas."

"Neither do I."

"Mr. Tygh! They're like candy."

"Really?" He shook his head. "Ugh."

Naomi laughed. "I'll share mine with Tater."

Who was her new shadow.

"Not me, baby?" Wat fluttered his eyelashes dramatically.

Naomi giggled. "Silly Daddy. You give me my food."

"True enough." Wat winked. "Let's get some bottles heated up, and then we can look at the other room."

"Sounds good." They bustled around, and Naomi got to look at the bedroom.

"Daddy! It has flowers."

Tygh had forgotten all about the mural along the one wall. It was a little faded, but it had clearly been a kid's room.

"Can I please have this room as mine, Mister Tygh? I'll be so very careful. I swear."

"Of course you can. And I bet Tater stays in here with you. He's a great fan of sleeping. He does snore a little, though."

She wrinkled her nose. "So does my daddy."

"Naomi!" Wat laughed. "Okay, let's go feed. I sent that list." They got down to the business of feeding and burping and diapering, and lord, that was a lot of work.

But it was damn good work, and Tygh was glad he'd offered to help. This was just another part of caring for everything on a ranch.

Chapter Nine

Wat walked Emma up and down the hallway of Tygh's house. She was stressed out by yet another change, and her baby belly was hard and unhappy.

Still, he didn't want the big (surprisingly hot) cowboy to be grumpy at him. They were forming a friendship, and he didn't want to screw it up.

He had thought he'd make friends with some of the other cowboys, but it hadn't happened. He spent all his time at the main house, dealing with the kids, making lesson plans, and just connecting.

He hadn't had time to be a young guy, having a beer, chilling out.

He never had been, to be honest. He'd married young, had a baby young, and then spent years in school.

Naomi was sound asleep, though, and so was Miss Maggie, the big dogs watching over them like that was their only job in life. Naomi had a cot-sized mattress on the floor and the Pack 'n Plays were in there too, and it was so darn cute.

He patted and walked, bounced and walked, trying to

keep Emma quiet and encourage her to burp. "If you'd just relax, baby girl, this would go better."

She pooted, and he laughed, because that was a good thing, right? Poor baby girl. This was all so hard on wee ones.

Naomi thought it was all a big adventure, and Maggie already adored Tygh, so...

"Tygh's been good to us, huh? Letting us all stay while the big house is buggy." Holding her was like holding a brand-new infant, and she soaked up attention, much like her big sister.

She cooed a little, as if making sure he knew she was listening.

Tygh's door opened at the end of the hall, the big cowboy looking out. "You okay?"

"Sorry," he whispered. "Little bit here has an upset tummy. We're trying to walk it out."

"Ah. Well, that's not good, but as long as nothing is *wrong-wrong*." Tygh watched him, leaning on the doorjamb. "Let me know if you need me to take over."

"I will." He bounced Emma, listening to her poot again.

"Better out than in," Tygh said with a chuckle.

"That's my philosophy on babies."

"And generally dogs." Tygh chuckled. "Same kind of idea. They can't tell you that their tummies hurt."

"Exactly. And they count on us to make all things right."

"They do." Tygh yawned. "Do you need anything?"

"No. No. I'm good."

"I'm gonna grab a drink." Tygh squeezed past him in the hall, that big body brushing against his, which was... a little weird. Not in a bad way. Not at all, which was what made it weird. In fact, it made his nose quiver, because he caught the scent of musk and some kind of spice, and it was super nice.

It made him want to feel it again, if he was honest. Preferably when he wasn't holding a baby.

Tygh came back a few moments later with a bottle of

Sprite and a bag of chips. At his raised eyebrow, Tygh laughed. "Don't judge me. There are no dogs in my bed for the first time in forever."

"Oh, and those two are big. They both deserted you?" He might have to get him a dog, now that Naomi was sleeping in her own bed again.

"They're in there with your girl."

"Oh, right." He chuckled. "It gets later every second."

"You want me to take her?" Tygh asked.

"I'm—"

"MOMMY! Daddy, help us!"

"Fuck." He shoved Emma to Tygh, then ran for his girl. "Naomi!"

"Daddy! Daddy, help me! It's Mommy! She's coming to burn me!"

"No, baby. It's a dream. Just a dream." The dogs were frantic, jumping up and down off the bed. "Move, guys. Naomi. You're fine. It's a dream."

He hated this part. Michelle had been killed by a falling beam on the second floor as she was heading for the bank of windows, and she'd clamped down on Naomi's arm, trapping them in the house. Thank God, that the firefighters had been inside already, and had saved his little girl.

"Tater. Biscuit. Down." Tygh never raised his voice, but the dogs went to him, sitting next to him. Tygh held Emma, who was hiccupping sobs, and Maggie started to cry next, so Tygh went to her.

Maggie reached for Tygh as soon as she saw him, and Naomi sobbed in Wat's arms.

"Shh... shh... I have you. It's just a dream. You're okay. Just a dream."

Tygh walked in circles, bouncing Emma and Maggie, one in each arm. The dogs wagged, but stayed put where Tygh had told them to sit, waiting to see what would happen.

And Naomi finally calmed down.

"Daddy..."

"I got you, baby girl. It's just been a lot today, huh?"

"Is Cowboy Tygh going to make me leave because I cried, Daddy? I want him to be my friend."

Oh, sweet baby.

"I'm right here, Naomi. I'm not making you go anywhere. I have nightmares too, sometimes." Tygh's quiet tone was perfect, helping Naomi to stop shaking. His heart broke for her.

"Oh. I'm sorry. Nightmares are bad. I will let you borrow Daddy in your bed, if you need him. He's the best."

He blinked, then glanced at Tygh, who stared at him, cheeks going red.

"Uh... Thanks, kiddo. But I bet you might need him tonight, huh?"

"Uh-huh. For a minute. Did I scare the babies?"

"Emma was up already." He didn't want her to stress it.

"Okay." She sniffled. "Can I have milk?"

"Warm milk?" At her nod, he stood, lifting her up. "Sure, baby. Mr. Tygh was about to have a snack, right?"

"I was."

"Oh." She gave Tygh a once-over. "You have both babies, and Emma's sleeping."

"Uh-huh. But I did have a Sprite and some chips. Maybe we can go pick them up before the dogs get them."

Tygh must have dropped everything when Wat had shoved Emma at him. Which was infinitely better than dropping the baby...

"Yes. Can I put you down, baby, so I can take Emma and put her in her crib?"

"Uh-huh. I'll go get the chips for Mister Tygh." She wiggled to get to the floor.

He let her slide to her feet, and Tygh got the dogs to move, but not to follow yet. "Will she be all right?"

"Yeah. She's down to one or two a month. They were every few hours at the beginning." It made him so damn sad, and he didn't know how to keep the dreams from horrifying him.

"Yeah. They'll get to where they're once or twice a year." Tygh sounded very certain of that fact, and he wondered. Hell, he wondered a lot about the man, but he wasn't sure if he should ask, or if he should let Tygh decide to tell him about it only if unprompted. But Wat could tell there was experience talking there.

"I pray that's right. I'd hate for her to suffer forever. It would kill me, you know?"

"I do." Tygh shook his head as Naomi reappeared. "I'll tell you my sad tale of woe, but maybe not now, fair?"

"Sure." Okay. Okay, cool. If Tygh could help Naomi, he was willing to pry.

"Chipses."

"Thanks, kiddo. How about we go get that milk, huh?"

Wat took Emma to settle in his room, but Maggie wasn't letting Tygh go for love or money.

"Warm milk. Do you know that?"

"I do," Tygh said. "I'm pretty good at not burning it." They walked to the kitchen, the dogs padding behind them, nosing Naomi every so often, clearly worried.

"I had a night-scare, puppies. I'm sorry. Still be my friend?"

Both dogs sat and let Naomi love on them, and he had to smile.

"That's the best thing about dogs, Naomi," Tygh said. "They live for this moment right now. If you make it okay, they're just fine."

"Yeah? So they'll forgive me? I can't help it."

"I know. They know it too. They never get mad at me."

Naomi climbed up into a chair as Wat pulled the milk out of the fridge. "What do you dream about Mr. Tygh?"

"Something bad happened to me when I was a kid. It wasn't a fire, like yours, but it was pretty rough. I don't dream about it much now, but for a while, I did. And when I do, the dogs like to make it better." Tygh got out a pan and put it on the stove.

"I'm sorry. I don't want you to be sad. Do you need a hug?"

Oh, his baby girl was a dear, empathetic little girl.

"I would love one." Tygh went to her, and Naomi stood on the chair to give Tygh a hug.

Tears stung his eyes, and Wat turned to the milk, pouring it into the pan so Naomi wouldn't see him blinking and ask if he had something in his eyes. She made his heart so happy, even as he wished he could take from her all the crap that had happened to her.

She made him proud, and he hoped it meant he was doing a decent job raising her.

"Thank you, kiddo. I needed that."

"Are you still going to have chips?" Naomi asked.

"Actually I was thinking graham crackers. Can Naomi join me, Wat?"

Oh, that was a good pick. Not too much sugar, but still a treat.

"Absolutely." He would take one himself, but he hadn't been asked.

"Well, then, we should all have some."

He grinned. Tygh was starting to feel like a mind reader. "I would love one. Sounds good, huh, baby girl?"

"Uh-huh. Can Biscuit and Tater have a cookie?"

Oh, look at those ears perk up.

"Half of one. Wat, can you get one out of that jar with the paw prints?"

"Sure. I'll break it in half. Does that work?"

"That's great. They don't need too much."

Wat grabbed a dog biscuit and broke it in half before handing it to Naomi. He already trusted the two big mutts not to nip his girl when they took them. They were sort of amazing dogs. And Tygh was great with them like he was with all animals.

"They like me, Daddy. Did you see?"

"I did, honey. Good job. You're very kind."

She nodded, so serious. "I am."

Tygh snorted, going to pour the milk into heavy mugs.

They all sat to have their cookies, even the dogs, and Naomi was nodding off over her milk in no time. Maggie was asleep again, and the dogs went out, then came in, and it was time to go back to bed.

"Do you want me to take Maggie and Emma to my room, Wat?" Tygh asked.

"Oh, if you could take Maggie, I'll keep Emma and Naomi in with me. Tomorrow, we'll try again." He hated to make Tygh crazy.

"Sure. I don't mind at all." Tygh grinned. "It's hard to be in a new place."

"It is. Thank you."

"Let me move the Pack 'n Play. You need me, you just holler, okay? If you leave the door open, the dogs will just come and go, or they can stay in with me."

"I'll leave the door open." He reached out, offering Tygh his hand. "Thank you. Seriously. For everything."

Tygh shook his hand, a faint smile crinkling his eyes. "You're welcome. Hold that thought for when I can't find my boots tomorrow or something, and I'm growling."

"Or when three girls are rumbling about being hungry at once. I hear you."

Tygh let him go, leaving his hand oddly tingly. "We'll figure it. Night, y'all." Tygh took Maggie and left, humming something tuneless on the way.

Naomi was curled up in the bed, and Emma was at peace in her temporary bed, so he snuggled up next to his baby girl.

"Love you, Daddy."

"I love you. Sleep."

"'kay."

He closed his eyes, knowing tomorrow would be another crazy day.

And tonight, he had hot puppy breath to contend with.

Chapter Ten

"Just let me come over there and—"

"No way, Tygh. Two of the guys have come down with it, too. I'm dealing fine. I just need to know the dose on that antibiotic for Miss M."

"I cannot believe she got that cut infected so fast."

"I think she was looking for you." Gareth chuckled. "Or Dani and Naomi."

"God help us." Day four of this ranch mini-pandemic, and Tygh was going to lose it. He needed to be able to do his job, but he was stuck at his place with two babies, a little girl who wanted to know how everything worked, a clueless-as to-how-hot-he-was Wat, and...

Well, okay, so the worst part was not being able to do his damn job. He was a freaking vet, and he couldn't get to his patients.

Maggie caught sight of him, and she started crawling for him, brows creased, lips pursed.

"Hey, baby." He reached for her with one hand, and she came scooting right over.

"Did you call me baby?"

"No, Gareth. Maggie. Give Miss M five of the sulfa tablets in some sweet feed twice a day. If it needs to go to shots, I'll mask up and come over." He let Maggie lift to sitting with his hand.

"I'm on it, Boss. Have fun."

"Hush you." He hung up and sat down, encouraging her to pull herself up to standing. Watson was encouraging her to use her muscles, bounce a little bit. So he would work on it with her too.

She cooed at him, her sounds starting to approach words, and he would bet she'd been making good progress when whatever had happened occurred.

"I know. Did you have a good breakfast this morning?" Wat was changing Emma, who was stinky-butt girl these days.

"Ba. Babababa."

"Uh-huh. I bet you did. I had a burrito. From frozen." Not fun, but he'd had to get up early to take a shipment of hay.

"Ba. Baba. BabababaBA!" Her smile was pure glee.

"That doesn't sound very yummy," Wat said. "Do you want me to make you some lunch?"

He glanced up to see Wat and Emma standing over them. "You have enough on your plate, man. Where's Naomi?"

"Playing in her room with the dogs." Watson gave him a warm smile.

"I've never seen them stay inside so much." He grinned back. "What did you have in mind for lunch?" He could eat, at that.

"I was going to make soup and sandwiches. Do you like chicken noodle?"

"I do. I have veggie beef too. In cans, I mean. I'm not much on making soup. Now, grilling? I am a king. And I can do pancakes." They hadn't managed to eat much together, the kids eating way earlier than he usually did, and Wat going ahead and having food with Naomi while he worked with his animals.

Wat always made sure there was food for him, though. Just waiting there.

"Oh, don't let Naomi hear that. She loves pancakes."

"I can make them for supper. Trade off with you." He would come in early tonight. He liked to see Naomi smile.

"That would be great. Do you mind if I put her down too? She likes to be on the blanket."

"I can watch her," Tygh said. "Her sister and I can do it."

He walked Maggie over to Emma, her little legs working hard.

"Look at her go! She wants to learn this, doesn't she?" Wat sounded so proud.

"Yep. She's ready to get back to growing up." He got that so hard. She was a fighter, all the way, and he was going to do whatever he could to help.

She tilted her head back so she could see him, and her smile stole his breath. Then she toppled over against his leg, knocking out her breath, and she started to whimper.

"Uh-uh." He swept her up in his arms. "That was just a little spill. Nothing a cowgirl like you can't handle." Not that she wasn't allowed to cry. But she didn't really want to, he didn't think.

She calmed immediately and snuggled right into his arms. That was it. She needed a little support.

"She has your number."

"She really does." He rocked her back and forth, patting her back. She was so tiny.

"Daddy! I read a story to Biscuit and Tater, and they liked it!" Naomi came trotting into the room, the dogs trailing her, adoring her.

"Ee-a-la! They did? That's amazing."

Okay, that was adorable. Listen to Watson being all New Mexican.

"They did! And they let me rub their bellies. Can I go to the barn with you this afternoon, Mr. Tygh?"

He didn't even blink. He was getting used to Naomi's stream-of-consciousness talk. "You ready to meet everyone? If your dad says yes, I guess we can, since your boots came in."

"Please, Daddy? I need to know how to take care of the animals. Please."

"If Tygh is okay with it, then I am. I'll stay with Maggie and Emma, huh? Maybe work on my lesson plans."

"Okay!" She twirled, bonking Tater with a book. "Oops! Tater. I'm sorry."

Tater did that wagging, head-down thing dogs do when a human stepped on them or hit them by accident, like they had to apologize.

"You have to be careful, sweetie," Wat said. "You're bigger than him."

"Yes, sir. I'm sorry. Tater, I'm sorry. I will remember to watch out." She actually teared up, but then she firmed her lips.

Tater just licked her arm.

Naomi giggled then, shaking her head. "Dogs are silly."

"They are. That's what makes them so awesome. Want to come read to me too?" Tygh offered, patting the floor with his free hand.

"Yes! The baby is crawling away." She eased Maggie back into play.

"She's on a tear today," Wat murmured. "I'll start lunch."

"Is Miss M okay?" Naomi asked.

"Gareth says she cut herself, but she'll be fine. If he doesn't think she's getting better by tomorrow, I'll go see her and wear mask and all."

"That's so sad. I hate when they're hurted. Do you ever cry?"

"I do." He was a cowboy, and they always said cowboys didn't cry, but he wasn't gonna lie to a kid. Not one who'd been through what she had. "Sometimes you have to. Sometimes you have to suck it up because it's not the right time, but that's usually when there's an emergency and there's not time."

"Yeah. Well, if you need someone to hug you, I will always. You just have to hold up your finger like this." She held up her index finger like she was hailing a cab.

Wat made a soft sound, and when he glanced over, Wat's shoulders were shaking like he was sobbing.

"I can get behind that, honey. Now, I want to know all about, uh, *Hank the Cowdog*." God, he'd read those. They'd been around forever. He had no idea there were new books, but it looked like there were.

"Daddy got it for me when we knew we were moving to the ranch. I knew Tater and Biscuit would like it."

"You're a good friend." He let her lean on him and read as he caught Maggie by the foot. And here he'd thought he'd be bored.

Maggie rolled over and gave him the stank-eye before she giggled and tried to get away again.

"Come here, little scooter." He lifted her, putting her on his lap. "Let's take a break, huh?" He stood her back up, letting her dance, holding on to him. He wanted to work her legs. Wear her ass out.

"Is she dancing?" Naomi asked, standing and copying Maggie, bouncing up and down.

"She is. You like to dance, huh?"

"Uh-huh!" She wiggled all over, her one hand waving, flipping her hair like someone in a TikTok video.

Suddenly music started, Wat turning it on from his phone.

Maggie blinked for a second, and then her little butt went to town, rocking and bouncing and dancing.

He held on and let her, and Naomi sang along with whatever this was, but it was kind of a crime against nature. Not anything he knew.

It didn't matter, though, because Little Maggie was having a ball, and her baby sister was fascinated, a huge grin on her face.

Watson came out of the kitchen, boogying right down with the kids, and he hooted. "Go, Wat!"

"Go, Daddy, go!"

The dogs disappeared through the doggie door in the face of this human madness, but everyone else was laughing to beat the band.

Tygh had never seen anything so goofy, and he'd had a mule that had been in love with a tortoise.

Naomi plopped down when the song went off. "Whew! That was fun!"

"It was." He kissed Maggie's nose, and in return, she licked his chin.

Okay, that was gross.

Not giraffe gross, but still...

"Let me go stir the soup." Wat was flushed and out of breath, and Tygh had this crazy thought that Wat would look like that after having sex. Only naked.

Whoa. Down boy. Wat had been married. To a woman.

That was a clear sign. So he quashed that feeling hard and pushed back to helping Maggie get up and down, her little legs working hard. He was amazed at how much weight she'd put on in just a few days of good eating.

"What kind of soup, Daddy?"

"Chicken noodle."

"Yay." Naomi plopped down on the floor next to Emma. "Hey, sister. You are a good baby."

Emma grunted, clearly agreeing.

"Soup smells so good, man," he told Wat. He needed to not get used to this. This felt suspiciously like having a family.

"I doctor it a little bit. I'm glad to do it."

"Well, I appreciate not having to heat up another burrito." He shuddered, and Maggie squealed at him.

"You like that, little one? Burritos?"

Maggie squealed again, bouncing and focused.

"Well, she's not ready for that, but some noodles? Sure." Wat smiled at him. "She's in love."

"She's my girl." He wanted to take it back as soon as he said it, because she wasn't, was she? As soon as the big house recovered, Maggie and Emma would go back to Ryder and Kase.

"She is. She trusts the hell out of you."

"Daddy, you cussed."

"I did. Sorry, baby girl." Wat rolled his eyes and winked.

Naomi tsked, but then flopped down on the floor on her back. "So hungry."

"Is your daddy starving you?" Tygh teased.

Naomi nodded, so dramatic. "Bueno to death."

"I'll make sure you get extra noodles, mi'ja," Wat said.

Naomi grinned at Tygh. "He loves me very much."

"He really does." He let go of Maggie with one hand to fist-bump her.

"I really love you too, Mr. Tygh. Let's have soup!"

He swallowed hard but passed it off. "You got it, baby girl. Let's do it." He rose, lifting Maggie and letting Wat come to grab Emma. They all trooped to the kitchen, where there was chicken noodle soup and ham and cheese sandwiches.

"Looks great, Wat."

"Thank you. I aim to please, huh?"

"You do." It was simple, but it was super nice to not eat a sandwich in the barn or hanging over the sink.

Watson smiled at him, and that eye contact didn't feel... simply friendly. Wishful thinking, right? It had to be. But man, he wanted more.

But if wishes were horses, they'd all ride away, right?

And God knew, his life had never worked like that, so why should it now?

Chapter Eleven

L iving with Tygh was surprisingly easy. Wat held Zoom lessons for the kids, played with the babies, and fed everyone. Naomi followed the dogs around, Maggie followed Tygh around, and Emma spent most of her time in a sling against his chest.

That little one needed food and contact, and she was going to get it.

And there was something about Tygh... it was... the man hadn't seemed friendly at first, but then he was exceptional with Naomi, had opened his home to them without hesitation, and was... fun.

They played cards for hours, they both watched weird competition shows on TV, and were morning people.

It was the oddest situation, but it was also normal. Simply the most normal thing ever.

If only Wat could stop thinking about what it might be like to kiss him.

Was that weird? It felt weird, but it also felt as if it were a natural progression. Michelle had always teased him that at least one of his freebie fives was a dude, so he so bi. He'd always laughed, but these days...

Hell, these days he was happy when he could sneak off for a private shower and he got a hard-on. He'd worried that part of him was broken, and if it was Tygh he focused on, so be it.

Speaking of which, he was just pulling orange juice out of the fridge when Tygh walked in, pajama pants slung low, feet and chest bare despite the chill that was starting to invade the morning air these days, hair standing up in short, messy spikes.

"Good morning, sunshine. Coffee?" Orange juice? Snuggle?

"God, yes." Tygh slumped down into a chair at the kitchen table.

He poured a cup and handed it over. "How'd you sleep?"

"Mmmph." Tygh took a long sip. "Hot. Hot hot. Uh. I slept. How are you?"

"Good. I woke up at four and fed Emma and got a long shower after she went back down." That was enough.

"That doesn't sound like a lot of sleep." Tygh blinked at him.

"No? Well, who was up with Naomi when Biscuit farted in her face last night and she cried?"

Tygh flushed. "Me. Since my dog was the criminal..."

"See? It's a trade-off."

Chuckling, Tygh stirred sugar into his coffee before taking another sip. "True enough. I like that."

"Me too. I can't tell you how—"

"Papi! Papi!" Maggie's shriek was wild, and Wat ran in to get her and swooped her up before she woke Naomi up. "No! No! Papi!"

As soon as Tygh appeared, she started struggling and reaching for him. "Papi! PAPI!"

"Hey. Hey. Maggie Mae. I got you." Tygh gave him a

slightly panicked look but took Maggie, holding her to his chest and rocking her. "I'm here."

"Papi," she sobbed, clinging to him. "Papi."

"She must have had a nightmare. She's not feverish."

"She must have." Tygh kissed the top of her head. "Breathe for me, baby girl. You're okay. It's okay."

He would bet Tygh used that tone with injured animals. Little kids had that in common with dogs and horses. It wasn't the words. It was the voice and the body language and the promise of relief from whatever was hurting them. Tygh had that down pat.

She relaxed for him, going still and heavy in his arms.

"There. There you are. Better. You want a bottle?"

Her thumb crept into her lips, but she nodded.

He shook his head at Tygh when he reached for it. Better to let her now and work on getting her to stop in a few weeks.

Tygh sat back down with her, humming in his deep, rumbly voice, and he went to make a bottle for her.

She took it from him with a smile when he brought it over, holding it with so much more strength. He breathed a sigh of relief. Night terrors sucked, but she was rebounding fast, and she was eating so well. When he made breakfast for Tygh, he would make her an egg too.

She caught Watson's gaze, then patted Tygh's chest.

"Is that your Tygh?" he asked, and she pulled the nipple from her mouth.

"No. Papi."

Well, then.

That was going to be interesting when she went back to Ryder and Kase's house.

Tygh grinned. "That's my girl."

Lord. He patted Emma's back as she started to fuss. "Let me go see if she needs changing."

"Do you need me to do anything?"

"Just hang out with Maggie for a minute?"

"That I can do."

He went to change Emma on his bed, getting her all dry and happy. She kicked and wiggled, exercising her baby body.

He grabbed her little feet and started bicycling her legs, making her giggle. She stared up at him, her mouth working as she blew bubbles, and she reached for him with her bitty hands.

"Someone loved you. What happened to you, baby girl? I wish we knew. But then again, maybe not. Maybe it's better if no one can ever tell you." He just talked to her all the time, getting her used to hearing nuance and the rise and fall of language. "It doesn't matter, because you are loved now."

"Who are you talking to?" Naomi came in, frowning. "Oh, her."

"Yeah, Emma. Is that okay with you?"

"No. You love her more than me?"

He glanced over at his baby girl. "What? No! Love isn't pie. Because I love her, doesn't mean that I don't love you more than life!"

"You promise? You hold her more than me."

"You weigh a lot more than her, baby."

"But I'm your baby."

"You are. And I love you so much I can hardly breathe sometimes. But Emma has had a bad time too, and she needs to know there are good people. How about I see if Tygh will watch Emma for a bit today while we sit on the couch and have a movie?"

She grinned at him. "For reals?"

"For reals." He kissed her cheek. "You know, if you ever need attention, you just have to say. I love hanging out with you." And even though he was in love with these two little girls, his baby was his heartbeat.

"I love you too, Daddy. I just got sad." She looked so happy now. "What's for breakfast?"

"Eggs?"

She made a face, and he remembered Tygh saying he could make pancakes.

"Maybe we can ask Tygh to cook?"

"Oh. I bet he can make pancakes!" She went bouncing off. "Papa Tygh!"

Papa Tygh. God help him when this all dissolved like a soap bubble. He got Emma all snapped up, lifting her to put her back in her sling. But he brought her little carrier seat too, so she could sit without him.

She curled into him, fingers fisted in his sweatshirt.

Damn, he was screwed.

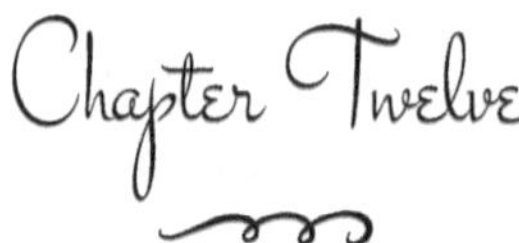

Chapter Twelve

<*How's it going, Boss?*>

Tygh texted Ryder on the eighth day, just checking in. It was like a revolving door over there. Someone would test negative and move to the non-sickie part of the house, and someone else would get worse.

<*Oh god. This is insane. Granny is still hacking, Elijah just tested positive, and Gram is refusing to leave their side of the house. You?*>

<*Everyone is well. The girls are getting attached.*> He thought it was important for Ryder to know that. Shit, Maggie was calling him Papi.

<*Yeah? Is that problematic? I can see if Jennifer can find another foster family.*>

<*No.*> That was automatic, and to his surprise, fierce in his heart. <*No, it's okay. I wanted you to know is all*>

<*It's fine. They need to know they're part of a family. Jennifer knows they're with you and Watson.*>

<*Cool. I'll keep you posted.*> It cracked him up how Ryder texted everything. Kase would rather call.

Which, speak of the devil. His phone rang moments later, Kase's name coming up.

"Hello?"

"Hey, Tygh." Kase sounded like he'd swallowed a frog. "I just got off the phone with Jennifer. She wants to do the weekly check-in on the girls. Do you think Wat would be willing to take that call?"

"I'm sure he would." That made sense, right? Wat was the one who was trained to know if the girls were developing and settling and stuff. "He's teaching until three today. Dani is back in the Zoom world."

"Okay, cool. I appreciate it."

"How are you feeling, man?"

"Like crap. I swear, my lungs feel like they have lead weights in them. But the doc got us on that pax-whosit, so we're hanging in. That stuff leaves a poo taste in your mouth, though."

"Sounds like something I want to avoid. How's Nell?"

"Mad as hell that she has to stay quiet and rest. She and Dani both miss y'all fierce. Dani is very worried about Miss M."

"Gareth reports all is healing well, and no one else has come in injured since the season is slowing down. Knock on wood."

"Yeah, your mouth to God's ears," Kase said. "I'll tell Jennifer to text Wat then, and pick a time after three."

"You got it."

"You guys need anything?" Kase asked.

"I put in another order with Ryder last night." Diapers went fast. So did formula with Miss Emma. Maggie was still supplementing with rice cereal and other stuff, but she was really getting into real food, which Wat said proved she'd been eating well before all the shit went down, whatever it was.

She was such a fighter. He adored her.

"Good deal. Are y'all okay? Living the good life?" Kase started coughing again, the sound rough and raw.

"We are. We're doing good, I promise. You need to rest, buddy. You sound like hell." He sent a little note of thanks to the universe that he hadn't come down with it. Two negative tests later.

"I'm just tickled the babies are safe with y'all. They needed immediate love, and our hands are filled."

"They are. And we got this, Kase." He'd taken the foster training the last time the ranch employees had done it, and God knew he understood the system from the kid's side.

"Papa Tygh, can I go see the goats?" Naomi was right there at his elbow. She was supposed to be doing her schooling...

"Aren't you supposed to be in school?" He pulled her close for a hug.

"I'll let you go," Kase said. "Gonna go try not to expire."

"Good deal, man." He hung up, smiling down at Naomi. "What's your dad up to?"

"Changing the babies. We're having quiet time. My arm itches." She showed him her stump, which had a fuzzy purple sock on it. It was healed up now, but sensitive to the cold, so she "decorated" it. "Can you check it?"

"Sure, kiddo." He sat her down and peeled back the sock, checking for any redness or scabs. Then he felt it, making sure it wasn't hot and that the skin wasn't raised or rough anywhere. "Feels fine. I bet it's just an itchy day."

Her arm was looking pretty good, really. The surgeon had done a good job of working on it so it would fit a prosthetic. He just hated that it had taken so many surgeries for her.

"I have that bag balm. You want some?"

"Please." She giggled and glanced up at him. "The end of my arm looks a little like a bag, huh? See?"

She bent her elbow and relaxed the muscles, letting it dangle.

He chuckled. "That's a neat trick." He got up to get the balm he used on every dry, rough, or itchy skin.

She followed him, skipping and happy, singing her song. Naomi was pretty well-adjusted for a kid who'd been through as much as she had. That came from her having a parent she knew loved the hell out of her.

She was a basically joyous child, and she adored her father. How could he resist that?

"Here we go." He rubbed salve into the stump, happy to help.

"Oh, yay! Thank you." She beamed at him, slipping the sock back on. "Daddy was right, you do rock."

"You're welcome, kiddo. So, goats, huh? That's not exactly quiet."

"Emma and Maggie needed a nap. I colored, but I want to be outside."

"Okay." He texted Wat. *<OK if I take Naomi to the goat pen?>*

<Sure. Thanks. She starts bugging u, holler>

<Will do> She was really a lot like Dani. She did was she was told, and she took such joy in the animals.

She was more active than her counterpart—more sure of herself, and that grew every day. Naomi was turning from a shy child to a confident little girl who was a force of nature.

"Hello, goaties!" Naomi called as they walked up to the pen. "How are you today? I'm here to give you scritches."

There was a great chorus of bleating, and his goats all rushed to the fence to greet her. They did love having a kid around. Pun intended. God, he cracked himself up.

"You guys be good. No knocking her down."

"I can get back up," Naomi said loftily.

"But they can also learn to behave." He winked at her, then opened the gate.

"True. That's important, huh? For babies, too." Oh, that question felt heavy...

"It takes human babies longer, to be sure. They need so much more help." He chose his words with care while he caught Turkeybutt Lovejoy before she could land on Naomi straight out of a happy sideways leap. "Goats are born with their eyes open, able to stand. Human babies can't do that, so it seems like they need a lot more attention than more grown-up kids." He gave her a sideways glance. "But more grown-up kids can ask for what they need."

"Yeah? Like what?" She went up to Grover and started scratching around his horns.

"Like if they need hugs or maybe some time out with their dad?" She and Wat maybe needed to go into town and go to the library. He should suggest it to Wat, offer to watch the littles. They weren't in quarantine, after all. Just not going to the big ranch.

Yeah, that was a good idea. Wat could take her to lunch too.

"Uh-huh. Because sometimes I worry that he thinks the babies are neater than me. I'm neat, huh? Still?"

"You are super neat, kiddo." He poured a little pellet feed into a metal bowl. "Want to give everyone a treat? Just a handful each."

Naomi gave him a look. "A you handful or a me handful?"

"A you handful is fine. And I'll hold the bowl so they don't overwhelm you."

"Thank you. Do you think I should get a new hand? Daddy says I can, but... do you think I need one?"

"Well, you wouldn't have to wear it every day if you didn't want to, but I bet it would make some things easier. It might make some things harder. But you're a smart one, and you can learn to use it." He wanted to encourage without pushing, and he understood all of a sudden why Wat said parenting was hard.

"Yeah. I don't know. I don't want more doctors. Maybe when I'm ten."

"I can see that. You've been through a lot." He watched her feed voracious baby goats. They nibbled food out of her hand, then nibbled at her shirt, seeing if it was edible, setting off a spate of giggles.

"They smell the bag balm, I bet. It smells like their mom."

"I smell like a goat?" Her laughter rang out. "Maa! Maa!"

That set off a round of goat noise, the youngest ones leaping and kicking all over the pen.

"So silly!" She just giggled like a loon, and he had to laugh, because her joy was infectious.

"Okay. Want to go see someone super special?"

"Ooh... yes please." Her eyes lit up, shining for him from under her copper curls.

"Okay, come on. I wanted you to get a little more used to the animals before you met her, because she's had a tough time." He led her into the cool darkness of the barn, and he heard Beatrice the chicken start to cluck in that warning way. She took her job guarding the quarantined animals very seriously, and Bobette the alpaca was still very new and recovering.

"What's wrong with her, Papa Tygh?" she whispered.

"She was left on an abandoned farm to starve, and her feet got really messed up. We're working on healing them and getting her back to a normal weight. Hey, Bobbie girl. How are you?" He kept his voice soft, friendly. And he didn't make any sudden moves.

She came up to the fence, eyes focused on Naomi, dancing and worried.

"She's just here to say hi, lady. She's a good one. You'll like her. Say hi, Naomi, but keep it low and easy, okay? She's been really scared for a long time."

Naomi sucked in a breath but nodded nice and slow. "Hi, Bobbie. I'm Naomi. I want to be friends." She didn't reach out, and Tygh was super pleased with her restraint. "I'm sorry that someone was mean to you. I promise I will never be mean."

"That's a good promise, Naomi. Sometimes it's hard when these guys fight you out of fear, and you have to remember it's not their fault and that you still have to be patient." He gave her a sideways look. "Kind of like babies."

"It's easier with animals," she said immediately. "She has such pretty eyes."

"She does. I love her eyelashes." Okay, enough of pushing about the babies for now. He'd convince Wat to have a daddy-daughter day this week. It was only fair. He could keep the littles. How hard would it be to strap Emma to his chest and work away?

Wat did it all the time. He would have to be careful not to get her bitten or kicked.

It was only for a couple of hours. Lunch and library—nothing huge. Hell, he could stay in the house and work on paying bills or something.

He talked to Bobette, and soon enough she was nosing over the gate, sniffing Naomi and taking a treat from him.

"So what's wrong with her feet?" Naomi whispered.

"Well, unlike a horse, alpacas have soft feet and toenails. They need to be trimmed every six weeks or so. Hers were not, and two of them got infected. We call it impacted."

"Oh..." She frowned. "I know *infected*. It hurts."

"It does. So you get it, right? How she's a little unhappy."

"That's so sad. How do I help?"

"Just teach her that people can be good, and I'll do the rest." She was such a good kid. She really was. He liked her a hell of a lot, and he'd never thought he and kids would get along.

"Okay. Can Dani and Nell come play soon? It's been a kagillion years."

"Soon. A few people at the big house are still really sick, though Dani and Nell are okay now and are on the other side of the house." That had to be a living hell, but this virus wasn't something to mess with.

"Oh yeah. We have school together."

"Yeah. Well, soon they can keep you company." He hoped. This shit needed to run its course. He wanted to get back to work.

"Yes. We need to run and play and dress up for Halloween."

God, was it almost Halloween? Holy crap. "We do. I need to get the hay wagon ready for the carnival. Did you know we have hayrides?"

"What's that? Is it fun?"

"We load a wagon up with hay and the horses pull us around while we're sitting in it. It's a hoot." He winked at her, easing her away from Bobbie. "I just need to give her some medicine."

"Okay. I'll sit over here and watch so I can learn how to do it." She climbed up on a hay bale.

"Good idea. So I just measure some of this powder out." He showed her the screw-top jar with the antibiotics in it. "And I put it in her feed. I don't give her a shot because she's a little jittery that way, and I don't want to scare her. As long as the powder works, I won't have to."

"Is the shot better?" Smart girl!

"It would work faster, yes. But there are all sorts of problems, from making her afraid of me, to making her feel sicker in the short term while her body fights the antibiotic and makes her very tired. I bet you know that feeling." She'd had more than her share of shots and antibiotics, he would guess.

She frowned. "Uh huh. Makes me feel icky."

"Exactly. This is easier on her body. Whatever she needs to be able to feel better."

"I like that. You're a good doctor. Sometimes doctors don't care how you feel."

"Sometimes they don't," Tygh agreed. "And sometimes they can't."

"That's what Daddy says. Is that a chicken?"

"Yep." He grinned at Beatrice, who had come out to say hi. "She guards the sick animals."

"Does that mean she pecks?"

He'd love to say no, but that would be a lie.

"She does sometimes."

"I'll stay over here."

He laughed. "Okay. I'll introduce you to some friendlier ones. And to our barn cat Geo if I can find him." Geo only had three legs, so he would bet he and Naomi became fast friends. He hoped Geo would give her someone to see herself in. "In fact, there's a jar of cat treats on that shelf right there. Can you reach it?"

"Prob'ly." She climbed up on the hay bale, stretching up tall. She balanced pretty well, rocking on her toes.

"Careful. Okay, now grab it down and shake it."

She did, and a smoky gray form came shooting out from one of the stalls, tail up as it ran. Geo had a distinctive gallumph to his gait with that missing leg, but it never really seemed to slow him down, and he'd managed to stay out of the way of coyotes and such, so he was a survivor.

"It's a kitty! Hey, kitty! I've got a nummy!" She shook the jar again.

Geo was all over her in seconds, jumping up on the hay to rub on her legs.

"Can you get the jar open?" Everything in the barn had to go in mouse-proof containers, but that might be hard for her to do.

She frowned and wrapped her arm around the jar, and used her hand to unscrew it. It was slow going, but he didn't push her.

"There!"

"Way to go! Okay, you can give him a couple of treats now." Geo purred up a storm, his tail waving back and forth at the tip.

She fed him, grinning at Geo and jabbering. Geo listened for a bit, headbutted her, then wandered off with his tail held high.

"He had three legs," Naomi said.

"He does. He had one get caught in a trap. Not on my land, but where he used to live."

"Oh. My momma had hold of mine. She wouldn't let go, even when I screamed."

Jesus. Her mom must have literally had a death grip on her. "I'm sorry, kiddo. That had to be bad. I'm very proud of you for not giving up."

"Daddy says that I am his brave girl. Don't tell him, but I was just little, and the fireman came and saved me. I wasn't brave at all."

He had to go give her a hug for that. "You're braver than you think, kiddo. Trust me." He kissed the top of her head.

"I love you too, Papa Tygh."

The back door opened, and Wat poked his head out. "Time for school again, miss. Come on."

"Darn it," she muttered.

"Come on, kiddo. It's time for me to take my afternoon siesta, anyway." Because he was turning into a lazy butthead. But he kind of looked forward to it.

"You and the babies." She winked at him. "I'll tell Maggie you're coming."

"She'll want to sleep on my chest." She loved to snuggle with him in his recliner.

"You're her Papa. Emma's too. She's just needing to hear Daddy's heartbeat so she can grow better."

He stared at her, because it sounded so good that his heart clenched. But she wasn't his, was she? Not really.

"Papa! Papa? PAPA?" Maggie stared out of the storm door, making grabby hands, her dark eyes focused.

"See? Her papa. Mine too, and the baby's. Come on, Papa Tygh." She took his hand to pull him inside, and he followed, feeling like he'd been hit between the eyes with an axe.

Okay, so he was Papa Tygh.

Now how the hell could he let all these little girls go back to the ranch?

Chapter Thirteen

Wat's phone rang when he was on his way back to Tygh's from a trip into town, and he fumbled for the hands-free button, which was kind of hidden behind the two great big coffee cups. He'd taken Naomi to the library, where they'd done a craft all about fall leaves, and then checked out a whole shelf of books.

She'd loved the sandwich and soup combo at the coffee shop, but even more, she'd liked picking out a coffee and pastry for "Papa Tygh". How sweet was that?

Well, the coffee was pretty sweet. He would bet Tygh added an espresso pod to it at the house.

"Hello?" Wat checked the rearview, but Naomi had on her headphones while she watched *Bake Squad* on her TV monitor.

"Hey, Wat. Ryder. We got the all-clear. The ranch is safe again, and we had a cleaning crew come in and sanitize every-thing, including the learning area."

"Excellent! Congratulations." And also, dammit. He had found a rhythm with Tygh, and they had bonded with the girls.

"Yeah. It's about damn time. So anyway, you can come back to work in-person on Monday. Dani and Nell have missed you two a lot." Ryder chuckled. "And no one will miss Halloween."

"Oh, thank goodness. Naomi is ready, and Tygh and I bought Maggie and Emma princess onesies." One icy blue and one icy pink. So cute. Maybe he'd get them a different one for the whole week before Halloween.

"Yeah? Are they adorbs?" Ryder sounded like he was typing, so that was a good sign, if he was feeling up to working in the office. "So I was reading Jennifer's summary of your call. We need to have a family meeting, I think."

"Oh?" Had he done something wrong? Surely not...

"That's very cautious of you." That warm chuckle spoke volumes. "No one is in trouble, but I do want to touch base with you and with Tygh before we do anything rash."

"Okay..." He had no idea what to say. "Tell me when."

"I'll have Kase set it up. He's feeling human again, so he'll get it all together."

"Okay. I—I have to tell you, I'm worried, man. Have I screwed up?"

"Not one little bit, Wat. But I think we need to be aware that the girls have been with you for a pretty good chunk, and they don't really know us." Ryder paused, and he let the man think. "It might not mean anything, but I just want to get face-to-face and chat about what we do next."

"That's understandable." And he wanted to talk to Tygh. Hell, he needed to get with Tygh, because...

Because it was the right thing to do. They'd been throwing themselves into taking care of these kids, and Naomi called them sisters, called Tygh Papa... How was he supposed to put a crowbar into that and pry it apart now?

And did he even want to?

Tygh was... Tygh made him feel things he didn't know if he wanted to. He found himself reluctant to go to bed and leave Tygh in the living room. He loved the way Tygh talked to Naomi, how Maggie loved him, how Emma turned to listen to him when he talked.

Tygh was a force of nature, and he was damned if he knew what to do about it.

"Good deal. Don't worry yourself so much. It's all good."

"Got it. I'm just coming back from town—"

"Well, no meetings will happen until Monday. But if you want to do Halloween stuff, we're all hoping to start tomorrow."

Which was Sunday. Okay, cool.

"I'll bring Naomi over to help and visit. She'll be excited." But he didn't want to bring the babies over and drop them off.

"Dani and Nell will be too. All right. Holler if you all need anything, huh? I can't tell you how much I appreciate all you've done." Ryder blew out a breath. "Okay. See you tomorrow, then."

"All right. Thanks." He hung up, trying not to freak out. His heart was pounding a million miles an hour. What if they'd made a complete mess of this foster thing? He couldn't afford to get fired. Not now, when Naomi was feeling stable and he was just starting to pay off some debt.

He glanced in the rearview again, but Naomi was totally focused on her movie, which was great. That way she wasn't asking questions.

"Siri, call Dad." His dad was a stable guy, one of the best humans on earth, and always full of good advice.

"Hello? Wat! How are you doing, mi'jo?"

"Oh, Dad... I think I've gotten myself into a lot of trouble." *And I don't know how to get out of it. I don't even know for sure if I understand what it is...*

All he knew was that he wanted to stay—with the little girls.

With Tygh.

"What's wrong? Do we need to come? Is everything okay with Naomi?"

"She's fine. She's doing really well, in fact. That's one of the reasons I don't want to mess up."

"Okay." Dad paused, always measuring his words. "Why don't you fill me in?"

"I— Dad, you know how I told you the main house got sick, and we are staying across the street with Tygh? Dr. Korden?" God, that was weird to say.

"Yeah. I hope everyone is recovering? You didn't catch it, did you?" Dad's concern was like a balm.

"No. No, we're fine. It's just... Emma needs constant contact, and Maggie wakes up calling for Tygh, and Dad, I don't want to— I'm a little in love..."

"In love with the girls? That's not unusual, son. I mean, they're sweet babies. I love all the pictures you sent."

"But I don't want to take them back." And he'd never felt like that before, like he was... theirs. "I don't want to go back."

"Ah." Dad paused again, and he could hear the tapping noise that meant Dad was rapping his fingers on the table while he thought. "What does Naomi think?"

"She calls Tygh 'Papa Tygh' and the babies her sisters. I should have been more distant, more objective, but I can't be."

"Oh, wow. So it's not just you. It's this Tygh fella too, huh?" Dad tched. "That's a situation, son."

"It's more than that." But how did he tell his dad that he was... feeling things about Tygh? He was—had been— married to the perfect woman. To the mother of his child, and now...

"Lay it on me." Dad didn't pull punches. "I mean it's a little early for a beer, but I have a burrito."

"I—I really care for him." He couldn't believe he was saying that. Out loud. To his father.

"For who? You mean the vet guy?" Dad's voice went up a little, but not alarmingly so.

"Yeah. His name's Tygh." God, help him. He was going to die. "I'm just being a dipshit."

Except he wasn't. He thought he actually… cared about Tygh. In a holding hands sort of way.

How did guys even date?

"Huh." Now he could tell Dad was chewing that over because he could hear his dad taking a big bite of burrito and chomping, probably to keep himself from blurting out something wild. Then Dad cleared his throat. "Well, that's different for you for sure, son, but that doesn't mean you're a dipshit if that's what you feel."

"I—I feel like I'm being unreasonable." His heart was telling him that he didn't do this. Had he lusted after a guy before? Sure. Hell, Michelle had teased him for years about having Channing Tatum on his freebie five, but that was sex.

"Don't discount your feelings for that, Wat." His dad chuckled. "Isn't your generation supposed to be like, less about gender? I see it on Facebook all the time."

"Oh, look Mr. Gen-X-I-Don't-Care-About-Anything-And-I-Wore-Eyeliner-To-Clubs-I'm-on-Insta." His cheeks were on fire, though. Christ, was this happening?

"You should see your mother. She's dancing with impatience to talk to you. Do you want her input too?" That was Dad-speak for *okay, I'm in over my head and I just got called out for it.*

"Sure. Sure, put her on." Like she hadn't been listening. Fuck.

"Cool." Dad handed off the phone like his ass was on fire, because Mom was right there in seconds.

"So what's all this now?"

"You were on speaker." He chuckled and shook his head. "You heard it all."

"I did. Are you going to try and adopt the new babies? They're both beautiful. Can you afford to raise them both?"

How the hell did he know? He wasn't dead broke—in fact, he had a college fund for Naomi from Michelle's insurance—but he was just a teacher. Who worked on a ranch. And he had a tiny house. Tygh had room, but that was ridiculous. That Tygh would let them stay.

"I'm not trying to burst your bubble, son, you know that, but you have a baby of your own to take care of, and she has special needs. Prosthetics are expensive."

He wasn't sure what trying to bust his bubble might look like, which wasn't fair. Mom worried, and she didn't want his life to be harder, but still—

Suddenly he realized she was still rambling on, and he wasn't listening, and it didn't matter if he listened or answered because she had to vomit up all this panic that had a basis in "why did you leave home" and "why did you go to Michelle's parents" and "let us help you and make sure nothing hurts you ever again".

"Mom, sorry, but traffic just got bad. I have to focus. Love you. Bye." He hung up, grinning as he caught sight of the single pickup heading the opposite way on the two-lane highway.

See? Traffic. Totally not a lie, right, Michelle?

He swore he could hear her laughing.

His phone chimed with a text, and he saw it pop up on the touchscreen of the car. *<Butthead>*

He chuckled. Maybe. But really, the next person he needed to talk to was Naomi. And then Tygh. Good thing he'd bought all the stuff for stacked enchiladas, which would be tostadas for Naomi, or flying saucers as she called them. The green chile was still a little hot for her.

She did like the smell, at least. That gave him faith that there was a New Mexican in her somewhere. She would grow into it. Michelle had let her get away with not having it in her baby bottle, which was what his mom swore she'd done to him.

He pulled in at Tygh's, the motion automatic now, instead of turning into the ranch. How had that happened in two weeks?

"We're home, Daddy! I want to read to the puppies. They would let me. They like reading." She wiggled and unfastened her car seat as soon as they parked.

"You know it." In fact, when Biscuit and Tater saw Naomi with a book in her hand now, they went right to the designated *"reading blanket"* to lie down and let her prop up on them. That was love. "Supper is flying saucers."

"Yaaay!" She bounced out of the car, grabbing her bag of books. He had the rest in his tote, which he took in, as well as the groceries.

"Need a hand?" Tygh met him at the kitchen door, grabbing the books.

"Papa Tygh! I got you a coffee and a bear claw!" Naomi got her hug and thank you before she disappeared.

"Hey. How was your day?" *How are the babies? Did you miss us? Did Ryder call you? Am I packing up my car in the morning?*

"Good. I got a lot done. Which I guess is good, since we're back to work at the ranch Monday, huh?" Tygh's back was to him, so he couldn't tell if that was good or bad or indifferent.

"Yeah." He didn't know what to say, how to start a conversation that basically went, "Can I move into your house and raise babies with you?"

"So." Tygh turned to face him, leaning against the counter where he'd set the books. "We need to talk about all this, huh?"

"We do. I want to. Talk, I mean. This is bigger than I'd thought it was going to be..." And he hoped it was for Tygh too.

Tygh's eyelines crinkled up, and his lips curved. "Yeah, I was just thinking the same thing. I mean— Maggie calls me Papa. How am I supposed to just pretend that's not important?"

"So does Naomi. They want to have a family meeting Monday. I want—" No. No, that wasn't how this worked. "What do you want?"

"Well, I was thinking. I got plenty of room here. There's no reason you and Naomi and the girls have to go back to the ranch. I mean, I'm foster certified too." Tygh watched him, those dark eyes not giving a lot away, but there was a seriousness to them that made his heart beat hard. "What were you thinking?"

"That we're creating a family." As soon as he said it, he worried on it, because they had been together for two weeks.

Fourteen days.

How was that a family?

Tygh nodded, but he stayed watchful, his chin set. "What does Naomi want to do?"

"I need to speak to her, but I wasn't even floating the idea without speaking to you. It is your home."

Tygh spread his hands. "It's much fuller with you here. I want you all to stay. *All* of you." Tygh chuckled, shaking his head. "I don't even know what that will mean, but it's true."

"I— Okay. Then should we talk to Naomi?"

"Talk to me about what, Daddy?"

Well, fuck.

"Come here, baby girl. Did you read the dogs a story?" He held out a hand to his daughter.

"Uh-huh. They love books about puppies. Did you know that, Papa Tygh?"

"I might have read them a couple over the years." Tygh looked at Naomi like she hung the moon. "They also like books about kitties, but not in the same way."

"Yeah? I wonder if Geo would like me to read... What did you want to talk about?"

"Well, no one is sick over at the big house anymore. So Mr. Ryder wants to know if we're going to come back to live."

"Oh." She stared at him and Tygh. "Do I get a vote?"

He nodded. "You do."

He wasn't sure what, exactly, she was going to say, but he was nervous.

"Okay. So, I want to stay here with Daddy, Papa Tygh, the animals, and my sisters in my room, and I want to go to school with Dani and Nell."

Well, that was clear.

"Also, I don't want a possisus yet. I like my different fancy socks."

"Okay. Well, we can let you grow up a little more." The doctors had said she might function better without one while she was still having growth spurts, but he would go where the wind took him there.

"Uh-huh. Do you need help with supper?"

"Not right now."

"Can I go watch a show with Maggie?"

"I'll come get you guys set up." Tygh sounded amused as hell.

He stood there for a second, then started working on the chicken for supper. His hands were shaking a bit, so he worked at not cutting anything important off.

"You okay?" Tygh walked back into the kitchen, steering the dogs away from him. Wat hadn't even noticed them until now.

"I am. I didn't realize how nervous I was until right now." Which was crazy, because he'd been fucking nuts.

"Well, you did great with her." Tygh leaned on the counter next to him, arms behind him to hold him up. "Are you good with it? Staying? It's going to be a lot of work."

"It is, but—we've got something working here. Maggie needs you most, but Naomi and Emma do too. And it's not a terrible commute…" And he could have the little ones in with him, free up the house for the ranch, and see Tygh more often.

"We do." Tygh gave him a sideways kind of look. "I'm—" He cleared his throat. "Full disclosure, then, Wat. You probably ought to know that I'm gay."

"And I—I know. I've never been with a man, and I don't know how to…date one, but… if you think that you might want to—" *God, Watson. Shut up. Shut right the fuck up before he decides you had a stroke.*

Tygh tilted his head. "Yeah? Well, we can work on that a little at a time. We'll have to get back into the swing of working and all first, right?" Tygh nudged him with an elbow. "But at least you get to watch Maggie and Emma during the day, so that won't be a terrible transition."

"And you'll be able to put Maggie down for her nap. She needs you." Wat tried on a smile. "You didn't run screaming. That's good."

Tygh snorted. "I ain't smart enough for that, I guess. And I'm a foster kid, Wat. I want to give them a good place to grow up. I know they'd be loved with Ryder and Kase, but I also know I'm already in so deep I can't let go." Tygh stood away from the counter, spreading his hands. "Is that nuts?"

"I have a daughter, I'm a school teacher, and I'm a guy that's got feelings for a man, real feelings that I want to act on for the first time. I think I win the top nut award."

"Oh, don't make me get that for you for Christmas." Tygh laughed out loud, startling the dogs. "Okay, what can I help you do?"

"I was thinking chicken enchiladas, so I'm poaching the

chicken in the broth. Naomi will want flying saucers, but I'm craving green chile."

"I am always ready for green chile. Though my grandma was way better at red. She made a red chile gravy to die for. She would roll the enchiladas, not stack them, but I still always got an egg on top." There was something so wistful about all that, and—

"But you were a foster kid?"

Tygh stiffened. "My grandma died when I was six and a half."

"I'm sorry. I don't mean to pry." He wouldn't hurt Tygh for anything, and some things were just private. "Forgive me, huh? I love red, green, and Christmas. Just so long as there's chile."

"No, it's fine. Just a bad memory. And not for when we're celebrating making this... more permanent." Tygh was smiling again, those dark eyes all lit up.

"Yeah. Yeah, do you think the Chiaras will approve? I mean, we did just sort of abscond with the girls."

"They asked you to do it. We had permission." Tygh sounded so sure, confident enough that he felt his spine lengthen and his shoulders drop from around his ears.

"Okay, good. So when we meet with them, we just say..."

"We tell them what we decided, and they nod and smile. I guarantee, they'll be good with it. We might have to negotiate your salary some since you're living offsite."

"I'm hoping so. We're right here, and this gives them more room to help, right?"

"It does. Someone else can have the little house, and we can do this." Tygh clapped him on the shoulder, the touch lingering a moment. "You want me to make the eggs, just holler."

"I'd love that. It's the best part, you know? My mom

makes a good enchilada." His folks were going to be... fascinated by Tygh.

"Yeah? You get along with your folks well?" Tygh glanced at him, his curiosity plain.

"I do. I mean, they're parents, right? We have our sandpaper places with each other, but we're good. My dad is an engineer, and my mom works in HR for the state health department. Michelle—that was my wife—she used to say we were painfully normal, unlike her family."

"Yeah? What's her family like?" Tygh seemed to remember his pastry, and he took a big bite.

"Her mother is a folk singer—sort of famous in the festival circuits—and her father is an inventor. He makes these wild things—the kind of stuff that ends up on *The Shark Tank* and *As Seen on TV*. They're totally off-piste, but amazing too."

"Wow." That had Tygh blinking hard. "That's kind of amazing."

"They are. And they were so selfless when Michelle passed, but we finally had to move on and get our own place again." His lips twisted. "I guess we're just not good at living alone."

"Let me tell you. Even if you are, it doesn't mean you want to."

"No. No, and it's hard to explain, but we were just..." How to explain this? "Instead of healing, we were... I don't know. Opening each other up."

"Like constantly picking at a healing wound and making it bleed?" Tygh nodded. "It happens. You and Naomi lived. Their girl didn't."

"Yes." He sighed. "They were never evil. They were too kind sometimes."

"Sure. Because together you all have guilt if you try to move forward before someone else is ready."

"Yeah, and I have to. I have Naomi. Michelle died saving

her. I owe it to both of them to keep living." Hell, he owed it to himself.

"You do. Naomi needs to keep growing and learning." Tygh hugged him, which shocked him immobile for a moment. "You aren't doing anything wrong."

He wrapped his arms around Tygh, letting himself just be right there for a second. It wouldn't last—there were children and supper and animals—but he had right now.

And that was really something special.

Chapter Fourteen

Tygh straightened his hat on his head, waiting for Naomi and Wat. He had Maggie in the truck already, and she was singing something nonsense along with her singing bunny rabbit stuffed animal.

"Are you guys coming?" He didn't want to keep Ryder and Kase waiting.

"Sorry, Emma had a poop-splosion, and then Naomi had to pee."

"Daddy!"

"What?" Watson popped Emma in after Naomi crawled in between them. "We need a bigger vehicle."

"We do. I'll talk to Ryder. He gets a ranch discount at a local dealer. We can go SUV." Tygh had plenty of money put back.

"Yeah? I can trade in the baby car. It's in great shape."

"If you're good with that, then sure. I need the truck for work, if I have to hit the road." Tygh liked that they were talking we and us.

"Yeah, and I'm just using mine to toodle. It's not big enough for three kiddos."

"Okay. Cool. Then we'll add that to our list." They had to be able to get three car seats in if they all wanted to go to town in the same vehicle. They headed across the road to the ranch.

They vibrated across the cattle guard, Naomi giggling softly. "It's bouncing my butt."

"It is. Ahhhhhh." Tygh let it shake his voice. His grandma had always told him to say that as they went over a cattle guard. He missed her so bad all of a sudden, the ache hard in his gut.

What would she think about this? Him wanting to raise babies, falling in—falling for a straight widower? A straight-ish widower? He knew Wat had been married to a woman, but the way he looked at Tygh... well, there was something going on there...

He parked in front of the big adobe's kitchen entrance. He would have to work on the ranch most of the day, but tonight, he would take another load of Wat and Naomi's stuff to his place.

Their place.

Naomi was over the moon at the idea of her own room at "Papa's", and he'd already promised to paint it for her this weekend.

He was not allowed to paint over the flowers, but she wanted the other walls to be pink, and she wanted sun and rain clouds on the wall with the flowers. And a unicorn bed.

She was something else.

"Can I go see Minnie?"

"Not without me, kiddo," Tygh told her. "How about you see Nanette and Mookie and Snuffy and Birdie and all while we talk to Ryder and Kase."

"And Dani and Nell will be so happy to see you," Wat put in.

"I *know*! They are my friends!" She squealed, and Maggie

started to cry while Emma started making a sound like a chicken.

"Hey, Maggie Mae. It's okay." He took her out of the car. "We're just visiting with Miss Nanette, huh? She loves wee ones like you."

"Papa." She clung to him like a monkey, and Naomi ran for the house as Wat scooped up Emma.

"I got you, baby girl. I do. I won't leave you here, huh? But I have to work today."

She frowned like she was trying to understand.

"You'll stay with Daddy, though, and Naomi."

"Daddy."

Oh, and Wat missed that! "Yes, baby. Daddy! He's going to keep you while I'm working."

"Daddy!"

Wat came around, bouncing Emma. "Did she say—"

"Uh-huh."

Maggie looked right at Wat. "Daddy."

"That's right!" Wat's eyes shimmered. "Did you hear that?"

"I did. She's wanting to stay with us, and I told her you'd be with her today while I was working. But you gotta stay with Nanette for just a tiny bit, baby, while we meet with the bosses." They started into the house.

"You want a cookie, Maggie? Nanette's got them."

She frowned but let him take her to Nanette.

"Mi'ja! I've missed you!" Nanette seemed exhausted, but her smile was real. "And see how you've both grown!"

"Hey, lady. Would it be better if we just took everyone to the living room?" Tygh didn't want to wear her out. They could watch the littles while they talked.

"I'm going to sit with Alba and all the girls. We're going to make dolls together. Naomi's already in there with Mimi."

"Okay. But you holler if you need us, right Wat?"

"Yep." Wat smiled. "I'll bring Emma. Be right back, Tygh." Wat carried Emma while Maggie went with Nanette, frowning over Nanette's shoulder at him like a tiny thundercloud.

God, that was harsh. He wanted to go take her, hold her, tell her she was fine. Perfect. And he would spend some extra time with her tonight, so she knew—

Tygh jumped half a foot when Ryder clapped him on the back as he walked up. "She's pissed."

"She is, and Emma's been listening to Wat's heartbeat for two weeks solid…"

"Yeah. He's coming back, right? You want coffee? Everything has been sanitized and all."

"Please." He needed to gird his loins for this.

"Excellent. Come on in. Y'all managed to stay healthy?"

"We did. I swear, we dodged a bullet, huh?"

"God, yes." Kase came in, pouring coffee as Ryder waved him to the kitchen table.

Miz Antonia and Jennifer, the social worker, were already there, and he raised an eyebrow. "Family meeting?"

"Yeah. She's sort of a part, huh?"

"Yep." Jennifer grinned. "I need to be in on any decisions about the girls, but it's not dire or anything."

"Sorry!" Wat hurried in. "Emma was fussing."

"She's used to being with you, hmm?" Jennifer asked.

Watson nodded. "We're bonding. She needs to form attachments and to believe she's safe with me."

"She does."

Ryder cleared his throat. "So, I'm getting the vibe that you guys are wanting to keep the girls."

"Yes." Simple as that. He was bonded with them. Watson was bonded with them. Naomi was too.

Kase sipped his coffee, peering at him with bright blue eyes over the rim of the cup. Then he cleared his throat. "That's a big commitment."

"It is." Wat looked at him, and he nodded. "We talked about it, and we're willing to go in on this together."

Eyebrows went up all around the table, but it was Ryder who asked, "What does that mean?"

"Exactly what it sounds like. Watson and Naomi are moving to my place. We have room—there are five bedrooms and three baths. It's a good-sized place."

"I see." That was Miz Antonia. "And is this a relatively permanent arrangement?"

"Well, we still have some stuff to work out, but this isn't as impulsive as it seems." Tygh kept it calm, because he could understand the confusion.

"And I wouldn't disrupt Naomi if it wasn't long-term." Watson sounded as cool as a cucumber. "Our—both Tygh and myself—our first priority is the girls."

"That's the perfect answer," Jennifer said. "I love that you're both certified. There's some paperwork involved..."

"I can't bitch, considering how Kase and I started out," Ryder put in. "But I hope you know we don't want you to feel obligated to do this."

"We're not obligated," Wat started.

Tygh continued. "And we want them. We are a family. Two weeks was enough to know that. Naomi knows they are her sisters."

"We adore them already." Wat grinned at him wryly. "I know it tosses a wrench in some things, but it's just across the road. So I'll still be available as needed for childcare."

"We'll need to talk about your salary," Ryder said.

"Or, we can leave the salary the same and give you a housing allowance just for the time being," Kase said. "That's an addendum instead of being a total renegotiation before next year."

"Oh, I like that." Wat nodded. "I mean, we don't—"

Tygh put a hand on his arm to keep him from blurting out

that they didn't need to give him more money. If they were going to get a new vehicle and such, then yeah they did need it.

Wat glanced at him, then gave a faint smile and nodded. "Well, we can work it out."

Ryder chewed his lower lip. "So what about if you have to go on the road, Tygh?"

Wat's gray-green eyes widened, that gaze alarmed as it met his.

"I imagine we'll have to ask for some help from time to time, but I'm only on call for emergencies these days." Sometimes, he did have to hit the road when there was an injury to a bull or a bucking horse that needed tending on the way back to the ranch, or if one of the working horses needed a retrieval.

"Oh." Wat relaxed visibly.

"Nice save," Kase murmured, and Antonia snorted.

"I'll need to do a home visit, Tygh," Jennifer said, scribbling things on her tablet with her stylus. "I know you've had all the training, but I need to see where the girls are living."

"Of course. You want to do it this morning, I can run you over while Wat works with Dani and Nell." He was the more flexible of the two of them. "If this all works for you and Kase, Ryder." He didn't want to just assume, even though it seemed like a done deal.

"We're fine with it as long as it's what's good for Maggie and Emma. And this gives us more room for at-risk kids, so who am I to complain?" Ryder's grin lit up the room. He was a solid citizen, for sure. "I mean, you have a lot of leeway with your job anyway, and Wat is set up to take care of all the kids, so they'd be with him most of the day anyway." He looked around the table. "Anyone have any reservations?"

"My only other concern is Naomi." Jennifer made more notes. "I know she's been through a lot. Wat, would you object to me talking to her?"

"Not at all." Wat didn't even tense up. "She gave us her

vote this morning. But I understand you need to do your due diligence."

"I appreciate that." She gave them a wry smile. "I love it when folks make it easier for me."

"Your job is hard enough, dear," Antonia said. "Now, I need to know I'll have my time with those girls. Me and Alba both."

"Of course you will." Wat beamed. "They'll need the attention. So will Naomi."

Tygh was damn pleased as well. He didn't want to deprive Maggie and Emma of the family they could have on the ranch. He knew Wat still had people, but he didn't. So how could he not be happy that the grannies wanted to be a part of those little ones' lives?

"I think that sounds grand." He sat back to take a gulp of his coffee, feeling as if he'd jumped a bunch of hurdles.

"Well, why don't I start with the house inspection so Wat can get set up for school?" Jennifer stood, and all of them popped up too. He was nervous, but they might as well get this over with, huh?

"Come on, Miss Jennifer." He stepped back to let her through, and Wat reached out to squeeze his arm, offering silent support. "Be back."

The others all nodded, and he led Jennifer out to the truck. "You want to ride with me?"

"That would be great." She climbed into the passenger side, waiting for him to climb in and get them going.

Tygh tried not to babble. Did she think this was a good idea or a bad one? Her recommendation meant everything.

"So are you good with this, Tygh?"

"Huh? Yeah, of course. I mean, Maggie already calls me Papa. I can't just turn her away."

"It's tough, I know, but I don't want you jumping into something because you think you have to."

"You gonna use my previous interviews against me?" When he'd been getting his certification because he worked with the kids on the ranch on occasion, he and Jennifer had discussed how he'd been a foster kid himself. Shit, he was eager to see how it worked from the other side.

"No, of course not. I just want to make sure this is all good with you. It can bring up some difficult memories."

"The foster system wasn't bad to me, lady. You know that." There had been homes where there were just too many kids, or maybe they didn't have everything they needed, but he'd never been abused, never gone hungry.

"Well, it's good that you want to pay it forward then."

"I do. And... And I want to do it with Wat." Whew. Listen to him, making that kind of statement.

That got him another one of those looks. "And is he willing to entertain the idea? I know he was married to a woman."

"I think he's got it in him, yeah. We'll just have to see." That maybe sounded flip, but it was true. Either way he wasn't gonna turn Wat out. Naomi needed a stable home, and Wat was right there with him being in love with Maggie and Emma. He could totally understand that. "Me and Wat have an agreement, lady, and I swear to you, I will take care of these babies—all three of them."

"I'm glad to hear it, Tygh. I trust you. I really do. But it's my job to ask the hard questions."

"I'm glad they have you on their side too." He knew not everyone was so lucky. He'd seen more than his share of kids come through his foster homes who'd had one too many people turn a blind eye. Hell, look at what had happened to Maggie and Emma, and no one even knew what their names had been.

"They do, but you know that you and Wat have the bulk of the work. Do you think Watson is up for it?"

"I do." In fact, he thought this was just the right time for Wat, who was ready to start life over again and stand up and be counted. He thought Wat felt as if he'd stepped away for a long time to help everyone heal from losing his wife. "You should see him with them, lady. He's just really good with all of the girls. And Naomi is a really well-adjusted kid, in no small part due to him."

He parked in front of his place. "Come on in."

"Yeah, that poor little girl…"

Tygh shook his head. There was nothing poor about his Naomi. That child was fierce, smart, and capable, and he loved her heart and her brain.

"What?" Jennifer raised an eyebrow as she moved past him.

"Well, I mean, she's been through some shit, but she's amazing. I feel awful for what she's been through, but there's no 'poor little' her in there at all. I'll show you her room. I have to go buy her paint colors today."

"Paint colors?"

"Pink. She wants me to paint the girls' room lavender and the playroom yellow."

"She has plans, does she?"

"She does." He flicked on the light in the bedroom. "I've got a new dresser on order for her too, but the bed will work, I think."

"Are you doing cribs for—"

"They're both coming today. Maggie's will transform into a toddler bed when she's ready. The clothes will stay in bins right now, until the anti-tip hardware gets here and installed."

"Good deal. You said the girls would have a different room?"

"Yeah, come on." He showed her where Maggie and Emma would share for now, then where Maggie had been in with him and Emma with Wat.

"I have two big indoor-outdoor dogs, but they're well-trained and used to kids. In fact, they've done library reading dog stuff. I think they must be out running…"

"I can see that you've been baby-proofing."

He nodded. "Maggie's not walking yet, but it's not going to be long at all, so we're just getting started now." That little girl wanted to motivate, wanted to follow her big sister.

"Can I see the bathrooms?"

"Sure. Come on." He took her to the hall bath. "We got one of those little bath things for Emma to go in the tub. My master still has a glass shower door, so we haven't been letting the kids in there at all unattended, even Naomi since she has some balance issues." He was babbling. He knew it. "I swear, I've talked more today than I have in two years."

"Hey, you let me come in, cold turkey. That says a lot. What are the kids eating? Is Maggie still having a bottle exclusively?"

He racked his brain. "She's been doing carrots and peas in puree. Eggs. Cheerios." What else? "Juice. Uh… Oh! Macaroni! She is all over macaroni noodles."

Jennifer cracked up. "Oh, I love that. I bet that is funny as hell."

"It is when you're not wearing it," Tygh teased. "But yeah. And Emma is really starting to catch up with her weight."

"And the constant contact?"

"She's beginning to relax and sleep for more than an hour or two at a time."

"You guys are really working on it." She nodded, walking him back to the front room. "I just need to see the yard."

"Oh, lord. I'll need your recommendations." That was still not even a work in progress.

"Sure. I'm assuming you have a fence and no pool."

"Both are true. No pool, and I had to put up a fence to keep the goats out when I use the grill. Which has a latch and a cover." He would never let the kids get near the grill. In fact, once everyone was mobile, he would possibly make an outdoor kitchen area that was not in their play yard. The flagstone patio was covered in chalk drawings from Naomi, and he'd promised her a little playhouse like Dani had.

"Hey, you have a patio and packed dirt. That's better than gravel on little knees."

"Yeah. Wat is talking about putting in a play place for them that has those locking tiles out of the foam stuff so it can be moved and cleaned." And God knew he picked up dog stuff every day...

"Oh, yeah? Especially when the little ones are still crawling—although we'll be cold sooner than later."

"It will. But in the spring, it will come in really handy. There's plenty of space in the house for a playroom, too. And they'll be over at the ranch most days."

"Yes. I imagine you'll be running little girls back and forth a lot. Naomi and Dani are fast friends."

"They really are." He thought that was the most amazing thing. He loved that they'd Zoomed every day.

"Do you think that Naomi will go to public school?"

"Watson thinks so. She'll be caught up by the start of the spring semester or at the least, next year. He really wants her to try."

"Good for her." Jennifer finally grinned at him. "I think you guys are doing an amazing job. And I'm rooting for you."

Relief flooded him. "Whoo. Lady, you have a poker face."

"It's my job. I was stunned when the guys told me they were sick. We lucked out with the little ones."

"You so did." They started back out to the truck.

"So when you go on the road..."

"Then we'll see what we have to do. I might be able to get one of the hands' wives to help out around the house for Wat." But it was rare that he was gone more than a week.

Usually less. He was the resident vet for a reason. "And Watson is a trained teacher, an experienced father, and he has help, whenever he needs it. I have faith in him, just like he trusts me when he has to take Naomi to the doctors in Santa Fe."

She nodded. "I'm glad you two have a plan. He seemed surprised you went out of town."

"We still have a lot to talk about. But we've got it." That he believed with all his heart.

"There's always stuff to talk about. It's when you've run out of things that you're in trouble."

"I'll keep that in mind." He parked back at the ranch, and he had to admit, he was relieved it was Wat's turn to talk. He needed to go breathe and work in the barn.

This wasn't his job. His job was horses and goats and sheep and bucking bulls. He needed a few hours where no one said anything to him. And where he didn't run off at the mouth like a fool.

"Well, I'll go find Wat. Thanks for being so patient." As if she got it, Jennifer left him at the truck, and he texted Wat.

<Off to the barn>

<K. CU@lunch>

<You know it.>

He grinned. Okay. Time to get to work. Maggie was going to be throwing a fit by suppertime, so he had to get it all in between now and then.

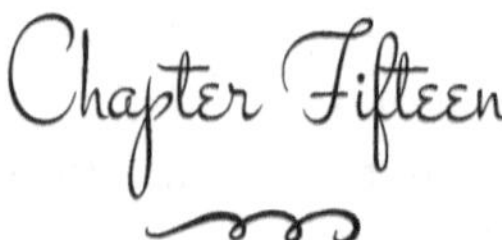

Chapter Fifteen

"Daddy, can I play with Dani until suppertime? You said you are packing the truck, and that's boring!"

"Baby, I don't know what everyone else is doing..." And Wat was exhausted, but he didn't dare show it. Not for a second. Today had been insane with school and Jennifer and the babies and a co-parent who didn't want to talk.

"Dani said she could." Naomi looked so hopeful.

"Let me just ask Nanette." Because Nanette would end up with them underfoot.

"Granny Chiara, can I play with Dani until supper?"

"If you play in Dani's room. Nell is with Mimi, and Nanette's gone home." She winked at him.

"I promise. I do."

"Just until I load the truck and the car, okay? Because we have to feed the babies and Papa Tygh."

"Okay, Daddy!" And she was off and running.

"Where is Tygh?" Antonia asked. "Isn't he supposed to be helping you load the stuff in the cars?"

"I'm sure he had a lot of work to catch up on." Wat hadn't gotten much out of Tygh at lunch…

"Oh, bah." She pulled out her phone, punching in something.

"I'll be fast. I swear. I don't need long and the babies are asleep." He was going to lose his damn mind.

She nodded, but then she was walking away, talking on her phone.

Okay, so first he would get all the clothes and stuff. Then the few breakables and family stuff. The food would go last. There wouldn't be perishables, but he'd been stocking up on canned stuff and snacks…

He didn't even get the first load out to the car before Tygh was there, grabbing the laundry basket from him. "You should have told me you were ready, Wat."

"I didn't want to bother you. I know you were busy." *And you didn't want to talk anymore.* Tygh had been pretty clear about that.

"I'm good. I was trying to get everything done because I figured Maggie would be ready for me to come home with you all for supper." Tygh took a load out, and when he came back in, three wranglers came with him.

"Oh. Hey." Wat couldn't believe they were getting help. He could believe it, they were good folks, but everyone wanted to go home.

"Hey, Wat." One of the wranglers he remembered meeting. Gareth? He'd been the one to spell Tygh here at work. "Just tell us where things go."

"I just want to load up as much as I can in the back of the truck and my rear. I'm going to put the babies in my little car, if Tygh takes Naomi in the truck."

"Sure." Tygh hauled out another armful, and it took the guys no time to get them all packed.

"We'll meet you over there," Gareth said.

"Oh, you don't—"

"Thanks, guys. That will make it go faster. I'll buy you a pizza, huh?" Tygh bumped hips with him on the way by. "Let me get Naomi, okay?"

"She's playing with Dani. Remind her she promised no drama." He loaded the two babies in the car and sighed. He couldn't believe that this was real.

Naomi came out with Tygh, her eyes wide. "Everything is in there!"

"Yep. Surprise." She'd expected to have more time. "The guys helped."

"Thank you, cowboys! You can all see my room."

A chuckle moved through the cowboys, who trooped over to a work truck parked nearby. "We'll see you there."

"Love you!" She waved her arm, then grinned at Wat. "Going to ride with Papa Tygh."

"Okay, kiddo." That would give him a minute to get his shit together. God. Still he appreciated the help.

"Yes, ma'am."

Maggie muttered at him on the drive, and Emma woke up at the cattle guard.

"Yeah, we need a smoother ride." He needed to feed them supper anyway, so it was no big deal, but they were both fussy by the time he parked. "Can you help me get them in, Tygh?" Wat asked. "I can feed them while everyone unloads."

"Sure, Wat." Tygh seemed pretty agreeable now.

"Thank you. Naomi, grab the diaper bags and your backpack, please?"

"Yes, sir! Daddy, sir!" She slung the bags over her shoulder and ran into the house, calling for Biscuit and Tater.

"We'll just haul, and you point us." Gareth went by with a kitchen load.

"That's a kitchen one." He got Maggie in her highchair

with a handful of Cheerios while he made two bottles and warmed up macaroni.

The house was suddenly full of cowboys and kids and the promise of pizza. The babies were having fits, both of them starving. So he added fruit puree and fed them, Naomi helping like a trooper. Tygh fed the dogs, and the guys hit the patio with beer once the cars were unloaded.

"I hope that's okay," Tygh said. "I didn't want you to have to cook."

"No, that's fine. I'll get the babies in the bath, while Naomi does her reading."

"Pizza is on its way. They'll head out after that." Tygh gave him a searching kind of look. "I can tell you're tired."

"It was a long day." And weird, with Tygh being so distant. It had been different at home and... and he hoped he wasn't making a mistake.

"Yeah. I got a little sideways."

"I'm sorry. It's a lot." Maybe too much. At least he would be able to sleep in his own room and... think.

"It is. But we got through the first big hurdle." And Tygh grinned then, making him laugh. That was... more hopeful.

"Yes, and thank God for it." He left Tygh with the babies and started the bathwater. He breathed in deep, letting the warm water get into his sinuses. Not hot like he would later for his own shower, but it worked.

"I'll help." Tygh brought Maggie and Emma in, one in each arm.

"Papa!" Maggie crowed, and Emma reached for Wat.

"I know. It's bath time. Hooray!" He chuckled and started stripping Emma down.

"Babababa." Maggie was making all sorts of words again now. "Baff."

"That's right! Bath! Bath for Maggie. Yay!"

"Ay!" she cheered.

He laughed, putting Emma in her bathing seat before getting Maggie in the tub. "You can go check on the guys if you want."

"You trying to get rid of me?" Tygh teased.

"I'm not. I was being nice. You do know nice, don't you?"

"Yeah. Sure I do." Tygh climbed to his feet, brushing water off his jeans. "I'll just go wait for the pizza."

Oh. Oh, dammit. He washed the babies, then got them both ready for bed with a final warm bottle.

By the time he was done with that, he started unpacking Naomi's things while she ate and got a bath herself.

"Hey, it's suppertime." Tygh came in, watching him from just inside the doorway.

"Cool." He wasn't hungry. He was nervous and uncomfortable and worried and he wanted to hide with a beer and a book.

"Hey, I'm sorry if I snapped." Tygh rubbed the back of his neck. "I wigged out some."

"Me too," he admitted, more than a touch relieved. "Want to sit and have a beer together after Naomi's in bed?"

"I do. The guys took their pizza and fled. So it's just us three for supper." Tygh grinned wryly. "They were great, though."

"They were. I'm so tickled. I appreciate it." He put another set of books in Naomi's bookshelf, the click and clack of the books hitting the wood familiar and comforting. "I wasn't trying to be ugly before. I was trying to make a joke. I'm sorry if it wasn't funny."

"I was just feeling kinda growly." Tygh sighed. "I mean, this is what we wanted, but I felt like I had to defend every decision we made. It was weird."

"Yes. And I understand why, but... it was exhausting. I appreciate you standing up for me and the girls."

"Ditto, honey." Tygh's smile widened. "Come on. I got you sausage and green chile."

Oh, Tygh remembered. "Let me get Naomi. She's just having a bath. I know she had some mac and cheese, but she would love a slice."

"Yeah, I got one of those little personal cheese pizzas for her."

"You'll be her hero." And Wat's confidence was making a comeback. Or if not confidence, then his ability to breathe.

"Yeah? I'm good with that." Tygh let him pass by, then followed, and that was disturbingly hot.

"Time for pizza, sweetie." He knocked on the bathroom door.

"'kay, Daddy! I'll be right there!"

"Like soon, kiddo." He knew she would linger in the bathroom if he gave her a chance.

"Soon, Daddy!" She sang it at him.

He grinned over at Tygh. "So-o-on," he sang.

Tygh chuckled. "Always one more minute, yeah?" He raised his voice. "Too bad she doesn't want a personal pizza with that dipping sauce she likes so much!"

The door opened, a head full of dripping wet curls popping out. "Dippy sauce?"

"Yep. You know I have your back."

"Get a towel," Wat ordered. "We'll be right there."

"I'll get drinks." Tygh gave him a broad wink and headed toward the kitchen.

"Thank you." He waited for her to come get help drying her mane of hair.

"Hurry, Daddy! Dippy sauce!"

"Let me spray in your tangle stuff. We can comb it right before bed." She loved the cups of dip that came from the pizza place. Ranch and marinara, with tiny lids. Tygh had taught her that their first week at the ranch.

"'kay. Papa Tygh remembered!"

He sprayed the detangler in her hair and sent her to the kitchen table so he could sop up the water on the floors and bring the soaking towels to the washer.

"Come sit," Tygh said, patting the chair next to him.

"Thanks. Smells great. Oh, and you got salad and garlic bread too."

"Yeah. Moving day. I thought we'd splurge."

"Salad is yucky."

He rolled his eyes at little Miss Getting Tired. "More for me, then."

"But I like garlic toast."

"I know, kiddo." He made sure she got a piece. "Careful with the dippy. You only get one bath."

"I will. So, Papa Tygh, did you have a very good day at work?" She put her chin on her arm, one eyebrow quirked just like her momma.

"I did okay." Tygh grabbed a slice of sausage and green chile. "Miss Minnie was glad to see me. Maybe you and Dani can come check in on her tomorrow."

"Oh, we can come at recess." She nodded. "Or at lunch, if you want to have lunch with us."

"I would love to have lunch with all of you." Tygh glanced at him. "To make up for today. I wasn't in the best mood. I'm sorry."

"It's okay. The first day back is hard. Daddy knows all about that. Nell pooped in her pants and cried."

"Yeah. Fun times." Wat chuckled, rolling his eyes. It wasn't the first time that had happened in a classroom; it wouldn't be the last. "But let's not talk poop at the dinner table, huh?"

"Sounds like a plan. I won't talk about medicating horses." Tygh grimaced, and he got the picture. Ew. Not for supper conversation.

"I like horses." Naomi dipped with her bread, so careful.

"I am reading about the island of lost horses. It's a little sad and a little scary, but so good. Have you read it, Papa Tygh?"

"Nope. I haven't. You'll have to tell me all about it when you're done." Tygh reached out to push a damp curl away from Naomi's mouth, and he had a little moment of "I'm doing something right". These two loved each other already.

"Oh, I will. What's your favorite book? Can you read it to me? Daddy's is *The Hobbit*."

"I like that one, but my favorite is called *Lonesome Dove*. We can read that one together when you're a little older."

Oh, he was glad Tygh said that.

"What can you read with me now?" Naomi asked.

"Have you ever read *Brighty of the Grand Canyon*? It's about a donkey," Tygh said.

"We have donkeys!" Naomi bounced in her seat. "Okay. You can read that one to me."

"I'll do that."

"More chewing, less talking, baby girl," Wat told her. He wanted his beer on the patio, and it was teetering on her bedtime really hard.

"Can I save half for lunch tomorrow?"

"Absolutely."

"Thank you. I'm tired, and I want to listen to my music."

"Thanks for telling us that instead of playing with your food, sweetie. Give Papa Tygh a kiss and I'll put you to bed." He would finish his pizza later.

"G'night, Papa Tygh. Love you."

"Night, kiddo. I love you too."

He just loved hearing that. He thought Tygh meant it too.

He stopped and got the comb before he headed into her room. The brushing and braiding went fast, and she jabbered at him about how she and Tygh were going to paint her room the entire time.

"Okay, love, I'm going to put on your music. If you need me, Tygh and I will be out on the patio, huh?"

"Night, Daddy." She patted the bed, and Tater brushed past him to jump up onto her mattress.

"I love you, baby girl."

"I love you, Daddy. Don't shut the door, okay?"

"Promise." He checked on Maggie and Emma in his room, traded out shoes for house shoes, and went out to the patio.

"Hey. I brought some of the pizza out." Tygh had a little cooler bucket of cold beers too. "She get off to bed?"

"Yes. Biscuit got the short straw of protecting us, huh?"

"They'll trade off once she gets sleepy." Tygh handed him a Bud Light.

"Thank you."

"She go down okay?"

He nodded and popped the top. "Like a dream. She was exhausted. It's amazing how much more energy she expends with the other girls."

"I bet they all sucked your energy right down. I know my head was killing me after talking to Jennifer." Tygh rubbed the back of his neck. "But we got through it. How did it go otherwise? Poopsplosion notwithstanding."

"Everything with Jennifer was good. The girls were tickled to be back to normal, and they all are excited about Halloween."

"Oh man, hayrides. I need to get all the equipment checked and start getting the horses used to pulling again. They stay lazy most of the year." Tygh sipped his beer, then licked foam off his lip.

"Do you usually drive? I mean, do you get trick-or-treaters out here? How does this work?" He wanted Naomi to have fun.

"We do a big party out here, and there's also a trunk or treat in town for the wee ones. It's earlier in the day. We do hayrides and apple bobbing and costumes and all the traditional stuff. In a safe way." Tygh's expression was just... sweet. That was the only way to put it.

"Oh. Oh, that's good. Naomi's at the perfect age for that, and the babies are too young to care quite yet. We'll just dress them up."

"The pictures are key at this age. I want them to have plenty to look at so they know they were loved."

He tilted his head, and it quivered on his lips to ask if Tygh had any, since he'd been with his granny for a while, but there was so much to that story that he didn't know. So he went personal on his end anyway. "We lost so many of Naomi's, but we were lucky there were a bunch on the cloud."

"That is amazing. What was her first Halloween costume?"

"Minnie Mouse. Her birthday is in November, so she was almost a year old. Michelle drew whiskers and a nose on with black eyeliner.

"Oh, God. That sounds amazing. She's so cute. What does she want to do this year?"

"Captain Hook."

Tygh stared at him a moment, then cracked up laughing.

"I know. She's already done it once. It was her therapist's suggestion because we were worried the hand would come off."

"Ah. Yeah. Well, that's smart." Tygh munched more pizza. "Should I tell the bosses to go easy on the bonfires? We can always do some alternative stuff, light up with electrics instead. No one will miss it, I bet."

"Let me sort of prepare her. I have to tell you, I couldn't quite look at that one I went to, and..." And the thought of Naomi near a fire made him want to scream, but he would not put his shit on his little girl.

"Well, we can feel her out and then take it to the Chiaras."

Tygh shook his head. "I wouldn't want to scare her for the world, and neither would they."

"I know. I can't tell you how much I appreciate that." It was one of the reasons he'd come to this ranch, and it was part of what he really liked about Tygh. The willingness to care for all the people there.

"Y'all are my family." Those words were simple. Sure.

Wat leaned toward Tygh, reaching out with one hand. "Thank you. I—that means a lot."

Tygh took his hand, squeezing. "I'm a grumpy old cowboy. Don't ever let that fool you into thinking I don't care."

"You're not old, cowboy. I'm just unnerved. I just, for all intents and purposes, tripled the size of my family."

"True. And we're still learning how to do this." Tygh let him go, but slowly, as if he was reluctant. "I keep forgetting it's like, two weeks."

"Yes, but it was a trial by fire. I—I've missed being a part of a couple." Even if he wasn't sure they were a couple yet.

"Yeah? I've never really done it. I mean, I've dated." Tygh's little grin told him even that might be an exaggeration.

"Always men?" He couldn't help but be curious.

"Yeah. I knew when I was a teenager." Tygh shrugged. "I guess that's why I haven't done a lot of stepping out."

He could see that. Tygh was a cowboy and a veteran and a veterinarian. And a lot of places in small-town New Mexico were still pretty conservative, no matter what the Albuquerque/Santa Fe corridor was like.

"Well, I'm not all that when it comes to dating, either, male or female. Michelle was my high school girl."

"Really?"

"Yeah. Really. I got her pregnant in high school. We got married, and she lost the baby the day we graduated." It had been horrific, but they were in love and determined, and they'd stayed together.

"Oh, shit, honey." Tygh's mouth dropped open. "That's awful."

"It was hideous. But we worked at it really hard. Both of us were super scared and depressed for a bit."

"I can see why. But go you for making it work."

"I'm a monogamist. Michelle would say that it showed a lack of imagination, but I would say that slow and steady wins the race." Because that put him in the best light, after all.

"It totally does. I'm a fan of the idea." Those lean cheeks went pink. "I'm old-fashioned that way."

"Yeah? I'm glad. How did you end up working here? Have you been here long?"

"I was on the road with the rodeo for a bit, and then I came up here and was a big animal vet who traveled all over New Mexico and Colorado." Tygh shook his head. "I got tired of being on the road, so when I heard they were hiring someone permanent, I threw my hat in. I've been *here*-here just over a year and a half."

"Oh, so not a terribly long time." He would still have been in the hospital with Naomi at that point. "Did you always know you wanted to be a vet?"

"Yeah. I mean, pretty much." Tygh chewed his lower lip for a moment the way he did when he was organizing his thoughts. "I went to a horse therapy thing the year after I went into foster care, and man, I was hooked. I knew I wanted to work with animals."

"That's cool." His girl thought horses were amazing, and he was grateful he'd landed in a space she could interact with them.

"It was good. Hard, but good." Tygh closed up the pizza boxes. "Do you have a ton of student loans?"

"No. I had a grant and scholarships, and I worked three

jobs while I was in grad school. Michelle ran a daycare in the house." What they hadn't had was life insurance.

He had it now.

"I was lucky that way too. I worked as a vet tech and at a boarding place, and I got a grant for need-based former foster kids as well as the GI Bill." Those long fingers tapped the table. "So that sets us up pretty well."

"Yeah. I mean, I'll be honest, I have some savings from the house insurance, but I don't have a huge amount. At least I have an education."

"You're great." The words seemed to just pop out, and Tygh blushed again. God, that was adorable.

"Thanks. I feel... like a giant bird that's trying to be... amazing." That was silly, but it was true.

"No way. The big birds are perpetually evil two-year-olds." Laughing, Tygh toasted him with his beer. "They're just smart enough to get into trouble all the damn time."

"Oh... if I'm not a bird, then what would you say I am?"

"All right, now don't get upset, because it's a compliment." One eyebrow went up and down. "But you're a kangaroo."

"Whaaat?" Wat sipped his beer so he didn't babble and ask what the fuck.

Tygh ticked off on his fingers. "Well, you're not from here, so you're kind of novel, but you're incredibly nurturing, you bounce back, and you'd stand up and fight like crazy if you had to."

"And I carry that baby around in a pouch all the time too!" He got it. He really got it. That tickled the hell out of him.

"You do. I carry mine around on my hip, so I'm more like a gorilla."

"Ha!" He snorted. "You keep trying to convince me you're bad-tempered, but I don't believe it."

"Not even after lunch today?"

"You were overwhelmed. I have dealt with social workers for all of my professional career. I know the drill." And he wanted to believe in what they had growing.

"I haven't had to see one but for the training since I was eighteen." Tygh shrugged. "I think it just got to me."

"It has to be hard." He burned to ask a million questions, but he knew from his work as an educator that some of the hard questions had to come in their own time. Tygh would let him know when the story was ready to tell. "Kase and Ryder seemed almost relieved, though. I think they're set up for children more than babies."

And Maggie and Emma were young for their ages.

"Right now they are, yeah. I mean, Charlie and Elijah are both pretty self-sufficient, but Dani and Nell are still a lot of work."

"They are." He was glad Tygh got it. "I feel pretty lucky."

"Me too, honey. Me too. Always know that."

He reached out and dared to take Tygh's hand for a second.

Tygh squeezed, and he thought they might lean in and maybe—

And Tater woofed and climbed to his paws, heading inside. Where they could hear Emma crying.

"I'll get her."

"I'll clean up." Tygh gave him a wry look, and they were off in different directions.

Dammit.

Chapter Sixteen

The water tubs were filled for bobbing for apples. The hay bales were on the wagon, and the tack was ready, the horses tested for soundness. The ranch bustled with activity, but Tygh had gotten all his early work done, and it was time to head into town. They would come back for supper and then the big ranch festival, but now it was time for the trunk or treat, and Dani, Nell, Naomi, Maggie, and Emma were all going.

They were amazing together. Naomi was Captain Hook and Dani was Peter Pan, while Nell was Tinkerbell, and the little ones were Lost Boys. It was adorable.

Better than that? Watson was dressed up as Smee complete with mop and bucket, and Dani was leading Birdie, who completed the look as Nana.

Tygh had gone for subtle, with a leather vest in faux croc print and a big gold pocket watch tucked into his watch pocket. The rest was just full-on cowboy. Let everyone guess he was the crocodile.

Watson got it.

In fact, Tygh could feel Wat's eyes on his ass, on his belly, on him, everywhere he walked.

After their near miss the other night, Wat was driving him nuts. Casual brushes against him in the kitchen, tiny touches to the small of his back as they passed in the hallway putting the girls to bed.

He knew Wat wasn't sure how to seduce him, and God help him when the son of a bitch figured it out.

He grinned, loading the baby seats into the truck. They'd talked to Ryder, and next week they'd go get a big SUV, but right now, they kept switching back and forth. Naomi was going to ride with the Chiaras so there would be room for everyone.

"Are you excited about the hayrides? Are you sure Naomi isn't going to bother you? She was so excited about you two making 'jack o' punkins'." He thought Wat was nervous about his baby girl going in another car.

"She's going to be great. I'm tickled as heck to teach her how to make creepy pumpkin faces." And he had battery-operated tea lights to put in for the pumpkins to glow, so Naomi didn't have to light candles. They'd decided as a ranch not to have fire at Halloween this year, even though Naomi had been brave and said she could take it.

Everyone had been sensitive with Naomi, especially once Kase had explained the situation to Elijah. That boy was determined that no one would be harmed under his umbrella of influence.

"She's not going to be scared on my watch," Elijah had declared and had enlisted all his buddies into coming up with alternate lighting solutions.

Tygh was fascinated to find out where Elijah ended up. The young man was not in any way a cowboy, but he was going to become someone stunning.

"I'll make sure everything is decorated right!" Elijah called, and he waved. He knew there would be a good mix of cute for the littles and scarier farther out for the later hayrides with the bigger kids.

"You ready, honey?" Tygh asked after Maggie and Emma were buckled in.

"I am." Wat climbed into the passenger seat. "Are you ready to hear how incredibly cute the babies are for the next hour?"

"Hell, yes." They were adorable in their scruffy Lost Boy outfits, and he loved how Maggie giggled every time she looked at her sister.

"I was worried the costumes would frighten her, but no. I guess Naomi wandering around like a nut for a week with a hook hand cured her."

"That and the pirate hat with the giant feather." Emma had watched that feather with rapt eyes every time Naomi moved her head.

"Yes. I imagine by next year, Maggie will know what she wants, so we'll enjoy this."

"We will." Tygh gave what he hoped was a crocodile grin.

Wat's cheeks heated, and he swore he saw a shiver. Score. Might as well amp that up a bit, right? Because Tygh was totally willing, if not anymore suave or anything.

But Wat had told him, straight up, he didn't know how to flirt with a man, so Tygh was going to have to take the lead.

They piled everything they might need in the back, though, and they were off, ready to hand out candy and show off the kids. The air was cold enough, but since it was still daylight, Naomi just needed her pirate coat.

They parked, and everyone tumbled out. Kase and Ryder —who were dressed as John and Michael, God bless them— completed the ensemble.

"Happy Halloween! Arr!" Naomi hollered, and everyone around them cracked up.

"Okay, guys," Kase said. "Wat, are you walking with me and Dani and Nell?"

"Yep. And Tygh will set up here with Ryder to hand out the early candy." Watson shot him a grin. "He has to work tonight."

"I do. So I get to sit on my butt and growl at all comers." Not that he would growl too much. Some of these kids were tiny. Good thing he knew a good many of them already.

"Daddy! Come on!" Naomi twirled, her loot bag ready.

"Coming!" Wat walked off with the little girls in tow, Emma in her sling, Maggie in a stroller, waving at him. He waved back, then got out his treasure chest and filled it with candy. It had been a party store find by one of the cowboys' ladies on a trip to Albuquerque. It held a lot, and it looked great, even if it was some sort of paper and paint concoction.

"That's great, man. How's it going with the girls?" Ryder's eyes followed Kase like a laser.

"Good. I mean, we have some nightmares, and Maggie is learning to throw some epic tantrums, but the doctor said they were both coming up to weight better on their last checkup, and they're pretty happy." He thought that was what Ryder wanted to know.

"Good. Good, temper tantrums are a measure of trust."

"Yeah?" Well, hell. He'd never known that. The foster system was different nowadays, though. Well, at least some of it.

"Yeah. Yeah, it means they believe you'll stick around, that you won't hurt them, that you're steady."

"I want to be, for sure." He searched for that pirate hat, and there was Wat and Naomi and the girls, who had quickly become his world.

"Good deal. I know Dani's glad to be well—she got her best friends both back at the house."

"She does." He thought it was so cool that Naomi and

Wat had become so close to Dani in such a short time. "I know she loves Wat as a teacher."

Ryder shot him a glance. "Dude, Tygh, I was talking about *you*."

"Huh? Oh, well, cool. You know I adore her, man." That was— Well, that was pretty neat, really.

"Yeah, she's going to be the one that wants to take over the ranch, mark my words." Ryder sounded pleased as punch.

"She has a real feel for the animals." He gave Ryder a sideways glance. "But who will run the rodeo company?"

"Nell. She's our business shark, I guarantee it."

"Not Charlie?" he teased, because that girl was in love with a barrel racer.

"Charlie has a lot of deciding to do. I want her to have all the options. I mean, I want all of them to. But I know Dani and Nell are my homebodies." Ryder grinned at a little bitty Pikachu. "Here you go, sweetie."

"Happy tricking treats!" she chirped, and lord, wasn't that cute.

"Tick tock," he growled.

She squealed, but she held out her bag so bravely that he gave her two pieces of candy.

"Thank you!" She skipped off to the next car, and then it was a steady stream of kids for about half an hour. They came in from all over, ranches and tiny mountain towns because the Chiara ranch was everyone's next destination.

"Oh, happy anniversary, Boss." Had it been two years since the foster program had started?

"Thanks." That beaming smile told him he was dead-on. "It's been a whirlwind, but the best kind. You're getting to know all about that, aren't you?"

"I am." Lord, was he ever. "The girls are this force of nature. I mean, I know that about baby animals, right? All of them. But these girls love me and Wat already, and they trust us."

"And Naomi talks about you all the time, too, Papa Tygh." Oh, now Ryder was teasing him.

"Hey, I'll take it. She's an amazing kid." Who was he kidding? He was all in. "Thank you for giving us all a safe place to figure this out."

"That's what a ranch is. It came from the Spanish, huh? A bunch of small places where everyone ate together in a central location."

"Yeah. It's a grand idea still." Tygh craved that family connection, for all of his protests of being a grumpy loner.

"Tricker-treat!" The cutest little bull and bullrider ever stopped by.

"Yeehaw, cowboy!" Ryder whooped, and Tygh cracked up. He was so getting one of those for his Maggie next year.

The kid galloped off with his candy, his dad chuckling, and he searched for his Peter Pan crew again, wanting to see if Wat needed help.

Kase was heading for him, holding Maggie who was screaming her head off.

"PAPA! PAAPAA!"

"Be right back."

"Go."

He met Kase halfway, grabbing Maggie into his arms. "What is it, baby girl?" She had lungs on her, that child.

"Someone dressed like a fireman had a siren that scared her." Kase handed her over. "She knew who she wanted."

"Thanks, man. Everyone else okay?"

"We're on round two because new people pulled in." Kase rolled his eyes before heading back to his kids.

"Hey, you." He bounced Maggie. "I got you. It was just a costume, huh? Like Naomi's hook."

Maggie didn't understand, but he knew she knew her

sister's name, and the tone of his voice was soothing. She frowned and jabbered at him, telling him all about it.

Damn, when she learned to talk, she was going to be nonstop.

"I know. It's hard. You're just so little." He got back to his chair, easing down with a wry glance at Ryder, who winked at Maggie.

"You missed a hippopotamus and a giraffe," Ryder said.

"Aw, well, we'll see them around, huh, Mags?"

Maggie made grabby hands at the candy chest, but he held her back. "I don't think you're ready for that, baby girl. But it does smell good."

In fact, he would probably devour a couple of Reese's as soon as Maggie settled. Which might be never, the way she was wiggling and dancing, laughing at the kids who came by.

"She's so much more interactive! I love to see that. She's so invested and focused."

Tygh's chest swelled, because that praise proved they were doing something right.

"Yeah. She's really opened up. It's—" He stopped himself from discussing how tough sensory deprivation was, even as a seven-year-old. Maggie didn't need to hear it. "She's a hoot."

"She is. You can tell, she knows you love her."

Maggie stared at Ryder, then grabbed Tygh's shirt. "Papa."

"I am your papa, baby girl. I am." That possessive word and grip made his heart melt.

"Not mine?" Ryder teased, and she frowned, full of thunder.

"No."

Ryder nodded. "That's a good girl. You know your papa."

She beamed then, patting his chest. "Papa."

"Whew." Wat appeared, only Emma and Nell in tow. "Can I leave her with you in the carrier? Naomi and Dani want to make another go."

Nell went right to Ryder to climb up on him. "Daddy, lookit! Candy!"

"Of course." He moved the stroller over, Emma knocked out, just snoozing. "You okay, honey?"

"These girls are intent on that candy…" Wat's eyes were wide.

"They're just the age," Ryder called, laughing. "Are you tired, Nellie-girl?"

"My feets are." She pointed to her toes.

"Are they? You walked a long way, huh?"

"*So* long." She agreed, pulling a long face. "Da says I can help give candies to the kids, though."

"You can. And tonight, you can ride on the wagon with Tygh for a bit. Right, Tygh?"

"There's room up with me, for sure." He knew from experience that the kids would rotate sitting up on the driver's seat with him.

"Yay! I sleeps with Mimi too?"

Ryder's eyes twinkled. That little girl was a hoot. "How about you and Mimi read a book and she rocks you before bed?"

"Okay." Nell leaned on Ryder's chest, and she handed out candy as the kids trickled by, but it was starting to taper off.

By the time Wat got back, he needed to shut it down and head out to the ranch so he could harness the team and check the route for anything pranksters might have done, though he would bet Elijah was on patrol for that.

Naomi and Dani were ramped up, but the other three were going down for the count, the three of them exhausted.

"Do you want to put the babies down at the big house and go hang with Naomi on the hayride?" Ryder offered, but Naomi shook her head.

"I'm good. Dani and me have Tygh, Daddy."

Wat's lips twisted, but he nodded. "Y'all will have to be good, eh? Tygh's working, and you two need to listen."

"We will! Papa Tygh knows how good I am!" Naomi bounced.

Dani gave them an angelic smile. "I always be good for Mister Tygh."

"Lord help us," Kase said. "Okay, let's load it up and go home. You girls stay out from under the horses okay? No getting around their feet."

"No sir," the two older girls chorused. "No horse feet."

"Arrrrr," Maggie growled, mostly in her sleep, he thought.

He glanced at Wat, cracking up as he buckled in babies.

"She's always wanted me to come with her before. She's growing up, huh?" Oh, poor Wat.

"You could always come anyway."

"No, I need to trust her. Let her prove she's a good kid." Wat grinned as they buckled in. "But it's so hard."

"I bet, but she'll be with me."

"Yes, that's the only reason I said yes."

Tygh squeezed Wat's leg. "I'll keep an eye on her. And Elijah will have a dozen teen boys in camo and sagebrush hats out there, popping out to keep everyone in line."

Wat laughed at that. "I bet. He's taking his responsibility very seriously."

"One less worry for Ryder and Kase. And I know they're worried about Charlie being away from home for the first time."

"Right? Two eighteen-year-olds on their own with their friends?" Wat's eyes went wide. "Trouble."

He hooted. "I was. God. I had just aged out of the foster system, I was about to go to basic, and I was working two jobs. That first Halloween I was an idiot."

He'd ended up very, very drunk and had woken up in a rural cemetery with two other boys and a girl with the sheriff's deputy shining a light on them to tell them that someone had reported a bunch of disinterred dead bodies.

"I was at home with Michelle. We had a huge fight the night before, and I'd slept at my folks. Embarrassing."

"Ouch. I was mistaken for a corpse."

"Whaaat?"

So he told Wat the whole story on the drive, and Wat was laughing like a loon by the time they pulled up at the ranch. Go him.

"I'll help you unload and put my chest of candy up at the porch, then I'll take the girls down with me, okay?"

"I'll make them go to the bathroom and surrender all but a few pieces of candy."

"Good idea. Kase will be all over that too."

"The last thing any of us need is those two hyped up on sugar. You think Dani will spend the night with us or vice-versa?"

"I bet she stays with us. But then again, Naomi might be seduced by Mimi stories." Alba was a comforting presence after a long night of buckling the swash, after all.

"Yeah. I can't say how much it means that they didn't have fires. She was going to be brave, but now she doesn't have to be."

"She's amazing, you know?" He unloaded Maggie, who murmured, "Papa" as he hugged her. "Do you need me to stay and help change them and all?"

"No, you go on. I know you have a full night of work ahead."

"Okay. Thanks, honey." He kissed Wat's cheek, feeling pretty damn daring doing it, and getting a gasp for his trouble.

"Have fun!"

Tygh headed back to the ranch, where Alba was waiting with the big girls, smiling. "Are you taking Dani or are we keeping Naomi? The guys are going to a hotel for their anniversary. They just don't know it yet."

"Then we'll take Dani. I feel like you'll have enough on your hands with Elijah's friends." He knew at least three of the boys were going to sleep over and watch scary movies. That way Dani didn't have to navigate a situation with lots of screaming and stabbing in the family room.

"Does that work for you, Dani?"

She nodded. "I packed my bag. Me and Naomi are having a party."

"Sounds fab. Why don't we load all that in the truck now so when it's late all we have to do is go to my place, huh?"

"I have carrots for the animals in the hurt barn so they don't get sad that they don't get to come play," Naomi said.

Alba chuckled. "Gareth offered to take them to see Minnie while you harness."

"I'm grateful."

"Of course. If you need me, please call. Antonia and I are on call."

"I will." He nodded, but inside, he was shaking his head. He and the wranglers would do this and let Ryder and Kase have the night off and Antonia and Alba wallow in the great-grandkids. "Okay, hayride ahoy." He took the girls, and Gareth met him halfway.

"Come on, ladies. Minnie needs a carrot."

That freed him up to do some serious wagon hitching.

It was time for him to deal with passels of children before having the first of God knew how many slumber parties of his life...

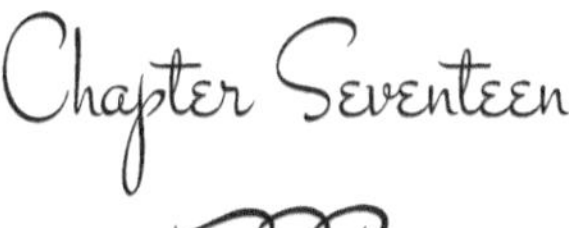

Chapter Seventeen

"Daddy! Can I spend the night with Dani? We're going to make Rice Krispie treats and watch *Descendants* and go to the Farmer's Market with Granny in the morning!"

Well, at least she asked this time... "Let me check with the Chiaras and Papa Tygh."

Ryder and Kase had a pregnant sixteen-year-old staying for a few weeks, and a teenage boy whose mother was doing thirty days in county, but they were settled. So he just needed to make sure they weren't running in all directions for the rodeo or something. The finals were... imminent, he gathered.

"Okay!" She twirled, because she was wearing a princess dress instead of the pirate coat. That was her thing this week.

He texted Tygh. *<The girl wants to spend the night here>*

<Good deal. We can have supreme pizzas and beer.>

<I'll talk to Ryder.> "Let me talk to Mr. Ryder. Just a minute."

He headed out, finding Dani dragging her father by the hand.

"Daddy! Tell Mister Wal you said yes!"

"I said yes." Ryder's eyelines crinkled in a smile. "We've got plenty of chicken fingers and tots, Rice Krispies, and the girls have a TV date with Mimi."

"That sounds great." Maggie and Emma would go down a little early and maybe he could get tipsy enough to make a move... "We're going to be home, should you need us. You can just call."

Ryder grinned at him. "We have clothes, a nightie, a toothbrush, and a Mr. Moose that lives here, so she'll be fine."

He got it. They had Dani's second favorite pillow, a copy of *The Tale of Despereaux* to read, and a cup she liked.

"Thanks, Ryder."

"You want me to take her up to the house?"

"I'd love that. Give me a kiss, baby girl. Papa Tygh will come say goodnight before he leaves the ranch."

"Love you, Daddy." She smacked a kiss on his cheek.

"Love you, sweetie."

"Love you, Mister Wat." Dani kissed his face too. "Thank you!"

"You're welcome, bug. Love you too. Have fun." He grinned as they skipped off, both of them dragging Ryder. The man looked as if he was waterskiing.

His phone buzzed, and he glanced at it.

<One more bull to check, then I can knock off early>

Oh, happy Friday. *<I'll get the littles home and order pizza?>* On Friday nights, it helped to put in the pizza order early, so either one of the town kids who needed money would deliver it or they could pick it up at an arranged time.

<Good deal. C you soon.>

He hummed, putting away the last of the school supplies and making sure the room was clean for the weekend. Wat liked to start Monday with good vibes.

"Are you girls ready to go home?" he asked Maggie and Emma.

"Papa," Maggie said immediately.

"Papa will be home soon." He put Emma into her carrier, then held out his arm to Maggie, who scooted over to him in her crablike walk-crawl. She was getting so much stronger, and was catching right up to where she needed to be, which was gratifying.

"Da." She raised her arms, so he scooped her into his embrace and then picked up Emma. Every time she called him Da, he took it as a personal victory. Papa had come easily to her, but Da had been harder. So he would take that and the warm glow that came with it.

"Let's go hooome." Wat sang as he got the lights off and the door closed and headed out to the freaking huge SUV he and Tygh had just bought. He'd never had a car that had new car smell, but this one did. It also had all the bells and whistles, and he was still in awe of them. His SUV hadn't been ancient, but he and Michelle had spent on luxuries for Naomi, like the media screen on the back seat, not the heated seats and individual air system and the screen that could calculate algebra and serve dinner in the dash...

At home, he got the girls in front of a cartoon, which was a sure way to keep them rapt until he got ready to let them play on the floor, loved on the dogs, changed clothes, and then ordered pizza.

Then he sat on his ass for a bit. Whew. Dani, Naomi, and even little Nell had been so ramped up for the weekend.

He also wanted time to ponder his approach with Tygh. Since that sweet kiss on the cheek at Halloween, Tygh had been driving him nuts. A touch to his lower back when they left for work in the morning. A too-close pass in the hallway, where their bodies touched all over. A late-night shirtless appearance in front of the fridge, pajama pants slung low enough to see the dimple at the top of Tygh's butt... God.

He jumped when the door opened, the dogs whining and

wagging instead of barking, which meant Tygh was home. Had he dozed off? Maggie and Emma were still corralled with him on the couch, but Maggie was wiggling down before he could blink.

"Papa!"

"Hey, sweet pea." Tygh hoisted her up to kiss her cheek. "How was your day, huh?" He grinned at Wat. "Happy Friday."

"Hey. I think I took a little power nap. Happy Friday."

"Do I need to order pizza?"

"I did. And Hannah Post is delivering tonight, so they're gonna bring it to us."

"Hoo yeah. Well, I'm glad to be off. The bulls were cantankerous. You get deluxe? Green chile?"

"I got a green chile, sausage, and onion, and a deluxe." He stared at Tygh. He wanted another of those soft kisses.

"Well, bring it on." Tygh came to put Maggie down, tickling Emma, who squealed.

She was putting on weight and was starting to catch up with her milestones. He was so pleased.

Tygh stayed bent down, and he got a light brush of lips on his forehead before Tygh straightened. "Let me go clean up, ladies and gent. I'll be back."

"I'll be right here." And he was buzzing, lightning shooting through him.

Tygh came back wearing an old almost-white pair of jeans and a big, soft sweatshirt, socks, and slippers. Oh, lord help him.

"Is there room for me, Maggie Mae?"

"Papa!" Maggie stood up along the back of the sofa, making grabby hands. "Papa! Me!"

"Careful, wee one." Tygh grabbed her and sat in her spot, laughing when Emma toppled over. "Whoops. Upsie."

He watched, smiling, loving how Tygh loved the girls.

"Up! Me!" Maggie laughed as Wat scooped Emma into his arms.

"There you go. What are we watching?"

"*Octonauts*. So the bulls were bad?"

"And stinky." Tygh shuddered.

"Yay. Emma must be part bull…"

"That good, huh?"

"You have no idea."

"Did they eat?"

Wat shook his head. "It was too early, and we crashed. But the pizza won't be here until six thirty."

"Oh, good man. Family time, food, bath. All that stuff has time."

"We have to make sure our littlest girls have their papa time." He winked over.

"Papa!" Maggie agreed, crawling up to bounce on Tygh's lap.

"Careful." Tygh shifted her away from important parts. "There we go. Did you miss me, baby girl?"

"She did all sorts of stuff today. We painted."

"Oh wow. Did you save me a painting?"

"It's on the fridge."

Tygh beamed. "I bet you're a great painter, huh, Maggie?"

Maggie gurgled and chirped, just telling Tygh what for.

He had to reach out, using Maggie as an excuse to touch Tygh's arm. Wat… needed the contact. Tygh had never looked so handsome. He was ready for more, and he wasn't sure what to do.

He had no idea what would happen if he did something and Tygh rejected him.

Tygh's breath caught, and he turned to stare at Wat, the expression in those dark eyes serious and sure.

He would have leaned over to kiss Tygh, but Emma

squealed and bounced, reminding him the kids were right there. Lord.

"Oh, you two are going to make your papa work for it, aren't you?" Tygh bounced Maggie, which jostled Emma.

She started crying, and he cradled her. "I got you. Sorry, honey. I know everyone was all keyed up today." He smiled. "I kinda am too."

"Are you?" Tygh's smile burned him to the ground. "Are you thinking happy thoughts?"

"I am." His cheeks burned white-hot. "Is that okay?"

"Oh, honey. It's great." Tygh chuckled, the sound low, intimate. "I like happy thoughts."

"Well, then, we'll have to explore them later." He grabbed his courage with both metaphorical hands to say it, and his whole body flushed with warm tingles.

"We will." Now was for the little girls, though, and Maggie's favorite song came on the TV, so they all sang along.

They had a rhythm with feeding and bath time, and soon they were easing two sound-asleep babies into their cribs, covering them up. How had this become his life? Oh, he'd loved Naomi as a baby with his whole heart, but after Michelle had died, he'd thought he was done having kids. And now he had two more...

"Hey, come on. Pizza will be here soon." Tygh put a hand on the small of his back, steering him out to the main room.

"Yeah. I hope Naomi's having a good time." It didn't seem to bother her to stay with Dani. Kase, Ryder, and the grannies were family. She'd decided that, and they had accepted her with open arms.

"I bet she is. Miz Alba is so good with them, and Miz Antonia adores her." Tygh went to plop down on the couch, patting the spot next to him.

Wat sat, his weight tipping Tygh closer.

Grinning, Tygh wrapped an arm around him. "I figure if I

kiss you, I won't be able to stop even for pizza. But man, it's killing me to wait."

"Yeah? I hear you. I want you too. I want to know what you taste like."

"Oh, damn, honey." Tygh turned toward him, and they both leaned forward, and the driveway cam chirped that someone was coming. "Shit. Let me get the food. You get us a beer?"

"I can do that." Along with paper towels, because grease and cheese.

They headed out to the patio, which was nice because Tygh had turned on the heaters, and before they settled, Tygh lit the firepit, which was just the right size.

"This is sweet." He sat, putting the beers down. "Smells good."

"It does. I was hungry and I didn't know it."

"You work your butt off." He pulled out a piece of supreme for Tygh and one for him.

"Thanks, babe. I try. Some days are busier than others. You have your own hands full, huh?"

"Yes." Right now he had two teenagers, two little girls, a preschooler, and the babies. That was a lot.

"You might have to get an assistant."

"I haven't even been here a year yet. That seems like a big ask." Especially since he was teaching Naomi and caring for Maggie and Emma on the job.

"Yeah, but if they get anymore foster kids, you need to, okay? Ryder and Kase are big on having the right tools and people to do the job. Oh, yum." Tygh munched his pizza, moaning.

Okay, that was... special. He swallowed hard and grabbed his piece of pizza.

Tygh grinned a bit, and he wanted to toss a napkin at him. Evil man.

"What...what do you do for Thanksgiving? Do you have it here usually?"

"I usually go to the big house. It's just me, and they have a big family meal for the hands." Tygh tilted his head. "Not just me now, though. Do you want to do it here?"

"My parents want to come out and meet the babies, so I need to ask Ryder if they have room for them and me and Naomi as well as you." They'd already talked about a hotel room versus his guest room, and they weren't taking no for an answer.

"Oh, honey, they have room for all. They set up in the event barn, and they do it up right. I'm sure they would love to have your folks. And if not, well, I sure won't go. I'm with you."

"We'll all go, then. I'll talk to Ryder when I pick up Naomi." And, most likely, Dani. Those two were something.

"Uh-huh. Trading back and forth." Ryder chuckled. "Man, the pizza is good tonight."

"That's because you're not eating with one hand, standing up and trying to field three little girls with the other hand."

"True enough. All we have is dogs."

And Biscuit and Tater were being uber polite, in a down command, waiting for their bites.

He tossed them each half of a pizza bone, licking his fingers clean. Tygh's moan made him stop, shiver. He stared at Tygh, who was looking right back, dark eyes alight.

"Hey." His heartbeat sped, and his cock started to fill.

"Hey." Tygh closed the pizza box. "You good for now?"

"Uh-huh?" Wat felt totally breathless. "Should we check on the girls?"

"Yeah. And then I intend to sit you on the couch and make out with you until neither of us can see."

"I'm totally in." Hopefully, he wouldn't cream his—Oh,

right. "I think I'll change into some sweatpants." That would be more comfy.

"I'll meet you at the couch, then." That glinting grin, and another soft kiss, made him want to hurry. Tygh took the pizza in, then went to check on Maggie and Emma while he changed.

His cock was half hard, and he couldn't help hurrying. He wanted to get the first, weird kiss over. He wanted to know they had chemistry, that they were a match. He felt it, sure, but what if they really got to touching and went... huh. Nah.

That would be awkward.

"Stop it." He cared for Tygh. He wanted that kiss.

He wanted more.

So he marched his ass back out to the couch and parked it, waiting for the promised making out. Eagerly.

Tygh sauntered out of the girls' room, then stopped, staring at him. "Well, hello."

"Hey. You want to come sit?" *You want to make out?*

"I do. I was just admiring." Those cheeks went pink, which told him Tygh was just as unsure maybe, and as turned on as he was. At least he hoped that was what it meant.

He guessed he'd find out, sooner than later.

Wat patted the sofa cushion next to him this time, and Tygh slid close. "I was pondering brushing my teeth. Did you?"

"No."

"Then we're safe."

"Garlic ahoy?" He couldn't stop chuckling.

"Exactly." Tygh leaned close, hand landing on Wat's thigh. "I don't want to knock you over."

"If you did, I'm sitting on the sofa, right? That's okay. I won't go far."

"True enough. I'm going to kiss you now, Wat. Everyone just needs to leave us alone."

"Okay. I'm ready." He'd been ready for a while, but his heart was still pounding as Tygh took his hand and leaned in.

Their lips met, the initial contact soft and kind of sweet, but one thing became certain. He didn't have to worry about chemistry. The press of Tygh's mouth against his made his lips tingle, made his scalp prickle with heat.

A soft moan slipped out of Tygh, gliding over his lips, and he inhaled it, letting himself be aroused, excited.

Hopeful.

One of Tygh's hands rose, sliding behind his head to grip the back of his neck, holding him there while the kiss deepened. Tygh pressed against his lips with the tip of his tongue, asking to be let in.

He didn't even hesitate. He might ponder on it later, how different it was to feel stubble against his face, to feel the calluses of a strong, square hand, but right now, he didn't need to.

Right now, he needed Tygh.

And Tygh seemed to feel the same way. Rough noises came from deep in Tygh's chest, and he crowded closer, still gentle but more insistent.

He turned fully, giving Tygh more of him. It felt as if there were embers in the pit of his belly, filling him with a spreading heat. When Tygh pressed his other hand to the small of Wat's back, Wat couldn't stop the moan that escaped him, his body bowing toward Tygh.

"Oh, honey. Look at you." Tygh tugged, nice and easy, and he dragged one hand up over a shoulder, the other hand around Tygh's waist.

They leaned together, and he had to admit, it felt odd to be the smaller partner, the one who was doing the resting against someone else's chest. But not at all bad.

In fact, his cock thought it was incredibly not bad, in an intense sort of way. He filled in a rush, his balls aching in a glorious manner. It had been a while, and he was tickled half to death by the feeling.

"Mmm. God, you taste good," Tygh told him. "I knew you would." Those fingers skated over his nape, stroking and teasing.

"I'm glad. I want—I want this to be good between us." He wanted it to be amazing.

"I do too. So if I push, or if I do anything you don't like, you tell me, okay?"

"Ditto. I don't want to push or be weird."

"Deal." Tygh sealed that with another kiss.

He wasn't sure which kiss had him straddling Tygh's thighs, seated fully in his lap. He was pretty sure he'd lost count. But God, it felt amazing. Tygh wasn't lying. They were gonna make out until they couldn't see. And he was ready for that.

Wat sank his fingers into Tygh's hair, learning its curly texture. It wrapped around his fingers, and he tugged, not enough to hurt, but enough so Tygh could feel.

"Mmm." Tygh arched under him, and he held on, riding the sweet heat underneath him. Tygh felt solid, all that hard muscle bunching and releasing, and he wanted to see and touch. Not only Tygh's face and neck, but all of him.

He slid off his T-shirt, hoping he was reading this right. "This okay?"

"This is more than okay." Tygh licked his lips, staring at Wat's chest. Then he reached up to touch Wat's pectoral, thumb brushing his nipple. "Oh, honey. You're amazing. Your skin is so damn hot."

His lips parted to answer, but all he could do was utter a deep moan.

Sorry, my brain is busy melting. Forgive me.

Tygh gave him a slow grin that meant he understood. Then Tygh kissed him some more, and they touched each other, Wat sliding his hands up the flat belly to feel all the warm skin and the dusting of springy hair.

Then he took the reins and started unbuttoning Tygh's shirt, baring that sweet chest.

Tygh shrugged it off when he was done, letting him have what he wanted. Lord, that was so pretty. Tygh was broad in the shoulders and narrow in the waist, and he actually had ridged abs. Like a six-pack. That was like a national treasure. Seriously.

He traced the ridges, imagining how good it would be, to draw his tongue along Tygh's belly, tasting the salt there. His mouth went a little dry as he thought about it.

"You're looking at me like I'm dessert."

"I know. I can't help it." He touched what he coveted so much. "I want to taste you too."

"You can lick anything you want."

He paused, arrested by that thought. "Anything."

Tygh nodded, dark eyes almost feverishly bright.

"I've never..." But he knew how good it felt, and he wanted to make Tygh feel it.

"We can work up to stuff like that, honey." Tygh stroked his hair. "I got you."

"I'm not opposed."

"No, neither am I." Tygh winked. "But we still have a lot to learn about each other, huh?"

"We do." He licked along Tygh's neck, and he could taste salt.

Better than that, he could hear the soft gasp that proved that Tygh had a hot spot right there, right under his ear. He poked at it with his tongue, making Tygh rumble and move under him, damn near unseating him.

Then Tygh turned them, laying him out on the couch and lowering on top of him to press them together and take more control of the situation.

Oh fuck, that was hot, and he arched, rubbing hard against Tygh's belly.

"So good." Tygh rocked against him, and he could feel the hard ridge of Tygh's cock against his thigh. Hot as a brand too, even through their clothes.

Listen to him, thinking in ranch terms.

Hell, he was impressed that he was thinking, full stop.

Tygh seemed to be pretty much running on instinct too. That mouth moved over his face and neck, and then Tygh slid to love on his chest, tongue brushing his nipples in turn, then running along his sternum.

The rasp of Tygh's stubble made him wiggle, and he couldn't believe how delicious it felt. He stroked the back of Tygh's neck, then down his back, testing all that muscle. He stopped at the waistband of Tygh's pants, but he wanted to go under the fabric to feel that tight butt.

"It's okay, baby. Touch me. I want you to." Tygh lifted his face, meeting his gaze. "I'm not scairt."

"No? Okay. Good." Was he? He wasn't certain, but he wasn't going to miss this opportunity. So he tugged, and Tygh lifted up so Wat could shove those pants down. He slid his hands over the smooth skin and tight muscles, then tested all that with his short nails.

It was enough to let him know that he was all in, that he needed to touch more, to feel every inch of that amazing body.

"I want to feel you too, Wat. Can we just get naked?" Tygh leaned back again to tug at his sweats. He got it. Skin on skin. Why the hell not?

Wat nodded. "Go for it."

"Thank you." Tygh stood to strip off his pants, then tug Wat's away as well. "Oh, aren't you pretty?"

Then Tygh took his cock, palmed it, and made sure that he felt it, as he stroked from base to tip.

"Oh, God." He was going to lose it. Tygh's hand was big,

square, callused, and so hot he might keel over dead from how it felt around him. He forgot anything but how good that was.

He spread, his hips jerking as he fought to—hell, he didn't know. Get closer? Come? Not come?

He had no idea.

Then Tygh's other hand flattened on his belly, holding him down, and he knew it was to get more contact. His body wanted to come.

"I'm about to start babbling," he told Tygh.

"I want to hear it."

Oh thank God. He wasn't the best at the stern stoic thing. Not at all. So he moaned, letting everything that wanted out happen as his balls drew up. He was going to go off like a rocket, and he didn't want to be selfish...

"I want to— You need."

"We have plenty of time, honey. If not tonight then soon. I promise. And you can give me a hand too."

"Promise. Not an asshole." In fact, he was a decent person, or he tried to be.

"Oh, hell, honey. I know that." Tygh gave him a wild grin. "If I thought you were a shit, I wouldn't be here right now, let alone living with you and raising kids." Tygh sobered a bit. "Which is nuts, right?"

"We both love the girls. We both want to try. We were both honest. That's adult, not nuts." Right?

"It is." Tygh kissed him, then stroked him in a nice, steady rhythm. "Not that I'm trying to ruin the mood."

"I don't think you could. I sort of want you madly, man. You've got amazing hands." And he'd been alone a long damn time.

"And you have the best damn skin. It just begs for my touch." Tygh proved that by petting his belly and thighs.

It was easy to let one foot land on the floor and spread, offer himself over. Tygh made him feel erotic, heated, sensual.

He opened up, and Tygh explored, touching his balls, then slipping behind them. He almost rose off the couch when Tygh tapped at his hole.

"Tygh!"

"Nothing you don't want, Wat," Tygh reminded him.

He laughed, the sound a bit hysterical to his own ears. "I want everything, though."

"Not this time. I'm woefully unprepared." Tygh's breathless laughter joined his. "This time, we just explore and love on each other."

"I like that." Love on each other sounded so much better than jack each other off or something. His belly pulled in tight when Tygh touched him there again, his breath whooshing out of him. He couldn't get it back either, so he started to pant, his hips rocking back and forth between the hand on his cock and the one on his ass.

"I do too. I got you, Wat. I see you. Come on, honey. Show me how much you want me."

How Tygh could keep up a steady stream of words, he had no idea. They weren't dirty so much as encouraging, and Wat let himself be led, his whole body on fire, but especially his lower half. He roared toward his orgasm, his cock on fire.

But showing Tygh how much he wanted was about easy. He bucked up, and when he pushed back, Tygh's finger pressed inside him, just enough to burn. That was all she wrote, and he lost it, his balls emptying in a rush.

He bit down hard on his lip to keep from shouting and waking the girls, a ridiculous noise coming from him instead. "Unnnn." He came over Tygh's hand, and it felt like he was back in high school, eager and devastated.

"So damn pretty."

He blinked up at Tygh, feeling dazed, his ears ringing. "Huh?"

"You're so damn pretty when you come." Tygh sounded...

smug. He had to laugh at that all over again, but then he shoved Tygh off him, catching Tygh unaware, if that surprised grunt was anything to go by. He felt amazing, and he was going to make Tygh feel the same way. He took Tygh's cock in hand, stroking hard, finding a rhythm that would do the job.

He set his mind to making sure that Tygh was over the moon. He wanted Tygh to feel as good as he did.

That face and chest flushed, Tygh's breath coming hard, and the cock in his hand swelled. It wouldn't be long. Not at this rate.

Today was a list of firsts, and he intended to enjoy them, learn from them.

Tygh moaned, bucking, and he glanced down to see where his hand was. What touch had done that. Right under the head, he thought. Right where a bundle of nerves made it feel squirmy good. He knew that from experience.

He used his thumb to work that spot, moving it nice and steady, rubbing until Tygh shuddered. Then he squeezed and pulled, and Tygh grunted, eyes closing as he came, shooting hard all over his belly.

"Hottest thing ever." The proof he'd made Tygh come was unexpectedly satisfying.

"Uh-huh." Now Tygh was the one who looked to be having trouble forming words. "Damn."

He grabbed his T-shirt and cleaned Tygh off before daring to move close again. Tygh dragged him in to curl up against that broad chest, then tugged a blanket around them.

"Comfy?"

"Perfect. You?" He was happy as a bug in a rug.

"I am so good right now." Tygh stroked his back. "That was amazing, honey."

"I thought so too. And no one is crying."

"I know. But let's not look that gift horse in the mouth."

Tygh patted his butt, and he had to chuckle. Some things were universal, he guessed. Soothing pats were one of them.

"I try not to look any horses in the mouth."

"It's kind of my job." Tygh sighed, holding on tight. "We can do this again, right?"

"Any time you want, Tygh," Wat promised. "Any time you want." And he meant it. That first-time awkwardness was out of the way.

Second-time awkwardness could hardly be more fun.

Chapter Eighteen

"Tygh, I'm going to need you to check Baby Huey every day. I need him in fighting form by the finals."

"Sure, Boss." Tygh got it. The damn bull didn't seem injured at all, and the films didn't show anything they could treat, but three days out of the last five, the bull manager had found Baby Huey out limping around in the mornings.

If he was injured, he needed to go into quarantine and try to heal up before the finals. If he was just being an asshole to get attention, then he needed to be left alone.

It was a fine line to walk.

Ryder clapped him on the back. "Good man. So what are you and Wat doing for Thanksgiving?"

"Well, we talked about it, and we were hoping you all had room for us," Tygh said. "We really want Naomi and the girls to feel like they're in the thick of it their first year here, and Wat's folks will be here."

"You know we have plenty of room."

"Cool. Cool, thanks. I'll ask Nanette what we can bring."

Ryder nodded easily. "Drinks, for sure. She always needs drinks. And if there's something from Wat's childhood…"

"I'll ask him." He would make mac and cheese. His grandma had been from Texas, and she'd made the best. One of the few things he had from her was a little recipe book he'd tucked into his backpack when he'd gone to the house the last time to pick out what clothes and toys he wanted. That and a piece of her jewelry, a black cameo with a chipped edge.

"Can you ride out with me this morning to see the bulls?"

"I'm good right now if you are." He pulled out his phone to text Wat. "Let me just tell Wat I'm not in the barn. The girls have snuck out on him a few times while he's changing babies. I've been stern enough that they seem to have learned their lesson, but the one day I'm not there…"

"Oh, God, tell me. Elijah was terrible about that the first three months he was here. One of the town kids told him he needed to prove how brave he was by riding a yearling. I swear, I thought I might just explode."

"I get that. I try not to shout at Dani or Naomi, because I know they've had a rough time, but I get scared and I sure want to roar."

<hey. Heading to the pasture. Watch the hooligans?>

<on it. have fun>

<Bulls> He knew Wat would get that. Bulls could be way less fun than horses or other smaller animals. But easier than bison.

Or ostriches.

Man, those dinosaur birds bit hard.

They headed over to grab one of the gator vehicles to run out to the bull pasture, and he loved the feel of what was essentially a souped-up golf cart. It made him smile.

"Things going good for you over at your house? Naomi seems to be doing great."

"She really is. And Jennifer is real pleased with Maggie and

Emma's progress too." His cheeks heated, because him and Wat? They were making amazing inroads themselves.

Wat was beginning to spend nights in his bed, and more and more of Wat's things were shifting to his room. They'd even had a shower together, though that had been ridiculous and had almost ended up with Wat getting a concussion. Their shower wasn't big enough for that shit.

They had babies and dogs too, which meant things like lots of being woken up in the middle of the night.

The wee hours of the morning.

"I can see it with Maggie, for sure. She's growing in leaps and bounds."

"She is. I swear, she learns more words every day." He was so proud of her. She was his brave girl.

"I know Jennifer was scared she was damaged, but she just needed her papa."

"She has me." He glanced at Ryder. "I know you know how that feels."

"God, yes. Charlie just... she kills me. She caught me by the heart the day she showed up, ready to defend her siblings from all comers, but so lost. I love her so much it scares the crap out of me." Ryder sighed. "And I feel like I have to watch her make mistakes now that she's in her first year of college and going a little wild, and I hate it."

"That sucks, man." And it told him what he had to look forward to. This parenthood gig was no light thing. But he was in all the way. Wholeheartedly.

"It does, but it also makes me proud. I know she'll come out the other side stronger. She's a good kid. She just has to test the waters."

"While you drown a little."

"Yeah. Kase is going to be that way with Nell. When she starts school and never looks back her first day, it's going to break his heart. But then, Dani is our girl too. And she's a homebody."

"She's a dollbaby. And she's going to care for your animals like no one else."

"She is. I just hope she learns to be practical as well."

"You know she will." That much he believed. Kase and Ryder and Ryder's grans—they were all imminently practical. They would teach Dani what she needed to know.

And he'd help. He loved that little girl to death, and he adored how she and Naomi were best buds.

"I believe she will," Ryder said, "but it seems like one step forward and two steps back."

"She's really a lot more grounded than when I first met her."

Ryder's grin broke out, fond as hell. "Yep. She's a little cowgirl."

They pulled up at the pasture where Baby Huey was being housed right now, hopping out to go to the fence and stare at the big Brahma cross.

"Hey, Huey!" Ryder called, then whistled.

The huge gray bull came meandering over, head heavy and swaying, hump solid. Those soft ears flicked back and forth, and he looked at them, liquid brown eyes calculating the fence, maybe.

"Hey, buddy. At least you're not limping today," Ryder said.

"Faker bo baker." Tygh thought the big guy was just looking for attention. "I'm telling you, Boss, he's just being a dick."

"I sure hope so. I mean, I know the films aren't showing anything, but—"

"But chronic soft tissue won't always show that way. I get it." And this bull was worth his weight in cash, if not gold. "I think he's smart enough to know that if he limps, he doesn't get loaded."

"Asshole bull. He only has to work sixteen seconds a week."

"They tend to be that way, though, don't they?" No matter what.

"They do. They're just smart enough to be trouble and full of testosterone." Ryder snorted. "Okay. We'll try loading him for this weekend. See what happens."

"If he balks, then we'll call in a specialist, but I really think he's just a prick."

Ryder chuckled. "I know he is, but he's good. While he's here, let's look at that futurity bull. I think he's in good shape, but I'd like you to clear him."

"Totally. How's he bucking? Are you keeping him or selling him?"

"He's doing well, but I might still sell him. There's an investment team who wants to buy him and then pay us to house and feed him. Win-win."

"Oh, I like that—you get to double-dip on him." That could be a good job, if you could get it.

"That's what I thought." Ryder took him to see a young bull who had some great conformation.

"You sure you don't want to keep him and breed him? He's awful pretty."

Ryder chuckled and nodded. "He is. I just need to see if he bucks under pressure and not just for fun."

"Well, it's a good thing that we know a guy with a rodeo company." Tygh almost managed not to roll his eyes.

"It is. With a practice arena and contacts in the bucking futurity." Ryder shot him a glance. "Smartass."

"Yeah well, without getting him in a pinch stall, he looks good. If you need me to examine him tomorrow, I'll get the guys to round him up." He didn't have any problems getting the cowboys to do as he asked.

"Cool. I'd appreciate that." They headed back to the gator. "So is it working out okay to have Wat at your place?"

"It's perfect. He's... he fits pretty well. I'm nervous about meeting the parents."

"You said they're coming for Thanksgiving?" Ryder got them moving back toward the house.

"Yeah. They want to see Naomi and Wat, of course, but meet the babies too."

"Family can be odd, but they can also be good. I would never have expected my gran to fall in love with Kase."

"She does like him a lot. It's obvious." He could only hope that Wat's people tolerated him.

"She does. I think you'll do fine."

"Thanks, man. I hope so. I don't want them to be like, what the hell? You know?"

"Do they know... you know, about you being gay?"

"I have no idea. I need to ask Wat, I reckon." They needed to talk about shit.

He got the side-eye. "That does seem... important..."

"Hush." He chuckled. "Wat and I are still working on that stuff too."

"Is he... I mean, that's important, man, that y'all are... compatible."

"We are. Trust me." He cleared his throat, because that came close to kissing and telling. "Not a problem."

"Fucking A." Ryder winked at him like he was sharing a secret. "I mean, we're dads, but... we're men too."

"We are. Thanks, Boss." He loved that Ryder got it, that he never had to worry about someone firing his ass for being gay. It gave him security, but more than that, it gave him the illusion of home.

Illusion? Was that the right thought? Ryder and Kase—

hell, even the ladies Chiara—never once gave him the impression this place was false. No, they worked their asses off to be open. Welcoming. Safe.

So he needed to give them that—full stop.

Ryder pulled up at the barn, then clapped him on the shoulder. "You're welcome. My advice is talk to your man about his folks sooner rather than later. Don't wait until they get here." Ryder winked at him. "That's when shit gets crazy awkward."

"I'll bring it up today." Maybe at lunch.

In fact, when Ryder waved and left for the house, he texted Wat again. *<Lunch today?>*

<Love to. Homeschooling co-op is picking everyone up for paint your own pottery at 1.>

<Then I'll come help get everyone off and we can have something yummy in town if you want>

<Oh, yay! I'd love that. You, me, and the littlest hooligans>

<Yeah. Let's make it a thing.> He could take the time. He was pretty well done with his work, since they had so few animals in quarantine, and he wanted to hang out with Wat, somewhere not in their house.

They could grab some Mexican food maybe. They ate pizza a good bit. Sanchez's Cantina would be a nice change. He checked his watch, then made one last set of rounds while he had time, doling out carrots and apples.

Soon enough he heard Alice Natchez's big old van rolling up to pick up the four homeschoolers to add to her three. Time to help load the kids.

He grinned at the excited yelling going on as he strolled up. "Hey, you guys. Let's calm down for Alice, huh?"

"Mister Tygh! Are you coming to paint pottery?" Dani asked, and Naomi giggled and shook her head.

"He's going to love on Daddy."

"I am. You guys go have so much fun, huh?"

"I love to paint!" Dani said.

"Me too!" Naomi offered him a worried glance. "Right?"

"Yep. It will be a blast, I bet." He knew Alice would be great at helping if Naomi needed an extra hand.

"Okay. Okay, right. I'll do something so much fun!"

"That's it. And Dani has been before so she can show you how it all works." That was Alice, smiling as she came to load the girls into her van. "That always makes it easier."

"It does. We'll be in town, if you need us."

"We won't, but thanks!"

"Wounded. Shall we go get the littles?" Wat asked.

"Mmmhmm." He followed Wat into the house to go to the school area, but he caught Wat in the hall to kiss him hard.

Wat's eyes flew open, and it only took a second before Wat grabbed hold of him, clinging like a limpet. That was just what he needed to get rid of his nerves, to remind him this was about him and Wat.

All the rest was next. They were making a relationship.

It felt really fine, and it was worth the work. He hugged Wat tight. "Much better."

"Uh-huh. Very much better. Hey."

"Hey. So I was thinking Mexican. What do you think?"

"Love it. The kids can have tacos and mushy goo."

"Or just refritos." Because he wasn't sure Maggie was up to tacos.

"Beans make them poot, but it'll work."

"Mmm. Angel poots."

They cracked up, because that child farted like a basset hound.

Or worse, a pit bull.

Those guys were intense. Especially with Mexican food.

Wat grabbed Emma, and he got Maggie who reached for him, waving her hands.

"Want to go to lunch with papa?"

"Papa!" That smile bloomed over Maggie's face.

"That's my girls."

"Dadda." Maggie beamed at Wat.

"We're both going with you," Wat said, his smile stretching his cheeks.

Emma sighed, her satisfaction obvious.

He grinned, ushering everyone out to the SUV. "We're going to have fo-o-o-od." He sang it, because that made the girls cackle. They liked his George Strait impersonation.

"FOOD!" Maggie cheered.

"Yep. We love food."

They strapped the kids in, and he headed into town, Wat humming along with the radio. He was pretty tickled with life himself.

"You seem happy. You having a good day?"

"I am. Baby Huey seems to be in good health. I've had a pretty light day. We're on at the big house for Thanksgiving."

"Good deal. Did they say what we should bring?"

"Just anything that's important for us to have. Drinks. I'll make Granny's mac and cheese."

"Ah. I bet my mom will make a green chile apple pie, and Naomi wants a cheese ball."

"What do you like?" They'd talked about this some, but not too much, and he was wildly curious.

"The mashed potatoes are my favorite, to be honest. And the rolls." Wat snorted, offering him a goofy-assed grin. "Lord, how do you say you're a carb addict without saying you're a huge carb addict."

"You really are," Tygh teased. "I actually like the turkey a lot. I love a roll with turkey, cranberry sauce, and gravy the next day."

"You and my dad. That's totally his jam."

"Yeah?" He paused, working up courage. "You think he'll like me?"

"My dad? You and he will sit together and grunt. My parents are totally practical people. Not like me at all."

"I don't think you're flighty, honey. Not at all." He loved Wat's creativity.

"No, but I'm… not completely grounded in reality, right?" Wat's chuckle was a touch embarrassed.

"You do damn well." He grinned, thinking how good Wat was with the kids. How patient.

How he was always looking for a way to make learning fun.

Tygh thought he'd lose his mind. He wasn't the most patient man.

"I was worried what your folks might think."

"What do you mean? Do you mean about us? Being together?"

"Yeah. I mean, you were with a woman." That had to be weird, right?

"Yes. I mean, they're smart, educated—they know bisexuality is a thing. And no, I don't know if either one of them is. I'd rather be blissfully ignorant."

"Oh God, I don't blame you." He checked the rearview. Emma was dozing, and Maggie was singing to herself. "I would want that too."

"I'm sure it's weird, but I didn't—I mean, Michelle won't care. She always knew that I was… that I was interested." Wat shook his head. "She was something else."

"She sounds like it." He probably would have liked her a lot.

"Yeah, but she would love how you are with Naomi. She would be jealous of how you make me nuts."

"She would, huh?" Tygh had to grin at that. "I do my best, honey. It goes both ways."

"Do you have any exes I need to worry about?"

"Not really, no. I had a few encounters, but nothing serious."

"I don't get it. You're amazing. How did you not get snatched up?"

"Me?" He made the last turn into town. "Honey, I'm a grump. Really. I put people off."

"That's nonsense. You're amazing." And Wat sounded as though he believed it.

"Well, I've been told I growl too much. You and the girls bring out the best in me. Like the animals do." He couldn't explain it.

"I'm tickled. I want to be... something cool."

"You really are." He reached over to press Wat's hand but had to let go to turn into the restaurant lot. It was a bit of a tight turn.

"Papa! Foo-oo-ood!" Maggie was absolutely joyful. His smart girl.

"Yep. Maybe we'll get a sopapilla, huh?" She loved them with a drizzle of honey. He loved them with a flood of it.

"You spoil her." There was zero heat in Wat's voice. He loved that she was growing.

"I do. But then, you do too. I've seen you sneaking her shortbread cookies." She still had to soak them in milk, but...

"Moi? Never say so!" Wat's happy laugh suited him to the ground. "My folks are going to love you."

"I sure hope so." It would suck if they didn't. He'd live through it, but it would be way easier if they got along.

After all, he was pretty damn serious about their kid.

Incredibly serious.

Chapter Nineteen

The house was clean.

The children were—in theory—clean. There was no particular reason either of the babies should be filthy, and Naomi had been warned to stay sparkly until her grandparents saw her at least two or three minutes.

It was the best he could ask.

Tygh had scrubbed the kitchen. Clean sheets and pillow-cases adorned the bed in the newly renovated guest bedroom, since he'd decided not to let his folks stay at a hotel. They'd gone with a Pendleton blanket theme and deep Southwest colors.

Hopefully, his mom would love it. His dad would be indifferent.

What mattered was that Tygh had cared enough to put out the effort.

"Whew. You ready for this?" Tygh came to wrap an arm around him, gazing out of the front window. The little girls were down for a nap. That way Naomi could see her grandparents first, before they met the babies.

"I am. I'm ready to stop worrying about it and have them here. I know it'll be fine, you know?"

"Yeah. Yeah, once we get the whole first half hour settled, it will be great." Tygh wore a good pair of jeans and nice sweater, which was a very good look for him. A touch weird, compared the stained denim, flannel, and thermal Henleys he usually wore, but hot.

Wat kept finding himself with excuses to touch, to stroke. He loved how Tygh felt in general, but today, he needed the closeness.

And it didn't hurt that Tygh was... fine to him. He could just stare at the pretty man for hours. Pretty. Tygh would laugh at that.

His phone chirped. *<Not left into the ranch, but right at the lane across from it?>*

<Yep>

"Okay, they're turning in."

Tygh took a deep breath and smiled. "Don't let me fall over and bust something in front of them."

"Right. And don't do anything too hot, because springing wood in front of them is... ew."

That surprised a laugh out of Tygh, and he hooted. "Got it."

He kissed Tygh's cheek, then called out, "Honey, come on. Nana and Pappy are here!"

Naomi came running out, her pink princess dress and brown cowboy boots combined with a huge cardigan he thought was Tygh's.

"I'm ready! I've missed them so much."

"Yeah? Me too." Truth be told, Wat had been too busy to miss anyone too much.

"You're going to meet them too, Papa Tygh!" Naomi came to hug Tygh, squeeze him tight.

"I am. I can't wait, kiddo."

His folks' car appeared over the little rise, then pulled in at the house, and they all went out with the dogs to meet them.

"Nana!! This is my new house!" Naomi waved, bouncing and trying to get their attention.

"Hey, sweetie. I can see that. It's very nice." His mom rubbed dog ears, then came to get hugs.

She smelled like jasmine and Ivory soap, and the familiarity of it hurt his soul, in the weirdest way, because he couldn't remember what Michelle smelled like anymore—not practically or in his heart. It was slipping through his fingers like sand.

He needed to make it a point to remember her with Naomi more often. Tygh wouldn't be mad at that, and he knew it. It wasn't that he didn't still love her, but—

"Hey. Baby boy. Where'd you go?"

"I don't know." Away into a past that still hurt.

"Well, we're here, so stick around." His mom beamed at him, then moved to grab Naomi. "Hey, you. I'm so glad to see you."

"Me too! You have to meet Papa Tygh! And my sisters! I have two little sisters!"

"I will have to meet everyone." His mom stroked Naomi's hair. "But give me a second to love on you, huh?"

"My arm is all healed." She held it up, the crocheted little sock Alba made her covering it.

"That's a very pretty sleeve," Mom said.

"Uh-huh. Mimi made it for me, Abue."

"Mimi?"

"Dani's granny. She has two. They're married, like Mister Ryder and Kase."

Mom stood there and blinked, while Dad grabbed Tygh's hand and shook. "Pleased to meet you, man."

"Nice to meet you, sir." Tygh sounded nervous, but he doubted his folks would know.

"Pappy. Hug me tight!" Naomi leapt at his dad, totally fearless.

He caught her, swinging her in a circle. "My little girl. How are you?"

"I am good! I have a best friend and new sisters!"

"Wow. That's so neat. So you like it here, huh? It's very pretty." He set her down, wrapping an arm around her.

"There's horses and dogs and pizza, too."

"Pizza?"

"Uh-huh. And goats and scary bulls and chickens and a classroom, and we're going to have Santa come here!"

"Wow." Dad winked at him. "Amazing."

"Uh-huh. I asked for a horse. I wanted a puppy, but Tater and Biscuit need me very bad."

"They're large." Dad looked at the two, wagging, drooling beasts as they all walked inside.

"She's always wanted a dog," Mom murmured. "So that's a win."

"It is. And they adore her."

"I can see that." She chuckled. "I like it here, Tygh. It's real pretty."

"Thank you. Would you all like a cup of coffee?"

"We would. Sweetheart, will you help Tygh while I go see Naomi's new room and peek in on her new sisters?"

Oh, Mom was good.

"I will." Dad nodded easily.

"Mimi helped me make cookies for you." Naomi was off like a shot, dragging Mom toward her room like a tugboat.

"So was I supposed to stay here or follow her?" Dad was way better at reading women, right?

Dad gave him a grin. "I think you were frozen out, son."

"I think you were supposed to stay here." Tygh chuckled. "Looks like she wants Naomi to be the one to introduce her around. Smart lady."

"Well, she is very proud of her new room. She and Tygh painted it together." And decorated it together. He hadn't been allowed to help.

"I bet. She looks great, Wat. So do you."

"Thanks. We're trying to make a routine. I think she's going to try public school after the holidays."

"Wow." His dad looked impressed. "I know she was pretty adamantly against that."

"She still is, but it's important that she tries." Wat shook his head. They had another month to argue about it.

"Well, good luck, then. This is a nice place."

"Thanks. I'm kind of in love with it," Tygh said. "It's even better now."

Wat's cheeks heated and he ducked his head. Okay, that felt good.

His dad chuckled. "I like the sound of that."

"I do too." In fact, he sort of loved it.

"Good deal." Tygh poured coffee. "What all do you take in it, sir?"

"Cream. I used to be black, but my stomach isn't what it used to be."

"Sure. It gets acidy." Tygh pulled out the cream to let his dad make up a coffee. "Have you tried that bulletproof coffee?"

"Nope. What's that?" Dad snagged a kitchen chair.

"It's coffee blended with MCT oil and grass-fed butter. It's supposed to be amazing for you..." But he thought it sounded tough.

"Ugh." Dad made more noises, making them both laugh. "No."

"No? We could try..." he teased.

"Now, if you offer butter on bread."

"Oh, now that's totally doable. With cinnamon and sugar, even." His dad had a soft spot for cinnamon toast.

"Yum. Yes please. And some for Naomi."

Wat nodded. "She never turns that down."

"I'll make enough for us all to have a snack. I expect we'll have Dani walkie-talkieing over any moment." Tygh rolled his eyes.

"Do they do that a lot?" Dad's eyebrows rose.

"Daddy! Can Dani come over and meet Abuelita? Mimi has to go to the store, and she can drop her off." Naomi dragged Mom into the kitchen.

"All the time," Wat answered, just managing not to roll his eyes. "That good with you, Mom?"

"That's fine. That's your best friend, right, nieta?"

"Dani is the bestest *best* best friend, Abue!"

"I'm so glad." His mom winked at him. "Oh, it's so nice in here. Thank you, Tygh." She took the coffee Tygh handed her.

"You're welcome, ma'am. Naomi, do you and Dani want hot cocoa?"

"With marshmallows, Papa?"

"With—"

"PAPA! PAPAPAPAPA!" Maggie yelled, which set Emma to wailing.

"Be right back." Tygh hustled out of the room and they could hear him talking to Maggie and Emma.

"She's got a set of lungs on her, doesn't she?"

"She does." He fought the urge to go see if Tygh needed help. He would holler if he did. "Emma's a little—"

"I'm going to help Papa with *my* sisters!" Naomi ran for the girls' bedroom.

"She's very proud to be a sister," Dad said.

"She goes back and forth between that and worrying that I don't love her as much as I did." He had no idea if that was normal; he was an only child.

"That sounds about par for the course." Dad didn't seem the least bit worried.

"Oh, good. I wasn't sure." He chuckled. "Tygh's no help there, either. He was a foster kid."

"So he had a number of siblings, sort of, and none at all in others?" Dad asked, and he guessed that was about right.

"Yeah. I guess it was different all over."

"Scary. Seriously, it's just scary." At least he thought it had been. Tygh didn't want to talk about it.

"Well, he seems like a solid type." That was a good thing as far as Dad was concerned.

"Like a rock. I—he's a good father, one hell of a man." And Wat was pretty sure he was in love. Like deep in love.

"I'm glad, son. I admit, we were surprised." Dad looked at his mom.

"I..." How did he explain? He'd always thought some men were hot as hell, but he'd never thought he'd act on it.

He'd never thought he'd lose Michelle either.

"Hey. I don't expect you to defend yourself or anything, because nothing is wrong. It's just unexpected."

He hugged his mom. "Thank you."

"I love you. I love my grandbabies. It's a thing." She kissed his cheek. "Now, does Tygh need help?"

"It sounds like it." There was wailing, Naomi giggling, and Tygh... well, not cursing. "I'll be right back. Make yourselves at home."

Then he hurried to the girls' room.

"Hey, there you are. Gimme a hand, huh? Emma needs changing, but—" But Maggie was clinging to Tygh's neck like a monkey, and Naomi was trying to pry her off.

"NO! Papa! NO!"

"Stupid baby. You have to share!" Naomi snapped. "We all have to share!"

"Easy, baby girl. Don't call names." He winked at Naomi and smiled. "But you're right. We have to share. I'm going to help with Emma. Do you want to watch for Dani?"

"Okay! I'll take Abue!" She ran off.

"Lord. She's swinging wildly, huh?" Tygh was like a fractious horse, eyes a little too wide, a little too bright.

"She's excited. Grandparents. Holiday. New sisters. New best friend."

"New papa..." Tygh murmured, and Wat nodded as he got Emma changed.

"New papa."

Tygh took a deep breath, then cradled Maggie in one arm, unlooping her with the other hand. "It's okay, baby girl. It's just Daddy's Momma and Dad. They came to see you. No one is going anywhere."

"It's Abue and Abuelito. They're going to love you."

Maggie sniffled, peeking at him from Tygh's collar. "Abue?"

"Yes! Do you know that word? Abue? She wants to meet you. She loves you already."

Maggie's lips pursed as if she was thinking hard, but she did nod in time. "Abue."

"Well, come on then, baby girl. We'll go meet her. I got you." Tygh bounced Maggie and she giggled.

Wat scooped Emma up, and they all headed into the kitchen where his folks and Naomi were waiting.

And Dani.

"Hey, kiddo," Tygh said. "You have all your stuff?"

"Yessir."

"Good deal. Naomi, did you introduce Dani around?"

"Yes, Papa Tygh."

"Excellent. This is Maggie and Emma."

"Abue," Maggie said.

Mom's eyes went wide, but she nodded. "Yes, baby girl. I'm your abue."

Maggie beamed and reached for her. "Abue!"

Mom took Maggie into her arms, her eyes misty.

"Lito, am I your girl?" Naomi asked Dad.

"Of course you are. I'm looking forward to meeting everyone, but you know I love you so much." He hugged Naomi tight. "You will always be my oldest nieta. Always."

"Thank you, 'Lito." She sighed. "I love babies, but it's hard."

Dani snorted. "It's always hard when they're cute babies."

Tygh laughed, nodding, and he supposed that was spoken like a true foster kid, even though Dani had been adopted.

"Yeah, they're cute when they're babies so we don't eat them." Naomi's words made him gasp a bit, but Tygh just laughed harder.

Someone had maybe heard that recently, and Wat stared at Tygh, who held up his hands, snort-laughing. "Wasn't me."

"Mr. Kase said that."

"Daddy says that a lot. Really a lot." Dani was so proud. "Especially about puppies."

"Ah." Wat nodded. "Now, that I can see." He grinned at his folks. "Kase is one of the owners of the ranch. You'll meet him tomorrow."

"He's one of my daddies. I love him very much. Very much." Dani beamed at his folks. "Both my daddies 'dopted me and my sisters and Lijah."

"I heard that," Mom said. "Can we all sit and have a little snack, Wat? I'm munchy."

"Sure." He got Emma into her highchair, and she squealed, knowing that meant food.

"What are we going to have, nieta?" Dad asked Naomi, who frowned for a second, giving him a long stare.

He nodded, encouraging her to remember the cheese and cracker tray in the fridge.

"Oh! Cheese and crackies." She twirled, barely missing some parts Tygh would probably rather not have hit. "Help me get it out, Dani?"

"Sure! Are there grapes? That's my favorite part."

"Of course! You're my best friend! Papa Tygh says there are always grapes here for you."

Mom was grinning at the girls with the *aw* face, and Dad was grinning at him. He thought they approved.

Now they just needed to get through Thanksgiving.

Chapter Twenty

Tygh got Maggie into the car, then made sure Naomi and Dani were buckled in. With Joe and Irene, Wat's folks, in there too, he'd have to take the truck over, which was fine. He had all the food.

The dogs hopped into the back as soon as he headed to the truck, and he grinned. "Okay, since it's a holiday. Some kind of livestock guardians you are."

Both beasts wagged at him, tongues lolling. Goofy critters. He loved them more than was necessary.

"Okay, you have to play nice with Mookie and the pack." They always did, but he always said it.

"Papa Tygh! You have to come too!" Naomi called out her window.

"I'm coming right now, baby girl. I just needed to get everything in the truck. I'll see you there." He waved as Wat eased out onto the drive.

He couldn't believe this was happening—that he had a lover, three girls who needed him, a family, a place.

It scared the fuck out of him, how much he wanted this.

Tygh took a deep breath, then hopped in the truck, which

smelled like mac and cheese and green chile apple pie. Naomi's cheese ball was tucked into a Tupperware container, and there were drinks for all, along with bottles for Emma and cheese crackers for Maggie, who might get picky.

The drive took no time, and he parked at the ranch house, making sure not to block anyone in. People would come and go all day.

"Let me help get the girls in and I'll come back for the food," he told Wat, meeting him as Wat stepped out of the SUV.

"Cool. Happy Thanksgiving, huh? Our first together."

"I know." He took a moment to smile at Wat, to reach out and touch his cheek. "Yay."

"Yeah, yay." Wat leaned in and, to his utter shock, kissed him right on the lips.

He gave his lover a wild grin, his heart pounding. Wow. Okay. This was happy all right.

"Papa! Papa, me!"

"Someone would like you to get her, Papa," Wat teased.

"I can see that. Maybe I should carry Emma..."

"Papaaaaaaaa!" The wail was real, and he laughed, because he would never disappoint his Maggie Mae.

"I got you, baby girl. I do." Tygh grabbed Maggie out of her car seat. "Hey, you."

"Papa! Up me!" She was all smiles, and he couldn't bear how happy he made her.

"Up-up!" He swung her around, laughing when she squealed.

Emma watched him, her gaze focused from her perch on Wat's hip.

"You want to fly too, Em?" He kissed Maggie before offering her to Wat's dad.

She frowned at him, but Wat handed her right over. "Go see Papa."

"Hey, sweet girl. It's okay. We can be a little more careful, huh?" He took her in his arms and rubbed their cheeks together. "See? I got you."

She gave him a sweet little open-mouthed kiss for his troubles.

"Aw, thank you." Whew. They maybe needed to trade off more often. Thank God, Maggie was fascinated with Joe's buttons.

Wat grinned at him, and then started carrying in food, letting Dani and Naomi help. The girls balanced as if they were on a beam, making sure not to tip the pie and casserole.

The place was packed—Grannies, the Chiara clan, cowboys, kids. There were piles of food, and it all smelled like heaven.

"Mom, Dad—I'd like to introduce you to the Chiara family." Wat started on introductions while he rescued food one-handed. There was lots of bouncing with carrying a baby.

Lots.

"Hey, there. I'm Kase, and this is Ryder." Kase grabbed stuff from him. "Come on in."

"This is glorious. Thank you for inviting us. Your Dani is a dear." Irene beamed. She was loving having more people to care for.

"You're very welcome. Come meet my grans." Ryder took his folks to meet Alba and Antonia, and Wat grinned at him.

"You good?" Tygh asked.

"I am. You? You doing okay?"

"I'm great." He could bust, in fact. He was a proud chicken.

"You are. They both like you."

"Yeah? Cool. Your folks are a hoot." Tygh liked them a lot. Sensible, kind people. He thought he could stand to have them as in-laws.

Which was kind of a huge thought.

It wasn't odd—they had babies they were raising, and he thought Wat was as determined to give them a permanent family as he was. But it was more than that, and Tygh knew it. He wanted to give them a family with Wat. He wanted to be with Wat. Full-on.

Maybe soon they'd have a night to spend some time, naked, together, touching and talking. Their lives were so busy with children and animals and the basics of day-to-day that Tygh hadn't had a chance to woo Wat, not really.

Not that he knew how to do that. He was more the nice-boots-wanna-fuck type, to be honest, and poor Wat was used to being with a woman...

"Tygh?" Kase touched his elbow, so careful. "Where'd you go?"

"Huh? Oh, I'm right here." He grinned. "It's been a busy couple of days. Smells damn good in here, though, man."

Emma reached for Kase, and he took her. "Look at you! Y'all have done some work. She's learning to trust."

Wat chuckled as he went by carrying some kind of cheese tray. "Put to work already. She's looking good, huh? I'm super pleased with how they're both progressing."

"She came to me, no stress. I'm stunned. Good job, y'all."

Emma frowned as Wat walked by without stopping, then looked back to Tygh with wide eyes.

He grinned at her. "You got this, chickie mama. We're here to have yummies." She loved her noms now. And Maggie was at the point where she would shove anything in her mouth.

"I got you, kiddo. I promise to keep you in sight of your daddies. Have you met the new kids?"

"More fosters?" Already?

Kase shook his head. "Orphans from Charlie's school. There are five of them."

Oh, man. College students could eat. "Did they bring laundry?"

"They did. Nanette told them to have at it because she's too busy cooking." Kase chuckled. "I'm going to put in a laundry building. I swear. That way we don't have to smell it."

"Oh, a laundromat would be a huge draw for the cowboys. They'd love that."

Ryder groaned on his way by. "Don't say that out loud..."

"I know." Kase laughed. "But still, it would save Nanette's mudroom."

"If Nanette would let me hire her an assistant..."

"You hush, Ryder," Nanette said as she bustled into the kitchen. "This house is my domain."

"You heard her, son!" Antonia's laugh cut the air like a razor.

"My life is ruled by women." Ryder grinned and threw his hands up.

"You're a lucky man," Wat intoned, nudging him with an elbow.

"Nanette is a queen among women. What can I do?"

"Go get the kids out of the horse barns? You know there is at least one of each of ours out there..."

"You got it." That he could do. Rounding up kids was a lot like rounding up animals or calling up dogs. Speaking of... He headed outside to whistle up Biscuit and Tater. They would draw kids in like magic. "Let's find Naomi, guys. Find her."

Sure enough, one of the barn doors was open a crack.

"Hey, boys, let's see what's up in here?" Tygh said loudly as he opened the barn door, letting the dogs spill in. He didn't want to interrupt something he didn't need to see.

Dani, Naomi, and Nell were all leaning over the top of one of the stalls, staring at one of the momma cows and her new calves.

Ah. His animal-loving crew. "Are you terrorizing Lola?" he asked them.

"No. We're being so good," Dani said.

"Babies!" Nell said, pointing and damn near tumping right over the top of the stall door.

"Whoa." He grabbed her and tugged her back. "They're adorable, huh?"

"So pwee! I 'nuggle them?"

"Hmm. Lola might not like that, honey. How about we give goat scritches?"

"Señor Stinky!" she crowed, and Lola lifted her head, snorting her displeasure.

"I know, Lola." He lifted Nell, letting the other girls climb down, and they headed for Señor's pen. He was a billy, but not a bully. He was a lover, in fact, and loved his chin scratches.

Nell jabbered and scritched, the big billy coming right over for feed and love. Goofy friggin' goat.

"Señor, Señor Stinky," the girls sang.

"Time for sausage balls!" Wat called from down by the house.

"Ooh." Nell bounced.

"No running, girls." Too many things to trip on and cut tender skin.

"You come?" Nell offered him a very brave smile.

"I do. I'm right with you." He took her hand, because sometimes he forgot she was so much younger.

"Thank you. The dogs run a lot."

"Where's Nell?" Lijah's voice rang out, tinged with worry. "Nell? Are you out here? Mimi's hunting you!"

"I'm here!" Nell skipped ahead, confident again.

"Nell! You need to say if you're going to the barn." Lijah swung her up in a hug. "Hey, Mister Tygh. Happy Gooble Gooble Day!"

"Goooooble!" Nell crowed.

"Happy day, bud." He tried hard not to call Lijah a kid. He took offense, like most teen boys.

"Thanks! I'm going out to play basketball with Marco and Ced after we eat. You can come."

"I might just do that." Who was he kidding? He and the girls would have a nap. He knew it. He was the king of finding a recliner and letting both girls snooze on him.

"Cool." Lijah grinned, then followed Nell inside. The kids were all gathered in the kitchen where the grans, including Irene, were doling out snacks, from sausage balls to Brazilian cheese bread puffs.

"Not too much," Alba said. "We have dinner midday."

"Can I have some?" His eyes went wide, because these were all his favorite things.

"Of course you can, Tygh." Antonia winked. "Once they're all watching a show, we all get to sit and have a plate of appetizers."

"Woo." He did a little dance, which made Emma giggle from where she was in a highchair. This place had all the baby stuff.

Emma slapped her hands on her high chair tray, and Maggie came up to him, wiggling and dancing along.

"Oh, hello." He grabbed her and danced her about, making her giggle like a mad thing.

"They really dig you," Ryder said. "For a grumpy, antisocial cowboy..."

"I did tell you that when you hired me, huh?"

Ryder snorted. "Now I know you were trying to get out of working Halloween and Christmas with the public."

"You know it. I'm raising a family with the people-pleaser."

"You are." Ryder looked at Wat, who was laughing with his folks, watching Nell gobble up a cheese bread. "I get it. I did the same thing. Kase was always more popular than me on the circuit."

"Yeah, but you were the champ, and everyone knew it."

Ryder puffed up a tiny bit. He got it. Everyone wanted to be thought of as good in their field. Maybe the best. Just like it felt amazing to be the official ranch vet with this outfit.

He was the man who made the decisions, and everyone coped. They didn't have a choice.

"Papa. Sance!" Maggie put her hands on his chest.

"Yes, ma'am. Dancing bear on command." He danced her around, watching all the grannies laugh at them. They could laugh. His middle girl wanted to dance.

"Papi!" Nell went to Ryder. "Dances?"

"Sure, baby girl. Let's dance." Ryder grabbed her up, spinning her around.

"Don't you dare make her throw up," Kase warned.

They all hooted at that, and before long, they were kidless, some movie about Santa on the TV. They'd all seen him at the parade, so they were primed.

"Cheese bread?" Wat asked.

Tygh opened his mouth for Wat to pop it in.

It wasn't until after he'd done it and was chewing that he realized what he'd done, and that Wat had fed him.

No one seemed to think anything about it, and the conversation ebbed and flowed around them. The apps were amazing, and as timers went off, they all rose in turn to grab things or baste them or change things out of the oven.

He'd never had this feeling at Thanksgiving in his life. He felt like an actual part of the family.

When Maggie climbed up into his lap, cuddling in and having him kiss her baby before settling, his world was about whole.

And he still had turkey and pie on the agenda.

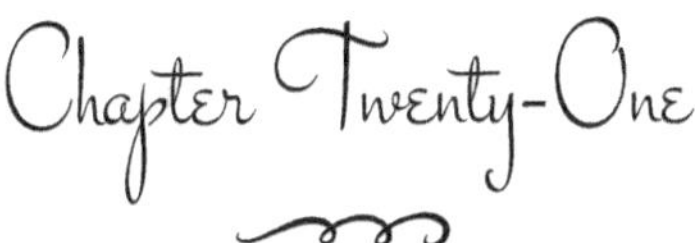

Chapter Twenty-One

"I am not going to the big school! I am not being with the big kids that have two hands! I am staying with Dani!" Naomi stared him down, frowning deeply. "You can't make me! I will move to the barns with Papa Tygh and Señor Stinky!"

His head was going to explode. "Go to your room."

"NO! I will NOT!"

She started screaming, so he picked her up, took her to her room, and closed the door behind her.

His head was going to explode, and he had two little ones sitting at the table, a lesson plan to file with the state, and dinner burning on the stove.

He moved the burned chile off the stove, then went to stare into the freezer. He needed something fast and easy.

The kitchen door opened and closed. "Feeding is— It's a little cold for a hot flash, honey?"

"It's rage."

"I HATE YOU!" Naomi screamed, then slammed her door back, and Maggie and Emma began to wail.

"Whoa. Okay, what do you want me to do?" Tygh came to

rub his shoulders, which felt like heaven. They were working on not immediately comforting the girls when nothing was wrong with them.

"Papa! Papa, up me!"

"She's in time-out. I burned supper." His head pounded, and he wanted to cry, but he was the dad, so he couldn't.

"Hey. I get it. What do you want for supper?"

"Something warm and easy and comforting?" He needed to sit.

"Okay." Tygh sat him at the table, washed up, and then got a teething cookie for Emma and Goldfish for Maggie, who instantly stopped crying. Before long, the scent of burned chili was replaced with tomato soup and grilled cheese. So it came from a can. So what? Tygh doctored the soup with some garlic powder and Italian seasoning and it smelled divine. "Should I see if Naomi is okay?"

"I'll do it. She'll be hungry." She'd gone quiet.

He headed down the hallway and opened the door, finding her sound asleep on her bed. He shook his head and eased the door closed.

Poor baby. She could have her soup and sandwich later, if she got up.

"So what happened?" Tygh asked when he came back to sit down.

"She doesn't want to try public school. I need her to give it a shot—she can't just hide at the ranch."

"It's not even Christmas yet. I bet she changes her mind a million times." Tygh chewed his lower lip. "I wonder what happened, though."

"I was basically with them all day. What could they have said?"

"I don't know. Maybe she heard something? Hell, maybe she just got watching Dani do something with both hands."

Tygh shook his head. "It's hard at that age in general. I imagine she's got it twice as tough."

And he was probably the worst father alive.

"God," he dropped his head into his hands.

"Hey." Tygh reached over to pull them away. "You're okay. It was a hard day, is all. Anything else I need to know?" That expression was all sympathy.

"She said she's moving to the barns with you." He went for the wink.

"Ah. Wow. But I like my house." Tygh dished up the food, the grilled cheese just right. Good man.

"Thank you." Wat winked over. "I'm not angry at you, or her. I just want her to understand what I'm doing..."

"I know. Trust me. I was prone to kicking and biting meltdowns. No noise. Just fighting. And I had one foster mom who would just put me in my room until I could talk. It worked, and it kept us both from being hurt."

"Yeah. She's so even-tempered, until she's not. It's like they're two different kids."

"Hormones, maybe? She did just grow almost an inch." Tygh shrugged. "You should ask your mom, huh?"

"I will. Mom will know about the vagaries of girl cooties, huh?" She wasn't near old enough to start her period, right? That was twelve or thirteen?

"She should, yeah. And if she doesn't, she'll be a sympathetic ear, right?"

"Yeah. You've met her. She's a force of nature, and she loves her grandbabies more than life."

Tygh gave him this weird little smile. "That's a granny's job."

"Yeah. It totally is." He couldn't let that smile go, because he wanted to know—hell, he needed to know all the parts, even the dark ones. "You said you lost your granny early on."

"Yeah. Yeah, I was pretty little." Tygh grimaced. "That was a mess."

"I'm sorry. Did—is that when you went into the system?" He didn't know how to say all the things he needed to, what to ask.

"Yeah. I was six and a half. I was living with her, because she was really the only family I had, but she wasn't well." Tygh sighed, shaking his head. "It's not a pretty story. You sure you want to hear this?"

"I'm not here for just the pretty stories. I'm here for all of them." Hell, his nasty story was still in the scabby phase.

"Well, she had a blowout during the summer, so I wasn't in school. I didn't know how to call anyone, so I was in the house with her for several days before someone checked on us."

"Oh, Jesus." He sat there, sort of blinking for a second. He couldn't fathom that—how scared little six-year-old Tygh must have been, how lost he must have felt. "That must have been horrifying."

"Well, it was pretty gross." Tygh chuckled, shoulders relaxing. "Let's just say it scarred me up pretty good for a bit. And then I bounced in foster care for a bit. Some places were better than others, but none of them were evil or anything. It was a tough when I first got into the system, you know?"

He reached out, holding Tygh's hand. "I can only imagine. I hope you had foster parents that helped, that loved you."

"I did. I had some great people who really cared, and who made sure I got what I needed." Tygh squeezed. "I'm not saying it was all hearts and roses, and I can relate to the kids who show up with everything they own in a trash bag. But I know it could have been way worse."

"These girls won't ever remember that. Being left behind. They'll have us, you know?" And he wasn't ever going to let any of them believe for a second that they weren't loved.

"They will. And we'll make sure they know how important they are to us. And Naomi is."

Wat nodded, still holding on. He wouldn't be able to erase that old horror, but he could accept it, let it not be a secret.

Let it just be an ancient fact, a faded scar.

"I guess I will." He winked, making the tease more obvious. "I may get her back into therapy. This is a lot to deal with. New home, new school, new sisters, new papa."

"It is." Tygh gave him a searching look. "Even if it's good, it's a lot of adjusting."

"Yes. This is good. We're a solid family, but she's gone from an only to an oldest in a heartbeat."

"And an oldest to a pair under three. That's a lot. Add in Dani and Nell, and she's got her hands full. I think you're both doing amazing." Tygh nibbled his sandwich, which was kind of hilarious. He was usually kind of a shoveler.

"I'm glad you're here, to do this together."

"I am too, honey." Now Tygh beamed at him, cheeks pink. God, that was amazing. That he made Tygh feel that way.

"I—at some point soon, we need to discuss Christmas. Michelle's folks want Naomi for a few days, I know, and I think Mom and Dad might too." But Christmas was his, dammit.

"Well, what about letting them have her before and after Christmas, but let her be here for Eve and day, at least."

"Oh, I was thinking more one set could have her the twenty-seventh and twenty-eighth and the other set to the thirtieth..." He didn't want to be without her that long.

"Oh, see, that's good. I don't know much about stuff like that." Tygh chuckled. "No one ever picked kids up for holidays where I lived, you know?"

"Well, this is just visiting grandparents, right? Not custody." And he wanted her to know her grandparents.

"Right." Tygh munched another bite. "I wonder if I'm

good parent material sometimes. My experiences are less than normal."

"We're all less than normal, somehow, I think." He didn't feel normal. He felt exhausted and utterly like a dad-fail.

"I think you might be right. You know, if you want to take a shower or a long bath or something, I'll hang out and see if Naomi gets up to eat."

"Honestly? I'd like to hang out with you for a while. I mean, if you don't mind..." God, was that weird?

It felt weird.

"I don't mind at all. You want to help me put the little ones down and move to the couch? I'll go change out of the work clothes and meet you there. Leave the dishes and I'll do them later." Tygh beamed as if Wat had made his night.

"Sounds like a plan." He helped with Emma, while Tygh got the already-snoozing Maggie into a fresh diaper. Then Tygh headed to the bedroom, and he went into the kitchen to pop the dishes in the dishwasher and threw a half-dozen cookies in the toaster oven. The burned chili pot he did leave for Tygh to do later.

He just couldn't.

Tygh came out to flop on the couch, groaning as he put his feet up. He sat next to Tygh and handed over the remote.

"I started cookies."

"Mmm. I can smell them. Hell, that will bring Naomi out if anything does."

"I kind of hope she sleeps." That did not make him an asshole. Not notty not.

"Or if she doesn't, that she's in a better mood, huh?" Tygh tugged him over into a soft kiss, surprising the hell out of him.

He slid a hand behind Tygh's head, humming at the feel of their lips pressing together. It made him tingle.

"Mmm... hey. Better?"

"Getting there, yes." He lifted his lips for another one of those kisses.

Tygh gave it, letting the contact go long, tongue slipping out to taste him. He sucked in a deep breath, his toes curling. It wasn't like 'whoa sexy,' but it warmed him up to the core.

"You taste so good," Tygh said against his mouth.

"So do you." And didn't it feel good to hear that?

"Yeah?" Those eyes crinkled right up again, the smile instant. "Good."

"Yes. Very." And it was time to let Tygh understand how good it was. He pushed closer, deepening their kisses, trusting Tygh with his passion.

Tygh turned toward him, one hand sliding down his back to keep them together, and the whole tenor of the kiss changed, going white-hot.

He moaned, and it was easy now, to open up, to be with Tygh and let his hunger swell.

They broke for air, panting, staring at each other. Then they dove back in, kissing harder.

He slipped one hand under Tygh's T-shirt, dragging his fingertips up along that fuzzy, amazing belly. Tygh moved down to grab his ass with that one hand, making him moan.

"Tell me we can go to bed tonight and make love?" Was that weird? Too gushy? Did men say that to each other?

"Hell, yes." Tygh leaned their foreheads together. "Not yet, I guess, huh?"

"No. Just in case." It was what? Six thirty? Seven? They had to wait a little while longer. "But I'm going to want you at nine, just as much."

He stroked Tygh's cock through his jeans.

"Uhn. Damn. Wat..." Tygh kind of danced under him.

"Mmhmm. I know." He nibbled Tygh's earlobe.

Tygh stroked his neck, then pushed down into his pants at the back, feeling his bare skin.

He didn't tense this time. He rolled his hips and thrust back into Tygh's fingers.

"Hot as hell, honey." Tygh kept touching him, loving on him, fingers sliding over him.

"I need you, cowboy. I need to spend some time with you, open and bare."

"Oh, damn. Yes. I need that too." Tygh moaned, arching against him.

He flattened his hand over the hard package in Tygh's sweats, using the heel to rub and give his lover some friction.

"Damn!" Tygh's explosive breath and hard body roll told him he was on the exact right track.

That was incredibly hot, so he did it again, snuggled right into Tygh's side.

Tygh started to hump his touch, body rolling in this slow, sensual rhythm that made his mouth dry.

He couldn't stop his moan, and it brushed his ear, making him dizzy.

Tygh pulled him in for another kiss, his hand still moving, and he felt ten feet tall, making Tygh so happy. Those noises were amazing, and he drank each and every one up.

He shoved his hand inside Tygh's sweats, needing to touch, skin on skin.

"Mmmph!" Tygh arched back, biting his lower lip. Wat thought it was to stifle a shout.

He muffled it with a hard kiss. No waking the kids up. Tygh made this agonized sound and hot, wet seed splashed into his hand and up over his wrist, Tygh coming for him just like that.

Okay, that felt hot as fuck. Very fun.

"What do you need, honey?" Those eyes were heavy-lidded, Tygh's lips swollen and his cheeks flushed.

"I am going to need you, but I want to wait until we can be naked, together."

"You sure?"

"Daddy? Can I come out?"

Tygh laughed softly. "You're sure. Let me go wash up."

"I'll take the kitchen. Coming, kiddo." He washed up in the kitchen after he and Tygh separated, then went to find his daughter.

She was waiting for him at the door to her room, lurking a bit.

"Can I have dinner? Please? My tummy hurts."

"Of course. Come on. Grilled cheese?" He wasn't going to meet anger with anger.

"Yes, please." She gave him a tiny smile, her eyes bruised-looking. But the nap had done her good. "Are you mad at me?"

"My feelings are hurt, more than mad."

"I'm sorry, Daddy. I'm scared about school."

"I can see that. New things are scary, but sometimes they're very good, and I'd like you to try it out for a semester, just so you know your options." He buttered the bread for her sandwiches. "You know you and Dani will still be friends, right?"

"I know." She said it in a tiny voice. "But what if they're mean?"

"Then you tell the teacher. You tell them to back off. You show them how you might not be exactly the same, but you do just fine, and you adapt." And he would defend his baby girl to the end of the earth, if he had to.

"I can try. I don't want Dani to be mad at me. Or for anyone to miss me."

"We'll be right here. You'll be her next-door neighbor. Think about it, but I think it's important to see if you like having a teacher that's not your daddy." And she was a social creature. She would thrive in a way Dani wouldn't in public school. That wasn't a criticism of either one of them.

That was just a fact.

"And if I don't want to go after a si-mem-ester?"

"If you don't want to go, you'll have the summer to think about it, and we'll talk about it, and together, we'll decide."

"Papa Tygh too?" she asked.

"What do you think about that?" He didn't want her to feel forced into it, one way or the other.

"Uh-huh. He's part of us now."

"He is." Relief filled him. He felt the same way.

"Then we'll all decide as a family, fair enough?"

She nodded. "But what if it is really, really bad? What if someone hurts me?"

"If that happens, your Papa Tygh and I will come to the school, and we will fix things."

"Okay." She seemed to accept that, and she ate hearty when he gave her soup and sammy.

"Hey, kiddo." Tygh came in wearing comfy sweats. "How's it going?"

"Better. Daddy says that you and me and him will talk about the big school after one simsestarry all together and decide if it's good."

"Okay. That sounds good. I'm glad you're going to give it a chance."

"I might need to talk about it again before I go. I get scared."

It broke his heart to hear her say that, but it also made him proud she admitted it, and that she trusted Tygh.

"Of course. We can talk together anytime. I want to listen."

"Thank you, Papa Tygh. Me too. And you too, Daddy. I love you." She dipped her sandwich into her soup. "This is good."

"I'm glad." He was. He didn't want to fight, but he knew

this was part of growing up, of change. He just wished it hadn't hurt so much.

Tygh put a hand on the small of his back on the way to the fridge to grab a beer. "Do you want anything?"

"No, thank you. I'm solid."

"Cool." Tygh grinned at Naomi. "Do you need anything?"

"Daddy gave me water. I think milk or juice might keep me up."

"Okay, kiddo. So what do we want to do this weekend?"

"Can we go Christmas shopping?"

"Sure." Tygh gave him a raised eyebrow. "Unless you have something else, honey."

"Christmas shopping is probably a great plan, huh? Maybe you can pick out your sisters' Christmas dresses."

"Oooh yes. Do I get one?" She looked so worried.

"Of course. We'll get some pictures taken, huh? You'll look so pretty."

She glanced at Tygh. "Do you think so too?"

"I do, kiddo. I think you're always amazing, but we'll get y'all dresses and do it up right." Tygh's grin held no small amount of relief.

"Or maybe I'll wear jeans and a fancy shirt."

"Works for me." He didn't care. He wanted them all happy.

"Can I get a hat like yours, Papa Tygh?" Naomi was chattering again now like always, the storm blown over.

"We'll see what we can find."

"Thank you. I want Maggie to have a purple dress and Emma to have a green dress."

"That sounds so pretty."

"Well, we'll start at the store for dresses, then maybe go to the western-wear place."

"And Papa, Daddy needs a purple shirt and you need a

green one. It's going to be so perfect." Naomi was so proud of herself.

"What color are you going to wear, love?" Wat asked her.

"Plaids. I love plaids and polka dots!"

"Oh, I like a nice Christmas plaid." Tygh got in the freezer and got them all a vanilla ice cream cup, which Tygh had told him his one foster mom had kept on hand to help with hard talks.

"Me too. Today was a hard day, but I'm glad we're all better now. Are you, Daddy?"

He nodded, because he was. He needed her to be able to communicate her needs.

"Good. Yum." She had let Tygh open her cup and was licking it like a cone. The wood spoons that came with the cups made it hard for her to do one-handed, but she managed, and he was proud as hell at how she adapted.

They cleaned up together, got her a bath, and checked on the baby girls, and then it was time for bed, and he and Tygh stared at each other for long moments, the silence just sort of ringing through the house.

Tygh held out a hand to him, and he took it, the callused, warm skin almost shocking against his. Together they walked to the bathroom, and like they'd agreed on it beforehand, they went through their pre-bed ritual before Tygh took him to the bedroom and started undressing him with a single-minded intensity that sent a shaft of arousal right through him, revving him up all over again.

He moaned, stepping into Tygh's space to kiss him, their mouths meeting hard, with very little fanfare this time. They both knew what they wanted, and they went after it, pushing to strip down and tumble onto the bed.

His fingers were fascinated by the planes and lines and swells of Tygh's body, and he simply had to touch. So he ghosted his fingers over one pec, feeling the tiny nipple there harden.

"Mmm... So good, babe. You have the softest fingers."

"Is that bad?"

Tygh chuckled. "No. I promise that's a good thing." One hard hand cupped his ass.

"Good. Because your hands make me a little stupid."

"Do they?"

"Uh-huh. Tanned. Scarred. Callused. Talented."

Tygh's cheeks went bright pink, and his smile looked so pleased Wat told himself he would compliment Tygh more often.

And if it caused Tygh to touch him the way he was now, sliding that free hand over his chest, then his belly to stroke his cock, then he wasn't going to be challenged to do it.

"Mmmm. Hot as hell, honey. I like it. Smooth as silk, too."

"I never thought I'd be with a man like this. It's—" Hotter than hell, a touch unnerving, crazy exciting.

"It's good, honey. As long as you want that person to touch you and it feels right? It's all good."

"Yes." He was so glad Tygh thought so and wasn't an all-or-nothing man. "You're good to me."

He pushed back into the kisses, his cock heavy and turgid, aching as he rubbed their shafts together.

"I feel you, honey. Tell me what you need. I want all of you."

"I'm aching. I need you." He needed to shoot. He needed to feel how much Tygh wanted him.

"I can give you anything." Tygh grinned. "But for right now, how about this?" Tygh slid down his body, mouth landing on his cock, and Tygh opened right up to suck him in.

His eyes crossed and he shoved his fist into his mouth to

muffle his cry. Someday soon, they'd send Naomi and the girls all off to be with the grandparents, because Maggie and Emma would get there, and then he and Tygh would really make some noise.

Right now, he was going to wallow in this moment of privacy and bliss. He grinned against his hand, then looked down at Tygh, the sight of that hot mouth on him adding to the pleasure of feeling it there.

God, he wanted to do this forever.

Wat's ass cheeks clenched, and his belly pulled in. He could barely breathe. His toes curled and he arched up into that burning mouth.

Tygh was relentless, giving him heat and wet pressure, licking, then sucking. And those hands were never still, skating over his thighs and his ass, then up to cup his balls or curl around the base of his cock. He felt a little like he might explode from the pleasure, his whole body on fire.

"I—I won't be able to hold on long, lover..."

"Mmmhmm." That didn't seem to bother Tygh at all. That mouth kept playing him, Tygh loving what he was doing. And it was working like a charm. Damn.

His hips began to rock, sawing back and forth, his desperation like a living thing. He was close. So close. And this was going to drive him right over the edge.

Tygh made encouraging noises, the vibrations adding to his desire.

He wasn't going to hold out, so he let himself go, his world rocking wildly underneath him. He bounced and writhed, and Tygh held him down and sucked him and he shouted, his balls emptying as he came hard for his lover.

Lover. Tygh was *so* that.

He hadn't wished for this, but it had happened. Somehow, it had happened.

And he was going to hold onto it with both hands. As soon as he could lift his head off the pillow.

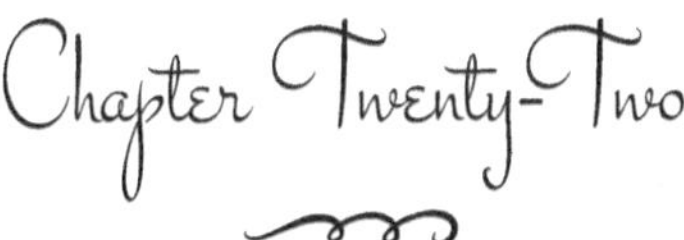

Chapter Twenty-Two

"Okay, so we have a purple shirt. We have ugly Christmas sweaters. We have a green shirt. So we need dresses..." Tygh ticked things off on his fingers. He'd never enjoyed shopping so much in his life, not even for food, which had been his big indulgence on his first real paycheck.

Man, he'd found out how much he hated fish eggs.

"And a plaid shirt for me, and I need presents for Dani and the sisters and Nell and Lijah and Charlie and the grannies and —" Naomi was going to pass out if she didn't breathe.

"And we might need a doughnut," Wat said.

"Foooood," Maggie called.

"Sister. Toys. We need toys!" Naomi corrected.

"Foooood!"

"She's a bottomless pit," Tygh said. "Girl after my own heart." They had Maggie in an umbrella stroller, Emma in her regular one, and Naomi was dancing, and all the ladies at the western-wear store were grinning at them.

"We'll go to the Walmart for gifts, okay? This is for clothes for our family picture, remember?"

"I do! I want pretty boots, Papa, and a belt with a sparkle buckle."

"Do you? Well, should we get some help?" He waved down one of the ladies he'd known since he moved to town. "Miss Belinda, this is Naomi."

"Hello, Naomi. It's nice to meet you." Belinda held out her hand to shake, and Naomi pursed her lips.

"I don't have a hand on that arm. Can we shake on the other?"

"Of course." Belinda never even blinked. She just took Naomi's hand. "So, sparkle, huh?"

"Yes, ma'am."

"I have a section just for you."

"Come on, Daddy! Papa! Bring my sisters!"

"Princess of the rodeo," Tygh murmured, and Wat nodded, eyes wide.

They followed along, Maggie singing as if she was in a parade. Emma giggling madly. They were all flying high, he guessed.

No one would guess these two babies were the same children who had shown up only a couple of months ago.

"Oh, Papa. Look at the belts!" Naomi touched a brown leather belt with flowers stamped into it and painted pink.

"That one is pretty."

"Uh-huh. Can I have it? Please?"

"Why don't we set it aside and see if it's the one you like best at the end?" Wat suggested. "You can get one pair of boots and a belt, and maybe a hat. We still have to get dresses at Walmart." And that would be a little drive.

"Boot-ses and belt-ses and a hat-ses for me!"

"Meeeeeee!" Maggie sang.

Naomi boogied, shaking her shoulders at Maggie.

"Yayayayyaaaaaaaaaaaaa," Emma added.

"That's right, baby girl. Yay yay yay." Wat's laugh filled the air. "We are lucky ducks, Papa."

"We are." He took some pictures with his phone, because damn that was cute.

"Now, about boots." Belinda just sort of let them all spin around her as if she was a maypole.

"Can I have pink ones? Dani has blue ones, and I want ones like that."

Belinda never even hesitated. "Ropers. I have just the thing."

"Yay!" They went through trying on boots, and he hung out with Naomi while Wat walked Maggie around out of her stroller, hanging on to her sister's side rail. He'd never really shopped with little girls before, and it was hilarious, but he was truly thankful for Belinda.

"Look, Daddy! I'm so pretty!" By the end, Naomi had a shirt worthy of a baby barrel racer, a pair of ropers, a belt, and a hat with a sparkly band.

"You are *spectacular*!" Wat beamed at her and snapped a picture. "I love the new outfit. Very cowgirl."

"Cowboy," she corrected.

"Cowboy." Wat didn't seem worried at all.

"Thank you." Naomi bowed. "Can I have it, Daddy? Papa?"

"Let's see what the outfit adds up to, kiddo," Wat said, and Tygh was glad he didn't just agree. He could afford it, no problem, but if Wat had a lesson about money management here, he wasn't going to step on toes.

"Oh." Her little face fell. "Right. We have to make sure there's pennies for the bills and the foods first."

Wat nodded to her. "And diapers and schooling and—"

She headed off toward the dressing room without another word.

Tygh glanced at Wat. "I can swing it, you know."

"I know, and I won't harsh her glow by not getting the outfit as well as the boots and belt, but she does need to remember that we're not made of money. I mean, this is her first spree in ages, and the last one was at the Goodwill, but we have a lot of medical bills."

"Sure." Hell, he hadn't thought of that. "We should talk about all that at some point."

"Yeah. I'm not setting—well, I was going to say the world on fire, but that seems crass." Wat rolled his eyes.

"Ouch." He winced dramatically. "Well, I'm doing all right, and we can totally combine forces." He'd spent for the house, but really, Tygh had incurred very few expenses over the years, so he could help with Naomi's bills if Wat would let him.

"I'm just trying to keep up and put enough back so if she says, 'Dad, I want that prosthetic' I can do that, you know?"

Naomi came out of the dressing room all put back together. "I'm ready."

"Where are your things?" Wat asked.

"I don't want them. Let's go."

"Hey." Tygh felt awful that she'd just left them all in the dressing room. "Let's get Belinda to add them up, huh?"

Her mouth firmed up, so stubborn. "It was fun to try them on, but I want a dress with sisters more. They have cheap boots at the Walmart."

Wat stroked a hand over her hair. "That's really good of you, sweetie. Why don't we take the girls outside and see what we want to eat?" He gave Tygh a meaningful look, which Tygh hoped he was right in translating to "get all that shit for Christmas presents." Because he so was going to have Belinda put it all away to come back for.

He chose to believe that was it, because Naomi was his baby too now, and she deserved a new kit. And she was a cowgirl. Maybe not as much as Dani. Yet. But they would be in 4-H before Wat knew what hit him and Tygh knew it.

In fact, Tygh wanted to get her riding on her own, learning the reins and having that freedom. He knew lots of ropers without fingers or worse. She could ride.

He would break that one to Wat, nice and gentle. Wat still worried about her with the goats.

"I want it all. Can you hold it, and I'll pick it all up when I come out to the feed store?"

"Of course. I'll just have Kenneth drop it off on his way through Monday. He lives that way." She started ringing up the bill. "What happened to her baby hand? Looks like a firework accident?"

"House fire. She was asleep with her mom." Tygh kept his voice pitched low, even though Wat and Naomi were gone. "It was bad, lady."

"Oh, that sucks. Her mom?"

He shook his head.

She winced. "Dammit."

"Yeah. She's adjusting pretty well, really, but she has her moments."

"Well, she was super good when her dad said they needed to think about budget."

"She was. I just want her to have her first chance to cowgirl up a bit, you know?" Tygh wanted to spoil her.

"Sure. I get that. It's not like we won't spoil our kids." Belinda had eight of her own, and something like twenty grandbabies already.

"Exactly." He grinned. "She's pretty level-headed, but all little girls need to dress up." He'd seen that over and over again in foster care.

"You know it. Every little one needs it. It makes them happy."

Yeah, he had a foster mom make him a purple superhero cape once that he'd worn until it literally fell apart.

"Okay, so I'll hold this for you until next week?"

"Yeah, I'll come pick them up on Tuesday, probably." No reason for someone to make a trip to deliver it.

"You got it. If you change your mind about delivery, call." She beamed, handing him one copy of the receipt, then stapling the other to the big bag she'd put it all in.

"I will. Thanks, lady."

When he went outside, Naomi was quiet, not pouting, but the exuberance had faded.

He hated to see that, and he wanted to get it back without pissing Wat off. He glanced at Wat, his lover looked pretty damn subdued, too.

"So, what do we want to nibble, guys?" Tygh asked.

"Daddy and I thought about tacos and sopapillas."

"I think that sounds amazing." He would so take them for Mexican food.

"Yeah. Maggie likes the meat and cheese."

"What do you want, kiddo?" Tygh asked, because she needed to have a say as well. They could always feed Maggie chicken nuggets or a cut-up hamburger from anywhere.

"I want a chicken flying saucer with no green stuff and two sopapillas."

"Oh, you want the sweet stuff." That relieved him. "Wagons, ho."

"What's 'ho' mean, Papa?"

"In this case, it's an exclamation. Like oi! Remember when we heard that in that British movie we watched? But this one means come on let's go or something."

"Wagons, oi!"

Okay, that was adorable.

Wat's soft chuckle was enough to relax him, to soothe him deep down.

They headed to the Mexican place, and the smell of chile made his mouth water the moment they walked through the door. "I do love me some chile," he said.

"Hey, I'm a native New Mexican, green chile runs in my veins!" Wat's laugh filled the air.

"No. Veins have bloods. I know this." Naomi rolled her eyes. "You have it in your belly."

"I want to soon."

"Hey, guys. Tygh, good to see you. Highchairs?"

"Two please," Tygh told Christina, the hostess who was always so cheerful. "And some coloring pages, right, Naomi?"

"Yes, please. With the mazes?" She did love her puzzles, didn't she?

"I think we have some of those." Christina waved down a server, and the chairs appeared not long after at a table big enough for all of them.

Chips and salsa, too. Woo-hoo.

"Is it angry today, Papa?" Naomi handed Maggie a chip to gnaw on.

Tygh tasted the salsa, and it was just hot enough. Not too much for Naomi. "Nope. No one was mad when they made this sauce."

"All right!" Naomi perked right up and dug in, grabbing her crayon as she chewed.

Wat touched the back of his hand, mouthing a "thank you" when he glanced up. Yeah. Naomi's mood had stabilized.

That bit of praise straightened his spine. He wasn't sure how he felt about that—about how those moments of approval meant the world to him.

"Papa!" Maggie slammed one fist on the highchair tray. "Peese!"

"Someone would like another chip, please," Wat drawled.

"She did say please." Tygh handed Maggie another chip, and when they ordered, Naomi got her flying saucer, which their server never blinked an eye at, and he and Wat ordered enchiladas and tamales and sopapillas.

"Oh, and an order of beans? The little ones will like that." Emma would get a tiny taste, and Mags would eat them up.

"You got it." She walked off.

His phone rang in his pocket.

Damn it.

It was Ryder, and he grabbed it. "What you need, Boss?"

"That damn showboat bull injured his leg."

Tygh blinked, trying to figure out what Ryder was talking about. "Which one now?"

"Hammer and Tongs. He's at the national finals."

"Okay, what happened? Excuse me, y'all. I'll be right back." He stood and headed out of the restaurant. "We're out for lunch and Christmas shopping."

"Shit. He's cut up. Tried to go over the rails with a rider on his back. Also might have swelling in a hock."

"Shit. What do you want me to do?"

"Well, you finish up with the fam, but I'll need to fly you out tonight so you can ride back with him tomorrow. We can't spare Jesse as we got too many animals at the finals."

Jesse traveled with the animals to major events, and he was really more of an animal paramedic. He did triage. The vets working the event would have stabilized the situation, but this must be serious if he was needed.

"Sure. We'll eat and then I'll head home. Everyone will understand. I'll fly out, make sure he's okay to travel, and bring him home."

"Thanks, man. I know this time of year sucks for you all of a sudden, and by next year, we'll get another traveling tech, at least, but—"

"Hey, it's in the job." And he didn't mind traveling. He hated that the bull was down though. "Wat will understand."

"I imagine so. But never underestimate the power of the

holidays." Ryder chuckled. "I'm sorry, man. You're the one I trust. I need him. If not to buck then to stud, so he can't get an infection and pop off."

"Of course not. Let me finish lunch, and I'll head back home."

He and Wat could take the kids out at some point next week. It shouldn't take him... well, tonight to get out there, a day to settle things, two days home. He'd be home by Wednesday at the latest.

That left plenty of time for him to break it to Wat that he'd bought Naomi all her western wear plus a bracelet that she'd stared at longingly at the jewelry stand...

"Sounds good. I'll get you on a flight out tonight. If that doesn't work, you and Vic can drive out, spend the night half-way, and then get there tomorrow."

"I'll fly if I can. That way, I can get there late tonight to check on him if he needs stabilizing before the drive back." Tygh started making lists in his head.

Maybe they could get the food to go...

"No rush if you're gonna fly. I'll get you a late flight since it's just to Vegas."

"Okay. Thanks, Boss. We'll be about an hour."

"You got it. Take the time you need with the kids and Wat. I'm not wanting to cut you off."

"I appreciate it." He hung up, and he stood outside for a moment, trying to get his bearings. This was the first time his new life and work had collided like this, and he felt like a rock had just been dropped on his head. Was this what they called adulting? He'd always sneered at that word, but Lord, now he got it.

Tygh took a deep breath and put on a smile, because Ryder was really being very calm and generous, and he went inside to finish his lunch.

Wat gave him a searching gaze when he sat down. "Is something wrong?"

"There's been an injured bull at the finals in Las Vegas. I'm going to have to fly out this evening to go get him." He'd talked to Wat about how sometimes he traveled to attend to an injured animal, but this was the first time since he and Wat had moved in together.

"Oh." Wat nodded. "Do we need to go now?"

He glanced at Naomi, who was crestfallen.

"Nope. We get to have our sopapillas. We might have to put off dress shopping for a few days though. Is that okay, kiddo?"

Naomi nodded. "If that's okay with Mr. Ryder. I love sopapillas."

"He specifically told me to stay and eat my lunch." He dug into his rapidly cooling enchiladas. "So are you going to see Santa this year with Maggie and Emma?" He wasn't sure if Naomi was too old for that or not.

"I don't know. If Daddy wants a picture. I was in the hospital last Christmas. They took my hand off."

"On Christmas?"

"The twenty-third. She had gone septic." Wat's voice was flat, as if that wound was still too open.

"Oh." Shit, he'd stepped in that. "Well, I guess we'll see how it goes on the day, huh?"

"Nonsense. I totally want a picture." Wat managed a smile. "I have the most beautiful girls on earth. I think that would be the best present, ladybug."

"Yeah?" She looked at her sisters. "Me too!"

"Yay." The sopapillas came, and that they could all agree on. Maggie loved them too.

As soon as they got finished, he loaded them in the car for the drive home. It sucked. They had been intending to buy things for Christmas, to decorate and celebrate and make merry.

It was going to suck to lose a week. But he would make it up to them. He would. And then he would talk to Ryder about that second road assistant. If he had to take on more around the ranch to make up for it, he would do that too.

Naomi read her book on the drive home, and Wat didn't say much.

When they got home and had everyone unloaded, Naomi went to her room with her book, and he took Wat to their bedroom to pack.

"I bought Naomi her western stuff," he admitted right away.

"That was good of you. She'll be over the moon." Wat winked at him. "Don't worry. The bull will be fine. You're an amazing vet."

"I'm sorry, honey. I know we had grand plans, but I'll be gone a couple of days, max."

"No big deal. We're closing up school this week. We'll be crazy busy."

"Are you sure? Do you need me to get someone to come over here and do the feedings?"

"Do you think Elijah and his friends would do it?"

"Yeah. And Grady can check in."

"However it works. I have a basic idea, but I'd have to wait until the babies are asleep."

"I know. And I don't want you to have to leave Naomi here to look after them and do the feeding. I'll get someone from across the road." He turned, reaching out to Wat. "I'm sorry, honey."

"For what? It's your job. I get it."

"I know. I don't know. I guess I just figured this holiday season would be all perfect." Tygh shrugged.

"It's never perfect. Trust me. Never." Wat winked, and Tygh thought his lover seemed tired.

"You gonna be okay? I didn't realize it had been so tough last year."

"I'm fine. Last year was the beginning of the real starting over."

"Well, aside from when I'm in the air, you can call me anytime, okay? I'll be happy to have the company." He didn't want Wat to feel alone.

"What do you need from me? Anything?"

"No. I'll throw some clothes in a bag, and I have a card for business expenses, so I'm solid." He did reel Wat in. "I could use some moral support, though."

"That I have in spades." Wat offered his lips.

"Oh, good." He bent to give the kiss he wanted to give, and take the one he desperately needed. He felt so weird, just up and leaving. It wasn't odd, but somehow, now, it was.

"Mmm." Wat hugged him tight. "Do I need to drive you to the airport?"

"No, I'll make a wrangler do it. You'll need to ease the girls into this."

"I will. We'll manage, Papa. We'll be busy."

"You will. I just want to be here is all." He chuckled, then packed a couple of pairs of socks and some undies.

"Do you want two or three shirts?"

"Three. Just in case things get messy. There's a good deal of poop involved in moving a bull."

"Especially a hurt one, I imagine." Wat got three button-downs and his heavy quilted vest.

"Yeah. There's added kicking with that." He put in one good pair of jeans and one work pair. Just in case. Sometimes the big names insisted on taking him to late-night pancakes or a breakfast buffet before he hit the road if the situation wasn't too dire.

Everyone wanted to know about the Chiara bulls.

Like he ever said a word.

Nope. He wasn't a business guy.

"I'll get your kit bag," Wat murmured.

Dammit. Things were weird. He hated it.

"I'm not mad. This is your job. That bull needs help. That's serious." Wat handed him his bag. "A wonderful cowboy taught me that."

"Yeah? Imagine that." That did make him breathe easier.

"I know. It's wild. The finals are almost over, then it's Christmas."

"It is. I'm ready, honey. I want to see all three of our girls having a ball." He zipped up his suitcase after he tucked in his kit bag. "Okay, honey. I got to go. Should I tell the girls goodbye?"

"Tell Naomi. Maggie and Emma are sleeping."

"Sounds good." He tugged Wat in for another kiss. "This was not how I wanted today to go."

"No, me either, but you're not being deployed for six months. You have an amazing job, and we have a fabulous situation here. Sometimes, we have to pivot."

"We do. Thanks, honey. You're a star." Grady pulled up outside, surprising him when he looked through the window. "Let me tell Naomi bye."

He went to knock on her door, smiling when she called for him to come in.

"I have to go, kiddo. I'll see you in a couple of days."

"Can I come? Please? I'll be so good."

"I'm sorry, kiddo. I'll be traveling back and sleeping in the trailer, probably." It was too cold for the KOA, but he hated the kinds of motels he could park a bull trailer at. The trailer should have a cab over sleeper.

"Please? I'll be the best helper, Papa. I promise."

She was breaking his heart. Her lips quivered, and she was

holding her little hurt arm like it was bothering her, cradling it against her chest.

"As long as it's not school time, you can go on the next trip, okay? I'm just not set up to take you this time. Can I have a hug? Grady is waiting for me. He's going to come over to help feed everyone while I'm gone, so I'll need you to work with him, okay?"

She blinked up. "Oh. Oh, Daddy doesn't know about how to milk Bandana and Tom Turkey scares him. I have to stay here to help."

Oh, thank God. "And Biscuit and Tater. You'll take care of them, right?"

"They are my *dogs*, Papa!" She acted like he'd wounded her, to the bone. "Biscuits at seven, supper at six, and dental chews at nine. Tater needs his pill at bedtime."

"That's my girl." He gave her the hug he so desperately wanted. "I'm counting on you."

"Love you, Papa." She smacked a kiss on his cheek.

"I love you too." He had to go, so he left her with a silent stay command to the dogs, who slept with her more often than not these days, and headed for the door.

He stopped to kiss Wat, who handed him his laptop bag, weighed down with his travel machine and... snacks.

"I know you get hangry," Wat murmured.

"Thanks, honey." He took a kiss. "I'll call once I get there." Grady honked slightly, and he sighed. "Okay, I'm off like a herd of turtles."

"Be careful. Take pictures of Vegas for us, if you get to see anything neat."

He doubted it, but he'd be doing his job, which up to the last few months, had been the most important thing in his life.

Tygh headed out of the door with a grin.

Damn, how things had changed.

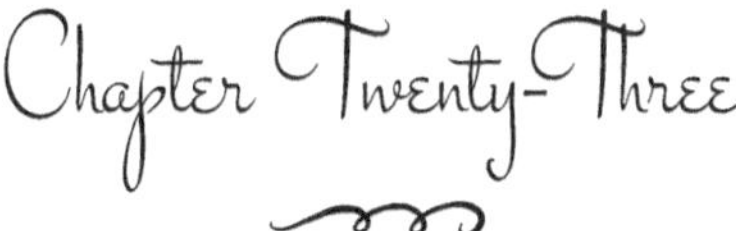

Chapter Twenty-Three

"PAPA! NO! PAPA! NO!"

Naomi stared at Maggie, one eyebrow lifted, in an expression that belonged to her mother. "Can't you duct tape her mouth shut?"

"What?" Had his sweet, innocent little girl said that?

"She's awful and loud and she never shuts up. We should do something."

"Naomi!" Wat blinked hard. "She's missing her Papa, and she can't help that. She was very scared when she came to live with us." He bounced Maggie in his arms, trying to calm her down, which was when Emma had started wailing.

"Uh-huh. When I was scared, it was because my mommy and my hand burned up in a fire! Papa Tygh is not dead, so she should shut up."

Wat wanted to cry, but he couldn't. He just couldn't, not right this second. He had three upset children, two barking dogs, and the donkey outside was calling to aliens or something.

Okay.

Okay, empathy, not aggression. Empathy.

"It is hard to hear her cry, isn't it? I hate that everyone is so upset." *I hate that I feel like a fucking loser, that I can't keep shit together for a whole day.* That his mom was hours away. That there wasn't a McDonald's he could just run to and make everyone smile with a hamburger or nuggets and a toy.

"It sucks."

"I'm sorry you're upset. I know you miss Tygh, sweetie."

"I didn't even get my dress!" She sniffled, and all of the sudden she was crying instead of growling. "I was supposed to get a pretty dress, Daddy!"

"I know, and we're going to go. School is out on Wednesday, so maybe we can go then. Or when Papa comes home. Maybe we can ask if someone can babysit and we'll just go on a daddy-daughter date." He'd do anything to make at least one of them shut up.

She sniffled hard but perked up some. "Okay. I would like that, Daddy."

"Well, there we go." He smiled. "Now, let's get Emma a bottle and Maggie a cookie, huh?"

"Can we go to McDonald's on our date?" And there it was. Speak of the devil.

"I think it's right next to the Walmart, huh? So we should be able to." He always hedged his bets and said should or I hope so or something. Promises could be broken so unintentionally, but it hurt little hearts when it happened.

"Okay. Yes. Daddy and daughter date. No babies." She stared daggers at Maggie. "You need to be good, sister. If you're not, Santa will not come for you."

"Oh, baby, she's too little to understand."

"Papa..." Maggie's sobs were heartbroken.

"Papa is at work!" Naomi snapped. "At work with the bulls!"

"Come on, little bit. Cookie time." She could gnaw out her feels. Naomi could use a snack too. They were all hangry.

He'd get Maggie in her highchair with some noms and then get Emma. It was tough to carry them both now that Maggie had put on so much weight.

God, he was tired.

His phone chimed, and he knew it was Tygh texting, but he ignored it for now. He simply didn't have time.

He felt like he was becoming see-through, like he was a too-often folded piece of paper hanging onto things by mere fibers.

God, he needed to grow the fuck up.

A knock sounded on the kitchen door as he got Maggie in the highchair, and he jumped half a foot, because he wasn't expecting anyone.

He opened it, the dogs wagging around, and it was Grady, the hand who was helping them out. "Hey, Wat. I was wondering if I could borrow Naomi. Mr. Tom is acting up, and I need her to distract him."

"Are you okay with that, baby girl?"

"Uh-huh. Come on, Tater. We're on Tom duty." She grabbed her 'work' coat and stomped into her rain boots.

Such a cowgirl.

He breathed a sigh of relief when she left. Then he went to grab Emma, who needed changing before she got her bottle.

His strategy worked, though, and once both littles were eating, he had a few moments of blessed silence.

His head throbbed, and he wished for a second that he could talk to Michelle. Just talk to her and ask her if he was doing the right thing or not. She would probably tell him to go with his gut. She always had. But Naomi was so mad...

Maybe he'd been selfish—taking her away from her grand-parents, forcing new sisters on her, a whole new life. What if—

Wat took a deep breath. No. She loved having sisters. She was really angry at getting her hopes up about some things and then having them dashed temporarily, but she didn't know how to verbalize that. It was his job to help her with that.

Every kid had this type of thing happen to them. She would be able to cope. She went to a therapist once a week.

Wat sighed, taking the empty bottle from Emma when she was done and putting both girls in front of the TV, Emma in her play area, Maggie on the couch. Then he slumped down in Tygh's old recliner, ready to rest his pounding head.

Maggie stared over at him, frowning deep. "Papa?"

"Soon, baby girl. Daddy promises. He'll be home soon."

She sighed, then wriggled and worked her way off the couch, coming to him, pulling at his jeans leg. "Daddy?"

Oh. Oh, dammit. "Yes, baby?"

"Up?" She opened her arms for him, and he leaned down and brought her into his lap, snuggling her.

Okay.

Okay, this was why they did this.

TYGH GAVE UP TEXTING WAT AND FINALLY JUST called. He was worried, to be frank. Okay, he was a lot worried. He was only halfway home, because the damn bull was developing an infection, and while he had supplies, he'd had to stop for several hours while he cleaned and debrided the wound from that front leg hitting the rail and slicing the underside, then administer the antibiotics, which caused a catastrophic stomach issue...

"Hey, you." Wat sounded exhausted, worn to the bone. "How goes it?"

"It's a giant cluster, honey." He blew out a breath. "I had to stop for a few hours and work on my patient. How are you?"

"Well, Naomi threatened to duct tape Maggie's mouth

shut, Emma is pulling at her ear, so I'm afraid it's an ear infection, and Maggie cried for a total of ninety hours today. I'm sure of it." Wat chuckled, the sound husky. "Add that to an influx of a family of four that are coming in tomorrow, a pregnant teenager who showed up tonight in flip-flops and a T-shirt, and Charlie coming home from school, so Dani and Nell wanted nothing of classes today? It's been a doozy."

"Ouch." Dammit. Wat was being overrun. "Well, I can push it now that the poopfest has slowed down. The antibiotics didn't sit well. I'm sorry, honey."

"No worries. Ryder is having apoplexy over that bull, so he has to be very important."

Important? Shit. This bull's semen was going to go for twenty thousand a straw on the low end. He needed to heal up and retire to a nice safe pasture where they didn't have to worry about him killing himself with his freaking acrobatics.

"Yeah. He's something all right." He blinked at the road, glad Wat was willing to talk. He was fighting the urge to nap while driving.

They were driving in shifts because everyone would be safer and more comfortable at home where they belonged.

"Are you thinking you'll be home sometime tomorrow? Is there anything I can do from here?"

God, Wat was a good man. All this shit going on, and Wat was still What-can-I-do?"

"Just hold down the fort. Do I need to call Ryder and Kase about getting you some help? Are you going to be taking on the new kids?" He hated that he was still so far away. He popped the air up a notch. "And I should be home tonight if I don't have to stop again."

"You be careful. I'd rather you home tomorrow and whole." Wat sighed softly. "The teenager just needs a place to breathe and make a plan, I think. The others will be hanging out with me on the short-term. I'm not on vacation officially until Friday at five, and I may still be on call for this one. It's a shitty situation."

Weren't they all, as a rule. Great situations didn't lead to foster care.

"Okay. Well, you call in someone if you need help. I know a couple of the wranglers' wives have worked daycare, and they could take the littles on, if nothing else. Okay." *I miss you. I love you.* The thought felt surprising, but right.

"I will. I have all three girls in bed with me. They miss you."

"I miss you too, honey. So bad. I want to be home with you and the kids." It was a physical ache how bad he wanted his life back. And wasn't he a weenie for being all woe-is-me for having to do his job?

He loved his job. He loved the animals. He didn't mind the travel.

But his babies were at home.

His man was at home.

His life was back there, and he wanted to be there too.

So he cranked up the air and kept his speed steady despite the urge to go faster. "I'll be home soon, honey. I love you."

"I love you. I do, you know? I mean, I'm in deep with you, and I'm not trying to dig my way out."

"Good." That settled something deep in his chest. "Call me if you need me, huh? I've got the hands-free, and God knows I have nothing but time."

"Do you want to chat? I'm just watching *Forensic Files...*" Wat took a deep, slow breath. "I can keep you company."

"I do. Please. I'm a little sleepy, but I'm really not in a place where I can stop anyway."

"Then tell me about your fantasy vacation. I want to know everything."

Chapter Twenty-Four

"Mister Wat, can I talk to you?" Charlie sounded so worried, so shy.

"Of course." Oh fuck. She shouldn't be pregnant, but... surely she wasn't pregnant. "What's up?"

"I'm going to be in so much trouble."

He blinked. "You're not pregnant."

"What? No." Her cheeks flamed.

"Sorry. It's on my mind with Brittany being new here. So what is it?"

"I sort of... I messed around a lot and failed two classes. I partied a lot, and I wasn't... it was so easy to be there with Leeann, you know?"

"Ah." He nodded, fighting not to grin. Failing classes sucked, especially if it was just negligence. But it wasn't life-threatening, and she could salvage her GPA if she wanted to. "So, what are you thinking about doing?"

"Running away from home and never coming back?" She winced.

"Maybe a little bit of an overreaction?" He nodded at a chair on the porch, because all the kids who would listen to their conversation were playing in the snow while Maggie, Emma, and the new littlest one Henry napped. "I mean, what's your plan to make it right? Have you thought about that yet?"

"No. I don't know what to do. They're going to be sorry they adopted me. Jennifer told them that they could wait until I aged out!" She blinked hard, fighting her tears. "I fucked up, and I'm so sorry."

Oh, sweet girl. "Sorry is a good start, and you know that those men love you, kiddo. Are they going to be pissed? Maybe, but you go in with a plan to make it right, or you ask for help making that plan. They want to help you. They're your dads."

She dashed away the first couple of wet trails on her face. "Do you think so?"

"I know so. You know how? I already love Maggie and Emma so much it hurts. I would do anything for them and Naomi. So you just have to cowboy up and own up to your mistakes. I bet Ryder tells you that all the time." He hoped his words were sinking in. Helping.

"He does. It's so hard to make yourself do things when there are so many better things to do instead."

"Don't I know about that." He winked over. "I think everybody figures that out in their own way. It's part of growing up." And didn't he feel ancient, with three little girls and his class of students.

"Yeah? You seem so steady."

"Oh my God. I was the good kid, and my first semester of college, I tore it up. I wanted to try everything. So I worked hard to pull up my GPA after that and get out with a three point seven. It can happen." He grinned. "You've done the first step. You've admitted you were a little nuts and you let things slide. But you need to tell your dads." He imagined they both would understand.

Hell, she was going to a community college. They weren't even out any money. She'd fix it.

"Yeah, biology? So not my thing. At least I rocked my math class, right?" She was perking up, and that was what he wanted to see. "Thanks, Wat."

"Of course. Good luck. Holler if you need me."

"I will." She got up to hug him, then headed off, waving at Dani and Naomi.

They waved back, then went back to whatever game they were playing that involved hiding behind piles of snow and running around as if they were being chased. It was kind of adorable, and he hoped they wore themselves to the bone. Adding three extra kids had been a challenge.

And even though Tygh was home, that bull was needing constant care, and the rodeo company was home for the holidays, so there was no way for him to breathe.

The poor man worked from six a.m. until sometimes eight at night.

Last night, Maggie had refused to let Tygh hold her, needing Wat to tuck her in.

Emma just seemed confused by the change in routine, but Maggie? She was done with this shit. And he still hadn't gotten his daddy day with Naomi. Maybe he should talk to Antonia and Alba.

Surely they would know someone who he could pay to watch the little ones one day. His oldest deserved that.

In fact, he would call up to the house now, dammit. They needed to pick out dresses for her and the girls before it was too late. He dialed the main house phone, hoping Nanette picked up.

"Hola. ¿Que tal?"

"Bien. ¿Como estas?" Wat waited while Nanette told him about cookies, gingerbread, and tamales before inviting him to supper tonight with the family.

"If Tygh is up to it, I'd love to. Actually, I was wondering if you had a list of babysitters. I owe Naomi a date."

"Ah. Si, si, I can call Bernadette. She will come. What day?"

"Well, we need Christmas dresses, so maybe tomorrow?" Time was flying.

"Si. I will ask. If not, I will do it with Miss Alba and Charlie."

"I would really appreciate it. I made a promise, and I won't break it."

"Then we will manage it for tomorrow. Take her to lunch and shopping, hmm?" She laughed. "I will put the older ones to work and the babies can watch movies and eat cookies, no?"

"Absolutely. I just need to give this to her. She deserves my time."

"She does. It's hard when new ones come in, even if it's exciting. Dani is making noises how it's no fair there's fosters at Christmas."

"Even though she was one, hmm?" He understood that.

"Yes. Time glosses that over, you know? She's adopted." Nanette chuckled. "The logic is not there sometimes at her age."

"Sometimes your heart tells you something, hmm? She doesn't love change." Wat and Dani got that. Naomi had to flex, constantly. She was amazing that way. He admired the hell out of his girl.

"It does. Let me call Bernadette, and I will call you back with the plan, no?"

"Thanks so much, Nanette." Yes. He'd done something right. Go him.

It was about time, too. He felt out of sync, out of time, and so friggin' tired. His to-do lists had to-do lists, and he wasn't close to prepared for the holidays, which were coming if he was ready or not.

Naomi was trying hard to be cool with it, but she wanted sparkly lights and happy music, and he wanted to collapse when he got home after opening a can of soup.

The door to the classroom building opened again, and he thought maybe it was Charlie coming back, but when he turned to look, it was Tygh, all tired and rumpled, but smiling.

"Hey, honey."

"Hey, stranger. How's it going?" He wasn't going to lay his shit on Tygh—the man was tired enough—but, man, he wanted to.

"Better. I think that damn bull has turned a corner. Enough that I have Grady on watch and I can have lunch with you all." Tygh gave him a kiss.

"Oh, that's good. Nanette is making cheesesteaks today." They were a favorite, and hearty and warm for any cowboys coming out for a meal.

"Yum." Tygh glanced out at the kids, smiling. "How's everyone doing?"

"Good. I'm not sure what they're playing, but they're having a ball. Freezing their butts off, but having a ball." In fact, he was going to have to call them in soon.

"Do I need to help get some towels and stuff?" Tygh's hand felt so good on his lower back, and Wat realized he was a smidgen starved for touch. He'd been getting kinda spoiled.

"That would be a huge help. They've been out an hour, and they've been so good, I've been reluctant to disturb them."

"Yeah, but they need to refuel, huh?" Tygh goosed him, then headed to the back cubbies to grab towels. It was good to see him, to be together for the odd moment.

He didn't know how to process all this, not really. He was used to tired, but not this type of bone-deep nonsense.

"Hey." Tygh set the towels down and wrapped him in a hug. "You look really tired."

"I am." He let himself lean. "I know you are too, though, so I'm not bitching. I get to take Naomi for a daddy-daughter date tomorrow."

"Oh, cool. I can probably take Maggie and Emma," Tygh offered.

"Nanette thinks she has someone to take them. There's the new fosters too, so it's a process."

"Yeah. The kids are all in flux, and Dani and Nell have to be worried about them coming in and disrupting things." Tygh gave him a squeeze. "I'm sorry I've been so out of the loop. I know Christmas is looming large, but I should be able to help more now."

"Yeah." He didn't even want to think about it. That list was so long it would wrap around him and squeeze him to death if he dared to stare at it full-face.

"You okay?"

He summoned a smile. "Of course."

"Hmm." Tygh seemed unconvinced.

"I just need to get organized." He was supposed to be off work right now, but that wasn't going to happen. Foster kids needed what they needed, and the Chiaras were going to ensure they got it.

"Okay, well, how can I—"

"Papa Tygh! Look!" Naomi did a one-handed cartwheel in the snow. It looked more like a frog leap, but damn he was tickled she tried.

"Wow! Who wants to dry off and go have lunch?" Tygh called.

"Me! Me, I'm ready, Cowboy Tygh." Dani shivered her way over to Tygh while Wat warmed up his icicle of a daughter.

"We were playing like we were super spies, Daddy!"

"Oh? Exciting!"

She nodded and grinned. "We're both going to be cowboys, but it's fun to pretend."

"I bet it is. I always wanted to be James Bond, huh?" Tygh handed out towels, and that bit of help made Wat feel like crying. Maybe he needed to talk to his therapist. He still had one online.

As soon as he had time, he'd get hold of Roger, schedule a session. He needed a little space to breathe, and he'd be fine.

"Daddy, we spied all over, and we had grenades."

"Wow. That's pretty amazing."

"Naomi can throw really well," Dani said. "She goes, 'I'm going to hit that rock, and bang—she hits it.'"

"Good aim, huh?"

"Yeah. She should get on a softball team. I would come cheer for her."

He almost mentioned her arm, but he didn't. If she played softball, great. If she didn't, also great. He wanted her to know he had her back. "If she wants to, we'll all be her cheering section."

"Yup." Dani giggled. "I like to cheer, but I want to be on the rodeo team."

"Can I do softball and rodeo both, Daddy?"

"If you want to and you keep your grades up, yes." He didn't have the foggiest fucking idea. He would have time, he guessed, to see what season each team did what and if they made reasonable accommodations for kids with challenges.

"Yay!" The girls started cheering and bouncing and, sure as shit, the three babies started wailing.

"Okay, you hooligans," Tygh said. "Run up to the big house and get ready for lunch. Take your boots off at the mudroom, or Nanette will have your hide. We'll be right up."

"Lunch! Lunch! Lunch!" the girls chanted as they ran off, and then Maggie came running.

Climbing out of her crib was her newest trick.

"Hey, sunshine. Can I carry you?" Tygh asked, holding his arms down for her.

She glared at him, but then her smile went to pure joy. "Papa! Love! Up!"

Tygh lifted her up, kissing her cheek. "You ready for lunch, little bit?"

"Eee!" That sound could pierce an eardrum, but it was crystal clear.

Emma sniffled when he picked her up, but she quieted easily, and he handed her to Tygh as well. He could double-arm it while he got the tiny one from their new fosters.

There was a burn mark on his cheek. Mom was in rehab after passing out stoned and setting the house ablaze. Just the thought of the baby caught in the blaze hurt his soul. And gave him a touch of PTSD, if he were honest. But he had to take that reaction out of it when he held Henry, because he needed to feel safe. Secure.

"We good, honey?" Tygh asked, nuzzling Emma's head.

"We are. I'm just a little scattered." He found his Tygh a smile. "Love you."

"I love you too. Lunch!" Tygh bounced the girls and headed up toward the main house, forging a path. That was Tygh. Just blazing a path.

If only he felt like he could do the same, but he was too damn tired.

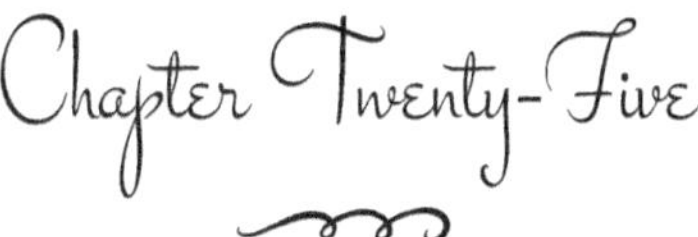

Chapter Twenty-Five

Tygh needed to get out to buy some presents. He knew what he was getting the kids, but he had no idea what to get Wat.

And he wasn't sure how to ask.

Wat had been... quiet. Tired. And they'd managed to get the decorations up at their house, but somehow, the seasonal cheer was lacking.

Tygh wasn't good at this relationship shit, dammit. He had no clue what to do to make it better.

He didn't think Wat was unhappy with him, not really. It was more run-down, worn through. And Tygh got it. They'd had a crazy couple of weeks. But how did he get Wat back to smiling?

"Why won't you listen to me?" Naomi came slamming in, snow blowing in behind her. "I said I don't want to get a new hand."

"I didn't say you had to!" Wat snapped back, closing the door against the winter weather. "I said you have to see the doctor when we go to drop you at your abuelos!"

"I'm tired of doctors, Daddy!"

"Well, tough. It's part of the whole healing thing, Naomi."

Whoa. Ouch. This was escalating fast. "Hey. What's up, you two?"

"Daddy never listens! I always have to go and do things just because I'm littler than him! Move here. Have sisters. Have doctors. I wish Momma had lived instead of you! She was nice to me! You should have burned up instead."

Wat almost crumpled, but then his expression hardened like ice. "Go to your room."

Naomi's eyes went wide. "I—"

"Go to your goddamn room!" Wat bellowed, the sharp sound ringing out.

"You are an ASSHOLE!" She was sobbing as she ran down the hall.

Jesus. "Hey." He stepped toward Wat, hand up.

Wat stepped back, wrapping his arms around himself. "God. I'm sorry. I just—I shouldn't have shouted at her, but that stung."

"Of course it did, honey." He wasn't sure whether to pull Wat into his arms or let him have his space. This was all new to Tygh.

Maggie and Emma were staring at Wat, both of them silent and scared, and Wat's shoulders slumped.

"Hey, babies. I'm sorry. I didn't mean to scare you."

"Daddy was just really emotional, guys." Tygh bent to kiss Emma on the forehead. "It's okay. I promise." Lord, what a minefield.

"It was a rough day. Dani had a meltdown about Naomi leaving after Christmas. It wasn't even about that. Charlie's having hard talks with her dads. 'Lijah isn't getting along with Brittany. Brittany is pregnant and scared. The family that just moved in makes Dani feel insecure." Wat poured a cup of coffee and sat hard. "School is officially over, and Naomi isn't getting a break because I'm having to take her over to the big house to help. I just—it's been an overwhelming day."

Tygh did straighten up to go hug Wat now. "I'm so sorry, honey. I can help more now." He was going to talk to Kase and Ryder about getting Wat some help too. If there was going to be an influx of new kids every few months, Wat needed an assistant. Someone to handle the more daycare-type duties. He knew the budget could take it.

Besides, Wat was a schoolteacher, not a babysitter. That was a big difference.

Wat leaned on him, sighing. "I need to go talk to Naomi."

"Not yet. Let her cool down. And get past you yelling at her. And you need to have a sit and maybe a snack. Then we can all sit together and talk."

"Yeah? I guess you're right. I'm just... I'm trying, man. I mean, I'm *really* trying hard." Wat was barely holding it together.

"I know. I can tell. And—" He took a deep breath. He'd been fixing to make it about him, and that wasn't helping. He'd been unavailable due to work and he had guilt, but Wat didn't need that. "Can I help, or do you just need me to listen?"

"I feel like a bad father. Like I've been selfish..."

"Selfish how?" He didn't mean to blurt it out like that, but Wat was the least selfish person he'd ever met.

"I moved her out here. I fell in love—with you and the babies. I changed everything, and I needed to. I was so tired of listening to both sets of parents telling me what I needed to know."

"Hey." Tygh squeezed Wat good and hard, holding on. "You did a good thing for you and for Naomi. I know she might not always see it, but right now, her big problem is being afraid to start school. And if she tries it this year and she can't do it, then she can try again next fall."

"I just know that she needs the social interaction. She's not an introvert. She loves people, and she and Dani are going to have to accept that they are different."

"They are. And Dani will get used to the idea too. There will be all sorts of stuff for her to get into without going to school." In fact, it was going to be harder for him, because he'd have her in the barns, constantly.

"I know. I just worry that I'm damaging Naomi permanently or something."

"Nope." He kissed Wat on the nose. "I'll make some food, huh? That will make us all feel better."

"I'll help. Then maybe we can go in together? Talk to her. I want to apologize for yelling."

"And she needs to apologize. She doesn't get to pull that out like a weapon."

"She's just wigged out because that new family had their house burn."

"Maybe, but that isn't right, regardless." Tygh didn't believe you just got to hurt someone because you were hurt.

Did it happen?

Sure. Of course. But it didn't make it right. And this was a great moment to emphasize that lesson. It had to be unutterably awful to be reminded of what she'd been through, but he knew from experience that lashing out helped no one.

Especially not Naomi. She was getting better at expressing her anger in more constructive ways, but this was all too much.

"I might need help with that," Wat said. "Sometimes, I want to give in just to make it easier. She's been through so much."

"I get that." He did. "I'll be the voice of mediation, huh?"

"Papa, the voice of reason and the whisperer of fractious animals."

"Yeah." He had to laugh at that, because Wat was already

feeling more even, he could tell. But things still needed to change, or that would fade fast.

He would have to go to the bosses and tell them what was up. No stress.

Maybe a touch of stress, but it was important to protect his family, and the Chiaras would understand.

In that family, you had to speak up to be heard. Things moved fast, and they had a lot on their plate. Seeing everything that was happening didn't really work.

Tygh got that; he was a foster kid. Speak up and get noticed.

He felt better now he had a plan in place, so now they needed to go talk to Naomi.

He started making tacos first, because Wat was making up with the babies, sitting on the kitchen floor and loving on them, offering them comfort. Maggie was telling him all about it, while Emma more wanted to be snuggled and held.

She was a lover, soaking up touch and care like a sponge. Maggie was way more the bossy big sister, but she was smiling in no time, happy to have Wat tell her it was all going to be okay.

"Should we get them fed and put down before we talk to Naomi?"

Wat nodded. "I think she's sleeping. That's what usually happens after an outburst, and she'll be able to listen a little better." Wat shook his head. "She's scared of the doctors, but this visit should be just a normal checkup. No amount of saying that is going to matter, though. She's convinced it's going to hurt."

"Well, sure. She's not had a lot of good from doctors, for all that it was for her health and safety, huh?" He put taco shells into the oven, then got out the stuff to make Maggie something easy. Eggs and banana slices. His tacos were too much for her, but he would give her a soft flour tortilla to tear up with her eggs.

"Yeah, but that doesn't matter, does it?" Wat sighed and shook his head. "And the therapist told me that it's normal for her to blame me. I'm safe. I'm never giving up on her."

"It still hurts like hell, huh?" It had hurt him to hear it, so Wat had to be stinging.

"It kills me. I mean, I know she can't understand, but I lost her mom too. Michelle and I were high school sweethearts, and for a few months there, I didn't know if I was going to swim up out of the darkness."

Tygh felt his heart clench. Jesus, he forgot that sometimes. "I'm so sorry, honey. I love you, for what it's worth."

"It's worth a ton. Just because I loved her doesn't mean I'm not in love with you." Wat stopped and glanced down the hall, then lowered his voice. "Can I tell you a secret?"

"Of course." He turned the meat down and sat on a chair to focus, to listen.

"We lost her, Naomi lost her hand. The house went up in flames, everything in it. All of that was awful, but the thing that I lost—just me, not her parents, my parents, Naomi—was my independence. Suddenly, I was living in her parents' house, and I couldn't work because I was at the hospital all the time. I was drowning."

He frowned. "Do you feel like you're drowning again here? I know it's been crazy busy, and you haven't had time to breathe. I need you to tell me if you are. I don't want you to ever have to feel that way again." He got the taco seasoning in and turned the meat to simmer so he could go to Wat.

"I feel... I'm tired. Not exhausted, but... this is supposed to be a little about us, right? You and me? And I know we started bonding over the babies, but—it's more than that. This isn't just two dads getting off when everyone else is asleep and the work is done."

"No." He looked right down into Wat's grayish-green eyes, loving how they had these flecks of gold. "No, this is about us. You and me. And I'm not sure how it goes sometimes, but I mean it with my whole heart."

"Yeah. I do too. I'm into you. All the way." Wat reached out one hand for him.

He took it and hugged Wat to him for a kiss. He needed the contact, and he thought Wat was ready for it now too.

They breathed into each other, nice and slow, focusing on just connecting for a second.

It was heady.

Wat's shoulders relaxed, his head drooping forward. "Oh, that feels good."

"It does. I love this, being able to be home with you."

"Me too. I mean, I'm glad things are taking a better turn for your patient so you can be here with me." Wat gave him a squeeze.

They changed the babies, and put them in their cribs, before heading to turn off the taco meat.

"Hopefully she'll feel like talking, huh? But if not, we'll just eat and talk tomorrow." Wat winked at him and inhaled deeply.

"That's it. We give her the space to know what to do. Then we poke her with a sharp stick."

"Let's go." Wat knocked on Naomi's door. "Baby? Are you ready to come talk?"

No one answered, and he frowned. Maybe she would answer him. "Naomi, honey? Are you okay?"

Wat frowned and tried the door, face going stony as he found it locked. "Tygh? Is there one of the pokey things?"

"Right here." Tygh reached up and pulled the skeleton key down from above the door on the frame.

"Hurry up. Please. What if she's hurt? Naomi! Come on, baby girl. Open the door!"

Wat was moving from concerned to panicked, and fast.

Tygh wrestled the weird little pokey key into the lock and opened the door. He'd never had to use the damn thing before.

"Naomi?" Wat rushed into the room, and when they didn't see Naomi right away, he checked the closet, but the sound of snapping fabric caught his attention.

"The window is open, Wat." The window was open, and there was a winter storm coming.

"What? It's too cold for that!" Wat rolled his eyes even as he said it, and he ran to the window, the gingham curtains flapping. "The screen's on the ground, and I can still see her footprints in the snow heading toward the ranch house. Dammit, the wind's really picking up."

"I'll call down there and tell them you're coming to get her." Little shit. What was she thinking? That road between the houses wasn't too busy, but it was getting on to dark and she could really get hurt. Of course, Biscuit and Tater were nowhere to be seen, so maybe they'd gone with her, followed her once she'd cleared the house. Tygh grabbed his phone out of his pocket, dialing up Kase.

"Hey, Tygh. What's up?" Kase was laughing, Tygh could hear it in his soft drawl.

"Naomi snuck out of the house, man. She's headed your way. I'll get in the truck and come get her, but it's cold out there. The dogs are with her, I think. Can you keep an eye out?" He knew Wat wasn't about to reward this behavior by letting her spend the night with Dani.

"Sure. Let me make sure she's not already over here. Those girls are pure trouble." There was no heat in Kase's words, just a soft, wry amusement, and he understood.

"Thanks, man. I appreciate it."

"Y'all tie it up?"

"Yeah. She has a doctor appointment coming up, so I'm sure that's the main thing."

"Ah. That's always scary." Kase made an odd sound. "Huh. Ryder?"

"What?"

"You seen Dani?"

There was a pause, then, "Not since I sent her to her room for pushing Nell. She not in there?"

"Nope."

"Danielle! Where are you?"

A sense of dread hit him like a train. "Someone check the barns."

"I'll go now." That was Kase. "Ryder, Naomi is with her."

"Fuck. Charlie! 'Lijah! I need you!"

"We're on our way." Tygh hung up, and then stared Wat. "Get the babies bundled up. We're heading to the main house."

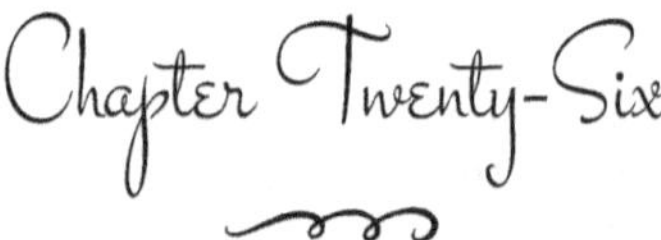

Chapter Twenty-Six

Wat stared at Tygh as if he'd literally grown another head. Was Tygh even speaking English?

Bundle the babies up?

What?

"Babe, they can't find Dani. We need to go to the big house. Now. Move your ass."

That last bit got through, and he started moving. Naomi didn't have her good coat, her snow boots. She'd get cold and come home, wouldn't she?

"Should one of us stay here?"

"No. If they come back anywhere it will be Kase and Ryder's, because that's where they are, somewhere I bet." Tygh was grabbing coats and boots and blankets.

Wat got the babies gathered up and the diaper bags in hand, along with phone chargers. He made sure the oven and stove were off, and by then, Tygh had the kids loaded.

Wat kept the window open, leaning out into the wind and calling Naomi's name. And he tried hard not to panic and puke or something when no one answered. That was his baby girl out there.

They got to the house, and Tygh immediately tried whistling up the dogs. "Tater! Biscuit! Come!"

"Should we call the police?" His heart was slamming in his chest, playing a wild tattoo against his ribs. "Should you call the dogs if they're with the girls?"

"Biscuit would take me back to them." Tygh shook his head. "But they must be out of earshot. I'm heading to the barn to saddle a horse. I don't want to take the ATV because it's too loud to hear them."

"I'm coming with you. They took Strawberry. Her tack is gone and everything." Ryder was bundled up to the gills. "My cousin Frank is headed to your place, Tygh. Granny's called the sheriff, but there's one hell of a wreck between us and them."

Took Strawberry. Wait. "The horse? They took a horse? She's only got one hand!"

"Well, between them they have three." Ryder's voice was rough with worry.

"I'm with you," Tygh said, glancing at Ryder.

Then Ryder looked at him. "Stay here and help Kase? There will need to be blankets and food and all sorts of shit when we get back with them."

He nodded to Ryder, but focused on Tygh, because Tygh was the man he had faith in. If anyone loved her close to what he did, it was her Papa Tygh. "You have to find her. You have to bring her home. I believe in you, cowboy."

"I will, honey. I promise." Tygh's expression was set and a little grim, but he knew that meant his game face was on, and that Tygh would move mountains to find the girls.

"Let's ride, buddy." Ryder led the way, and Tygh left him there with Kase.

"Let's get the babies inside, Mister Wat." 'Lijah and Leeann were right there. "Charlie's searching all the security footage to see which way they went. Everyone's looking. Everyone."

"Thank you." Should he call his folks? Michelle's? Would it just panic them, or would he be in a pickle because he didn't? He had no idea. Naomi had never even threatened to run away before. And she'd sure never had a horse to grab or a ranch to get lost on.

Alba was right there, to help bring the babies in and enfold him in a hug. "We'll find them."

"I hope so. She didn't even have her coat." And it was snowing. Fucking bitter.

"I bet she took one of Dani's." Leeann took Emma. "Come on, Mr. Wat."

'Lijah herded him inside, where Kase and Nanette were both on the phone. He plugged his in, then started unpeeling the littles so they didn't get sweaty and fussy.

Nell came wandering in, tears on her cheeks, and she held her arms up to Wat. "Hold me?"

"Of course, sweet girl." He wasn't alone. He wasn't dealing with this in a vacuum. He was a part of something bigger that he didn't honestly understand.

"I can help with the babies," Brittany offered, the teenager's belly as if she'd swallowed a basketball.

"That would be appreciated, and the Martin children are all a little scared, so if someone could get them soup and cartoons?"

"I'm on it," 'Lijah bounced and headed back to the center wing of the huge adobe. This was the Southwest version of the Winchester house. It just seemed to have grown organically and haphazardly.

"Wat. They'll be fine." Alba came to give him a pat on the shoulder. "I have milk ready to warm. Would you like some tea?"

"No. No, I need to do something. Maybe I should get out and drive?"

"In this mess? How far could you see?"

That was true, but what if they had taken the road?

"Grady is searching the road, Wat," Kase said when he got off the phone. "I hate it too, but the best thing we can do is be ready to mobilize once they find the girls."

"When was the last time you saw Dani? Naomi and I had a fight. I sent her to her room." He'd yelled at her. What if that was the last thing he'd ever said to her?

"I caught them on the cameras about twenty minutes before you came over," Charlie said. "So they don't have that much of a head start." She handed Kase a printed picture.

"I'll call Ryder." Kase headed outside, phone in hand.

"They had the horse and the dogs, so that's good, right?" Charlie asked.

Antonia nodded, her lips tight. "Strawberry will come home if the weather gets too bad. She knows where to go."

"Horses are so much smarter than us humans," Charlie said. She looked strained around the eyes and mouth, though. She took being a big sister very seriously.

"Ryder and Tygh are out there. They will find them." If he said it enough, he would believe them.

"Yes." Antonia shook her head. "And we'll hug them, then beat them to death."

Charlie barked out a hysterical laugh. "Hell yeah, Granny."

Wat had to unbend enough to smile at that. Yes. He wanted to tan Naomi's hide, despite that not being something he really did. She was never going to hear the end of this.

Ever.

He might put an alarm on her window. An Apple tag on an anklet. Bells around her neck.

They all fretted and paced, and Kase came in and out,

always on the phone with someone. No, Frank hadn't seen them or the dogs. Neither had Grady. They'd headed out across the pasture, not the road.

Emma started crying, and he handed off Nell and went to her, rocking her and trying to breathe.

"Papa?" Maggie said. "Sisser?"

"Papa went to go get sister, yes." Sister. She'd never said that before, he didn't think. God. He was going to lose his shit.

"Hold it together, Mister." Charlie held his gaze, serious as a heart attack. "No matter what. No matter how bad. You hold it together. It's your job."

Jesus. From the mouth of a kid who shouldn't have learned that lesson but had. He wouldn't disrespect that knowledge for anything. "Yes, ma'am. Holding on with both hands."

"Yeah. Me too."

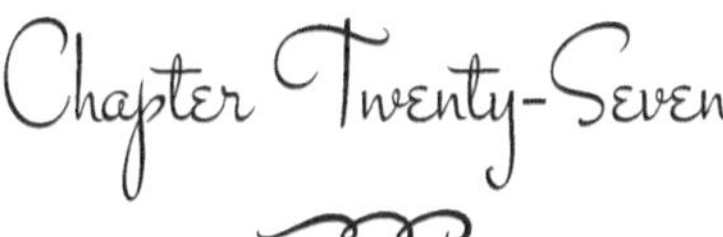

Chapter Twenty-Seven

Tygh and Ryder rode out, hats tilted forward against the snow, which was driving into their faces. They didn't try to talk through it, but every so often he called or whistled to the dogs, knowing they would hear him long before the girls did.

Jesus, what were they thinking going out in this storm? He'd run away from foster care more than once, but not like this. Naomi had to be really scared of what was coming to just up and leave on horseback in a storm.

And then there was Dani. That little girl knew better, knew how hard it was not to have a solid home.

Ryder had to be losing his fucking mind.

He whistled again, knowing they could be more than a half a mile from the house in the direction Charlie had pointed them. Their horses would be moving faster than Strawberry, who would want to be back in the barn.

She wasn't terribly interested in messing around in bad weather. She wanted home and food and warmth and comfort.

Tygh hunched his back against the cold wind that swirled

around them. Hell, he got that. He might be a block of solid ice by the time this was done.

"Do you think she's going to keep heading straight on or will she start to circle back, man?" Ryder yelled to him.

"Strawberry will circle back if she can! And the dogs will help!" He kept looking for prints, but the snow was coming down fast enough that he might not see them.

He whistled again, and he thought he saw the beam of a flashlight, swinging through the air.

"Dani!" Ryder's shout echoed in the air. "Dani! Is that you, baby?"

Ryder saw it too. It wasn't a hallucination. "Naomi! Naomi, Dani—wave the light again if you can hear me!"

He whistled again, praying that the dogs were in range.

A sharp bark came to him, and he knew that was Tater. Jesus, his old boy had to be hurting like mad, being out in this storm. He wasn't made for it like Biscuit was. But he'd stuck with his girl, and Tygh called to him. "Come on, boy! Herd!"

Wild happy barking filled the air, and that light waved again. "It's them!"

He pushed them to move faster, driving them toward the light.

"Dani-girl! Daddy's coming!"

Which was when they heard the wail. "Daddyyyyy!"

"Yes!"

"Naomi! Naomi, Papa is coming!" He popped the reins down on Applejack's back, hurrying them on. He didn't want to run the girls down, but as soon as they got close enough, Biscuit swam up out of the storm, keeping them from smacking into Strawberry.

"Daddy! We got lost! I'm sorry. I don't want to go have Christmas at Naomi's granny's!" Dani was sobbing, running to Ryder's horse.

Ryder slid down to grab her, keeping himself between her and the horse. "Oh, baby girl. You scared me."

"Naomi!" Was she still on Strawberry? "Where are you?"

"She's scared you're going to hate her," Dani told him. "She says she can't go home anymore."

"No! Naomi! Biscuit, lead!" His dogs would take him to Strawberry. "Strawberry! Barn, lady."

He heard a bark, then a wild whinny. Oh, someone was not happy. Not at all.

"I'm coming!" He nudged Applejack forward, and Strawberry damn near mowed them down, appearing out of nowhere, Naomi clinging to her mane with her one hand.

"Papa! Papa, help me!" Naomi seemed so, so tiny up there alone. "Make her stop!"

"Hold up, girl!" He leaned down to catch Strawberry's reins. "Okay, I got you. I do. Naomi, I'm going to come alongside you and put you in front of me, okay?" His heart was just thundering.

"I'm sorry. I just... I'm so sorry. I'm so sorry, Papa. I didn't mean it. I don't want him to die!" Naomi reached for him with her arm.

"I know that, sweetie. So does your daddy." He pulled her into his lap, wrapping Strawberry's reins around his saddle horn as he shifted her into one arm for a moment. "Biscuit, Tater, come." He had to hope the dogs would be okay. They were both half outdoor cold-weather dogs, at least. They'd have a warm fire and blankets and snacks when they got back.

And God knew he knew a vet.

"I'm just glad you're safe."

"I love you."

"Call home and tell them we have the girls." He held Naomi closer, keeping her warm. "I love you too, kiddo. We need to get everyone inside."

"Tater is limping a little, Papa." She hiccupped. "I'm sorry."

"He's just a little sore, baby girl. You just hush and stay up tight with me."

"I've ruined Christmas." She started sobbing, and that set Dani off too.

"You're safe. That's all we needed." They would have a long discussion about Christmas and about how people talked things out and faced up to their problems instead of running away, but right now, he needed her safe, warm, and dry, and he needed to get her and Dani home. And the animals as well.

That was his damn job.

It was so much faster getting home. The snow was blowing against their backs, the lights were calling for them, and they had the girls and the dogs and Strawberry.

Several wranglers were waiting for them when they got back, and a couple of them grabbed reins. "You get them inside. We'll rub these guys down and get them settled."

"Holler at me if anyone has issues," Tygh said.

"Will do."

He carried Naomi, calling for the dogs to come with him, because he needed to look at Tater's leg once he got Naomi to Wat to dry her off and warm her up. She was still crying, but it was a tired sniffle now.

Charlie came flying out of the house, dark eyes flashing. "What were you thinking, Dani! What's wrong with you?"

Wat was right behind her, eyes searching for Naomi. "I knew you'd find her. I knew you would."

"I did. She's pretty cold and scared, baby." Honey just didn't seem to cut it anymore with Wat. He handed Naomi over, and she started sobbing again as Wat wrapped her in a blanket.

"Shh. Shh. Come on inside where it's warm. Daddy has you."

"Don't hate me! I'm so sorry!"

"I could never hate you." Wat hurried her in, and Tygh left Ryder and Kase to deal with their kids.

He needed to check on his dogs, see that Naomi was in one piece.

At least he knew she didn't have frostbite on one hand... The thought surprised him, and he bit back his hysterical laughter. God, he was glad that hadn't popped up out loud.

"How's Dani?" he asked Ryder. Kase and Charlie had whisked her away, blankets and promises of a bath starting right off.

"Scared, ashamed, cold." Ryder was pale as a sheet, and the grannies came up, blankets and mugs of steaming tea in hand. "Charlie's melting down."

"I bet." He dried off as best he could, and someone handed him sweats to change into. Good thing they always kept something his size around, or he would look like a weird teenager who'd outgrown his clothes.

"Go change. Then we can check on everything else," Ryder told him, so that was what he did.

He sat on the pot for a second so he could change his socks, completely unsurprised to find his hands shaking.

He was getting alarms for all the windows. That way, if she tried to sneak out, they'd have some warning.

He took a few deep breaths, trying to calm the churning in his gut. She was safe. All the could-haves weren't in play anymore. That was what he needed to remember.

Now he needed to check on his dogs and his youngest daughters. Soon it was going to be Wat who needed him.

"Hey, guys." He found Tater and Biscuit curled up on blankets in the kitchen, where the oven was on, something that smelled like cookies in it, and two pots of boiling water sat on the stove. To heat the room, he would bet. "Let me see that leg, buddy."

Tater rumbled at him but let him check the foot out, but he didn't have any bad damage—he'd bet it was ice in that arthritic paw.

Little Nell came in with one of the wee, worried-looking foster kids that Tygh thought was named Stella. "Can we have a 'nana to share?"

"Of course you can, baby girl." He grabbed a banana and split it, making sure to get the strings off. Nell hated those things. "Think I ought to give Tater and Biscuit one too?"

"Thems like 'nanas?" Her eyes went wide.

"They do. I'll share one with them." He didn't want to eat anything, but it was probably a good idea.

"'kay. Sister's in trouble, huh? Her and N'omi?"

"She's had a rough night. And I know Mr. Wat and I will have to talk to Naomi about what happened. I bet your dads talk to Dani. But we're home safe, and that's what matters now." Look at him be all calm. He tore open a banana to share with the dogs, though, needing the little ritual of feeding them.

"Uh-huh. Here's safe and warm and home."

Little Stella nodded. "Uh-huh."

Oh, sweet babies. Suddenly, he needed to see Naomi, hold Maggie and Emma. Right now. He fed the bites to the dogs, then hurried to the front room of the ranch house, where Maggie and Emma were cuddled on the couch with Alba.

"There they are," he murmured.

"I know. I always feel that way. When one is hurt, I need to check on the others." Alba smiled at Nell and Stella, looking for all the world like one of those dried apple dolls.

"Little ones. Come and sit."

"Mimi! I gets a 'nana!"

"Did you? How yummy?" She got all the kids back up on the couch with her.

He picked up Maggie moments later when she reached for him, holding her against his chest. "Love you, baby girl."

"Papa." She patted his chest. "Da?"

"He's in with Naomi. She's changing her clothes."

"Sisser."

"Yes." He kissed her sweet cheek. "Let me say hello to Emma too, hmm?"

"Mmm." She went right back to Alba, clearly feeling all was right with the world now that everyone was done shouting and running around.

Emma was content to let the world happen around her, still. She didn't need any nonsense. So he bent to kiss her, and she made smacking noises.

Then he went to find Wat and Naomi.

"Sisser, Papa. Sisser sisser SISSER!" Oh God, wasn't that cute?

"We're in here, Maggie."

Tygh found them in the schoolroom, Naomi bundled up, eyes bloodshot from crying.

"I'm sorry for the trouble, Papa. I was wrong. I'm so sorry."

"I'm just worried about why you ran away, kiddo," he said, glancing at Wat. "Are you ready to talk about that at all?"

"I just... I'm mad about the doctors. I hate that they want me to get a fake hand like there's something wrong with me. I was mad, and there's nothing wrong with me!"

Wat gave him a faint smile. "Of course there's not, bug. I think maybe the doctors just want you to feel like everyone else."

And make more money, Tygh thought, maybe just a teeny bit cynical. But if she didn't want a prosthetic, she didn't have to have one.

"Well, I'm sorry you were worried and mad, kiddo, but

you know it was wrong to put you and Dani and Strawberry in danger."

She gulped. "And Tater and Biscuit. Is Tater okay?"

"He's fine. Just a sore paw. But it could have gone very wrong, so thank you for your apology." He hoped he was doing this right.

"I'm so sorry. Please let us stay. I just... everything is nice, and it's going to change. I thought Granny could help me..."

"Bug, your granny wants you to be happy and safe."

"I'm not going to ask you guys to go away." Tygh was a little shocked at the idea. "I'm your papa. I love you both, and your sisters too. Sometimes, change can be good. School might be awesome." He looked at Wat again, getting the tiniest nod. "In fact, what if you make new friends?"

"What if Dani's mad?" she whispered.

Jealous, more likely, but that was something that her dads would have to deal with, just like they would.

"Love and friendship isn't pie, Naomi." Wat's voice was calm now, patient. "You aren't less her friend if you make more."

"No?" She bit her lip. "I've never had a good friend like Dani."

"Well, if she's your friend, she won't stop being one because you go out and do new things." That he knew from long experience. "And I know Dani. She's a good friend. It may be hard for her to adjust, but she will."

She sniffled. "Promise?"

"I promise, baby girl." He joined them when Wat held out a hand, giving them a group hug.

Maggie pushed into Naomi's arms, snuggling in. "Sisser."

Naomi blinked. "She said my name!"

"Sisser!"

"She loves you. You're her big sister." Wat's eyes were

bruised, the lines around his mouth deep. "Of course she knows your name."

"Wow." Naomi laughed. "I love you too, Maggie."

"Can you take her to go sit with Mimi, kiddo?" he asked. He needed to check in with Wat. "We'll be out in a minute, okay?"

"Uh-huh. Come on, Maggie. Let's walk to Mimi. I bet she has cookies. Mimi always has cookies."

Wat sat there, silent as a stone.

"Hey." Tygh reached out to him, hand closing on Wat's shoulder. "I know you're not okay, but are you gonna make it?"

"Yeah. Believe it or not, this isn't in the top ten of bad things that have happened with me and Naomi..."

"Oh, baby." He hugged Wat to him tight, soaking up warmth and hopefully giving comfort. "I'm here, though. I hope it helps."

"I know. It does. You help a ton. I just... I'm afraid I'm not as good at this dad thing as I thought I'd be."

"Huh? Wat, you're amazing. You get through this thing all day every day and you keep on plugging. It's hard, but you make it look easy. I mean, damn." He meant every word too.

"I think I want to go home, Tygh."

"What?" Was Wat talking about leaving him? Heading back to Santa Fe?

"I'm tired. I want our bed. I want to nail Naomi's window shut. I want our fucking tacos and to be on fucking vacation!"

Relief slammed through him, and he had to fight the urge to laugh, because that would be hysteria again. "Okay, baby. Let's get everyone loaded in the truck." He pulled Wat to his feet so they could go stomp into their boots and get coats on and all.

They were sent home with cookies, an enchilada casserole, and a huge package of meatballs.

And when they all piled back into their own kitchen, the taco meat needed to be warmed up and wasn't even ruined. So Wat was going to get his tacos.

Did having kids mean every day was going to be this wild?

No wonder Wat was tired.

Chapter Twenty-Eight

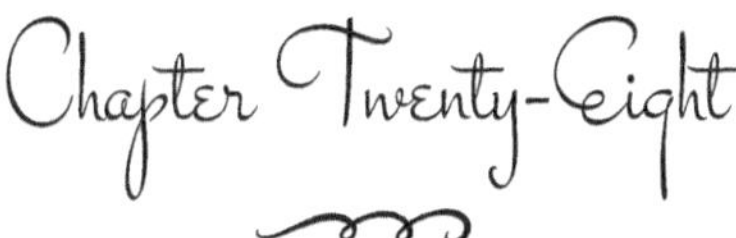

"Come on, guys. Let's get out of your wet stuff, and we can color." Wat's head was pounding. He had Naomi and Dani, Nell, Stella, Oliver, and baby Lily, plus two pair of the hands' kids who were out of school but their parents were working. He'd sung and played, read and had them outside to work off energy in the snow.

He was supposed to be on vacation, dammit.

He had been working on keeping Naomi busy, and she had been practicing saying, "No, thank you. I'm happy as I am." in the mirror so she could stand up to the doctor. He'd also promised to inform the doctor that she wasn't ready—not now, maybe ever—to discuss a prosthetic.

That seemed to be going pretty well.

Now Wat had to figure out how to do the same thing for himself. Stand up and say, "Hey, I'm supposed to be on my time off."

"Hey, I'm fucking tired."

"Hey, I have a master's degree. I am not a babysitter."

He sighed, hanging up dripping coats. They had a small wet area for that now thanks to Tygh, who'd put in that interlocking floor mat stuff, a curtain rod, and some shoe bins. It had been a lovely gift.

"Okay, everyone get a coloring page. We'll make cards out of them."

"Fun!" Naomi was being a trooper, helping the little ones get all set up to make what he was sure would be another mess.

He settled in his chair, forcing himself to keep his eyes open. He'd never been so fucking tired. Never.

Okay, that was an exaggeration. He'd had a ton of nights in the hospital that were worse. This was a normal, grumpy tired.

He woke up when Tygh put a hand on his shoulder, staring down at him when he opened his eyes. "Hey, baby. What are you doing over here? I was about to head home and Grady said you got called in?"

"Yeah. I've been in here with all these little ones today." And the kids had been good, really, but it was Christmas break.

"Damn. You were supposed to be home making cookies. I know you were looking forward to it."

"Papa. Look at the picture Maggie is making you," Naomi said.

Tygh glanced over his shoulder. "That's amazing, kiddo. When are you off-call, Wat?"

"Is that a thing? I'm not sure that's a thing." He didn't know if he could simply say no.

"It has to be a thing. You're supposed to be a teacher, not a daycare worker, right?"

He chewed his lower lip for a moment, looking over Tygh's shoulder at the kids, but they didn't seem to have heard. "Ideally, yes."

"Then we need to talk to them about daycare. I get that the grans are getting on and Nanette is a housekeeper, so they don't want to watch the kids, but you shouldn't have to do this alone." Tygh stroked his cheek. "Or at all. You're on Christmas break."

"I know, and I'm tired, babe. I'm bone-deep exhausted." And it felt like he was whining, but it was still true.

"Okay. So we need to fix it."

He started to open his mouth, but Tygh shook his head. "No, baby. You and me together. As a we. We'll talk to Kase and Ryder."

"Yeah? You think so?" He wasn't sure if he was supposed to feel this amazing release of pressure, but he did.

"I do. If they need just a sitter, you can get a job at the school or teaching online. Something that suits you." Tygh nodded. "In an emergency, of course we all do what we need to, but this isn't that."

"I keep thinking that. But I don't want to get fired or be unreasonable."

"No way. It's not like no one else was here. I just saw Kase. This is just we need someone to watch all the kids, so we'll call Wat." Tygh shook his head. "I know they're busy, but we have three kids of our own, and we need family time. And us time. And rest."

Hearing it from Tygh made him feel less selfish and weird. It really did.

"We do. I want to make cookies and look at lights and watch the *Grinch* with you and the girls."

"Then we do that." Tygh pulled out his phone. "Hey, Ryder. Yeah. Uh-huh. Well, it's time for us to head home, so— Yeah, Wat still has them. That would be great. Can we talk tomorrow, the four of us? Okay, cool. Yeah, we'll give you five." He hung up. "They're coming to pick up the kids."

"That was quick." Wat had to love that, how Tygh made things happen.

"Well, to their credit, I don't think the guys want to take advantage of anyone. They just get busy and forget who's dealing with what." Tygh rose to help him get everyone bundled up to go home with them or Ryder and Kase.

"Are we going home?" Naomi asked. She and Dani were both grounded from spending the night with each other until after Christmas day. Then they could have one night before Naomi left for two days.

"We are. We're going to make cookies."

"Yay!" She clapped her hand against her thigh. "Oatmeal scotchies for Papa, ginger snaps for you, frosted sugar cookies for me."

"Yep. We can all have a half-hour nap," Tygh said. "And then cookies and soup and bread, huh?"

"Yes, sir! I'm ready." Someone was ready to make Santa happy.

"Good deal." He checked Maggie's snowsuit and Emma's coat, and Ryder and Kase burst in after two more minutes or so.

"Wat. I'm sorry, man. We'll stay here in the schoolroom until Lanie and Kyra come get theirs, and then take our kids home. We thought you were getting spelled by the ladies." Kase made a face. "We got our wires crossed between the bunch of us."

"Thank you. I just... You know. I have some family things to do." And he was tired and needed a beer.

"Sure you do. And can y'all come on over about ten? Tygh said you wanted to talk." Ryder's expression went wry. "I bet I know what about."

Tygh put a hand on his lower back. "Is that okay, baby?"

"It is. Do you think someone could come watch the kids?"

"I will." Lanie came running in, her ropers thudding on the floor. "I'm so sorry, Wat. I misunderstood."

Wat hugged Lanie. "No one is angry, and I'm not quitting, okay? I just think we may need a daycare person."

"Yeah. I bet there's someone in town, and if not, someone

will want to be here." She waved Ryder and Kase off. "I'll hang out for Kyra."

"Thanks, lady. You guys all have a good evening. We'll see you in the morning." Ryder offered them all a smile. "No stress, right? We're just going to make a plan and enjoy our Christmas." Ryder grinned at him. "You're almost at your three months, you know."

Wat knew. At three months, they could adopt the girls and no one could take them. He nodded and smiled. It was just a few more days.

"Yessir." Tygh winked at Ryder, who laughed, and they each grabbed a little girl while Naomi skipped along beside them, singing "Jingle Bells," which was her favorite Christmas song at the moment. It felt amazing to head out into the cold air to be going home.

"I'm going to load the girls up in the vehicle. Naomi, are you riding with me or Papa?"

"Papa, please! We have to talk about your Christmas present!"

"Oh-ho!" Tygh laughed. "Well, I guess that works, huh? We'll do it." Tygh did help him get the littles strapped in.

"Hey, you. I love you." He felt as if he could breathe maybe, knowing that Tygh had his back.

"I love you too, baby. I'll see you at home, huh?" That look spoke volumes about what Tygh wanted to do later. After a nap and cookies, maybe.

He thought, maybe, a little afternoon delight would be better than an Excedrin Migraine.

Hell, even if it wasn't, he could totally have both.

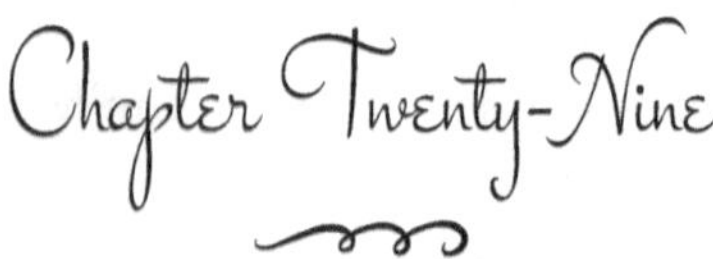

Chapter Twenty-Nine

Tygh wasn't worried.

He could tell Wat maybe was, but he knew Ryder and Kase enough to know that after yesterday, they would be aware what his demands were. Well, his asks. He wasn't one to demand, but for Wat, he might get heated.

Lanie was at the house with the girls doing popcorn stringing and a movie with her wee one and their girls, and they were waiting for Kase and Ryder in the big study at the ranch house.

Nanette had brought in coffees and pastries, told them to relax, and Wat was sitting and staring.

"It's gonna be fine, baby."

"I know. I just hate this kind of thing." Wat sighed but then grinned. "Adulting."

"Kinda sucks. But it's worth it for Naomi and Maggie and Emma."

"Are you ever stunned at how fast everything has changed?"

He caught Wat's eye. "Every day. And grateful as hell."

"Yeah? I mean, after the first of the year, we can petition to adopt the girls. Make them legally ours."

"We can." His heart kicked into a heavy rhythm. He wanted to talk to Wat about all of them taking the same last name, but that could wait.

"I'm so glad to hear that," Kase said on the way in.

"Yes. Those girls are a solid family, and they love you." Ryder brought in a pair of envelopes. "Merry Christmas Eve eve."

"Thanks, Boss." He tucked his away without looking, and saw Wat do the same.

"Okay, out with it."

"We need a daycare person," Wat said. "Maybe two. I'm happy to help, but I can't teach if I'm always on call to take care of the little kids."

God, Tygh was proud of him.

"I think you're right, but—" Kase and Ryder glanced at one another. "We'd like you to act as a manager of sorts. You'll get a raise, and you'll have the teaching duties for the school-aged homeschoolers, plus hiring and managing the daycare staff."

"Wow." Wat's eyebrows went up. "Seriously?"

"Wat, you've been steady as a rock, and you've proven to be really good with the foster kids. And Dani adores you. So yeah. And if you manage them, well..."

"Then you guys don't have to," Tygh said, laughing.

"Laugh it up, Tygh. You're getting two new assistants. And Grady wants to go for his vet assistant. An associate's, at least."

"No shit?" That was damn fine.

"You guys are inspiring," Ryder said, just as matter-of-fact as ever. "And with Wat not needing the house, that's an extra space for us. Plus, a daycare-slash-private school is a way to get the best cowboys in."

"That's true." Homeschooling was good for guys who wanted their kids not to have to ride a bus into town. Or gals.

Wat was still blinking hard. "We brought you some cookies."

"If you need time to think it over, you can tell us at the first of the year," Kase said. "Charlie was out yesterday, but she's agreed to be here to watch the kids, so you're on your own time except for checking on our prize bull, Tygh."

"No. I want it. I want to stay, and this is a good place for Naomi and the babies. It's a good place for me and my man." Wat met Tygh's eyes. "I want to be here at home, with you."

"I want that too, baby. Full time. Forever." He reached out to grab Wat's hand, so in love it hurt. This was what it felt like to be part of something. To be a family.

"Okay, then." Wat glanced over at him. "I think we should talk to Naomi about getting married. We have three girls. We want them protected, sure, but I want you to know I'm yours."

Kase actually went, "Aww."

"I'm all in. You beat me to the question, but yes, I want that too." He grinned at Wat, then the guys. "So romantic."

"Believe it or not, it is. We're a family, and we're in love. We have dogs, goats, horses, and that weird-assed polydactyl cat in the barn. We're pure romance."

That was the most amazing thing anyone had ever said to him. Merry Christmas to his happy ass.

"We're gonna take that offer then, guys." Tygh nodded once. "I like the idea of being married to a manager. Makes me sound studly."

"Hey, I'm marrying a doctor."

"Get out of here and go tell your kids," Kase said, laughing. "And take some tamales home with you. We'll see you the day after Christmas for a leftover feast, huh?"

"Yes. We promised Naomi that she could see Dani before

she headed to her grandparents for their visits, so that's perfect." Wat stood, shook Ryder and Kase's hands. "You all have totally changed my life."

"And we're grateful to have you." They shook with Tygh too, and Kase shooed them out the door.

"Come with me to the barn," Tygh said. "And then we can go. I just want to check on my patient."

"Sure." They took the tamales Nanette handed them, and Wat followed him out to the barn, his wellies sloshing. Naomi and him had gotten Wat cowboy boots.

If his man was going to be a cowboy, he needed them. Besides, Wat's butt was going to look utterly amazing with the lift the slight heel gave him.

Strawberry whickered when they walked in, so Wat went to her while Tygh checked on the damn bull. He was about ready to go back to the main bull area, which was a damn good thing. He was a strong beast, and Tygh didn't like him around the kids.

When Wat turned around, though, Tygh was ready for him, kneeling, even if he didn't have a ring for him.

Wat's pretty hazel eyes went wide. "Well, Dr. Korden! What is this?"

"I was going to ask you at Christmas, but... I want to marry you, Wat. I want us to share a last name. If you want me to take Torres, I will. But I want us all to be the real deal. A family."

"I think Korden-Torres has a ring to it, to be honest. And the girls can use either. That way we're taking each other's." Wat's eyes filled with tears. "No one's ever proposed to me before."

"No? Well, I am now, baby." He knew that was a yes, but he wanted to hear the word. "So, yeah?" He kissed Wat's ring finger.

"Yes. Yes." Wat stared at him, wondering. "We did everything backward, Tygh, but somehow we did it right."

"We did, baby. And that's all I can ask for." He stood, kissing Wat hard on the mouth.

He couldn't wait to go home and ask the girls for their permission too.

Epilogue

"**D**addy! Daddy, I got a doll house! A whole doll house that's just like Dani's!"

"You did!" He watched Maggie stare at her play kitchen, eyes wide. "You should show your sister her kitchen. She's a little overwhelmed."

Emma had her soft first baby and was gently gnawing on it.

"Okay! But then I can play?"

"Of course you can, baby. Maggie will catch on quick, but big sisters rock so hard."

Her cheeks went pink, and she nodded, then went to show Maggie how to make fake food.

"I love the matching jammies," Tygh told him. "I always saw pictures of that."

They had green striped ones that said *Daddy*, *Papa*, *Big Sister*, *Little Sister*, and *Baby Sister* in fancy red script. Wat was over the moon, and the pictures were amazing.

The girls had gotten their dresses, and Naomi was wearing her belt and boots and hat with her jammies. Wat thought she looked like something out of a 1950s Kodak ad.

The ring Tygh had given him was on his hand, and the felt Stetson he'd gotten was gray and gorgeous.

He'd gotten Tygh a fancy iPad with a cover and some veterinarian software. His practical lover had loved it, but he'd loved the hand and footprints of his daughters more.

And his boots. They were practical work boots, not fancy Santa Fe ones, but they were perfect for getting around the ranch.

"These are the best cinnamon rolls, Daddy." He thought Naomi might be on her third, so he would have to watch her.

"Are they? Good. Can you bring me and Papa one to share?" He guessed Christmas was supposed to be a day of excess.

"Uh-huh." She got them a big one on one plate and two forks. "Look, Maggie. You can make eggies."

"Eggies?" Maggie's eyes lit up.

"Just fake ones. We can have real ones in a bit, huh, Daddy?"

"We'll all need some protein by then, yes."

"She does love her eggs," Tygh murmured.

"Eggies! Papa! Daddy! EGGIES!"

Wat nodded, managing to keep a straight face. "Yes, ma'am. Eggs for you to cook while we're in the kitchen."

Emma waved her baby in his face, and he gave it a kiss.

"Pretty baby."

She giggled madly, and he had to admit, this was the best Christmas in a long time. And when he thought of Michelle, he could smile now. Her picture was on an ornament Naomi had made and hung on the tree, and Tygh had listened to all the stories about her, including her in their family too.

Things weren't going to be perfect. Naomi had to try public school, had to go away to see both sets of grandparents. He had to learn to manage employees and trust them with his daughters.

He had to learn how to be an openly bisexual man, someone who was married to a cowboy. They had to adopt their youngest daughters.

There was so much, but it was all right, because he was doing it for his family, and he wasn't doing it alone.

Tygh had his back, and more importantly, he'd proven to have their girls' backs. And there was love. So much love.

Goofy dogs, loud kids, lots of friends and family.

It was the kind of life people dreamed about. People like him and Tygh both.

The door had opened for him, and he walked through it. It had taken work, love, and a little faith, but it had happened.

They'd survived, they'd rebuilt, and they had found home.

Want More?

Interested in learning more about BA's cowboys? Want free fiction and news? Join my newsletter or follow me on Ream!

Western to the bone and an unrepentant Daddy's Girl, BA Tortuga spends her days with her hounds and her beloved wife, having mother-daughter dates, and eating Mexican food. When she's not doing that, she's writing. She spends her days off watching rodeo, knitting, and surfing Pinterest in the name of research. Following their own personal joys, BA and Julia heard the call of the high desert and they now live in the New Mexico mountains. BA's personal saviors include her wife, her best friends, and coffee. Lots of coffee. Really good coffee.

Having written everything from fist-fighting cowboys to rural single dads to werewolves, BA does her damnedest to tell the stories of her heart, which is committed to giving everyone their happily ever after. With books ranging from heart-warming stories of found families, to rodeo cowboys that are fighting to make a mark, to fiery passionate love affairs, BA refuses to be pigeon-holed by anyone but the voices in her head.

Also Available from BA

Gay Romance

BA's Cozy Cowboys (cowboys w/ kids novels)

Back in the Saddle

Cowboy Haven

Cowboy in the Crosshairs

Cowboy Logic

Cowboy's Law

In the Morning Light

Ranch Manny

Security Detail: an AusTex novel

Silver Buckle Linings

The Cowboy Contract

The Cowboy Guardian

The Cowboy's Texan

The Meaning of Life

Trial by Fire: an AusTex novel

Two Cowboys and a Baby

Two of a Kind

The Banished Series

In Wulf's Clothing

River's Edge

Aspen's Song

The Border Crossing Series

Bombs and Guacamole

Ammo and Enchiladas

The Cereus Series

Cereus: Building

Cereus: Opening

Cereus: Training

Cereus: Rescue

The Cowboy Wanted Series

Cowboy Healing

Second Chance Cowboy

The Foster Ranch Series

The Cowboy Contract

The Cowboy Guardian

The Cowboy's Texan

Leanin' N Ranch Series

Commitment Ranch

Finding Mr. Wright

Whiskey to Wine

Come Back Around

This Old Wind

Perfectly Seasoned

Love is Blind Series

Ever the Same

Real World

Midnight Rodeo Series

Welcome to the Pack

Tails and Whiskers

Above the Fold

Brownie's Sway

Thack's Angel

Here, Kitty Kitty

The Recovery Series

Refired

Slip

The Release Series

The Terms of Release

The Articles of Release

Catch and Release

The Road Trip Series

Racing the Moon • Steam and Sunshine

Under Pressure • Walking on the Sun

Roughstock Series

Blind Ride

And a Smile

File Gumbo

Back to Back

Pulled from All Sides

Coke's Clown

Leading the Blind

Mud, Movies, Bullets, and Bulls

Needing To

Old Town New

Rainbow Rodeo

Rough in Wranglers

Say Something

Seashores of Old Mexico

Soft Place to Fall

Stetsons and Stakeouts

Truth or Consequences

Wicked in Wranglers

Historical Standalones

Cabin Fever

Hammer and Tongs

Oranges and Peppermints

Paranormal Standalones

Baker's Dozen

Calling His Bluff

Forged in Magic

Long Black Cadillac

Luck of the Draw

Redemption's Ride

Roman and Cage

Setting His Sights

Things that Go Bump in the Night

Unearthed

Wolf Run

Lesbian Romance

Summit Springs Series

Christmas Bizarre w/ Jodi Payne

High Note

Honeymoon in the Cards w/ Jodi Payne

Tipping the Barrel

Contemporary Standalones

Bright Lights and Boobjobs

Games Girls Play

Historical Standalones

Bustles and Doeskins

With Jodi Payne

The Collaborations Series

Refraction

Syncopation

The Cowboy and the Dom Series

First Rodeo

Razor's Edge

No Ghosts

The Soldier and the Angel

The East Meets Westerns Universe

Temptation Ranch

Les's Bar Series

Just Dex

Hide Bound

Wholly Trinity

New Tricks

Merry Everything Series

Window Dressing

Cowboy Protection

Cowboy and Cupcakes

On the Ranch Series

Tending Tyler

Roped In

Diamonds in the Rough

Wrecked Series

Wrecked

Flying Blind

Special Delivery

Seeds and Sunshine

Pick Up Man

The Higher Elevation Series

Land of Enchantment

Keeping Promises

Bigger than Us

Heart of a Cowboy

Home Free

Hey, y'all!

Thank you for giving The Cowboy Guardian a try. I hope you enjoyed the story, and will consider leaving a review at the eBook retailer website where you made your purchase.

Don't forget to "like" my BA Tortuga page on Facebook to keep up with new releases, author news, special discount codes and sale announcements. And if you're interested in sneak peeks, rodeo pictures, and general fun, please come see the BA's Cowboys on Facebook. We'd love to have all y'all!

Yeehaw!

BA

www.ingramcontent.com/pod-product-compliance
Lightning Source LLC
Chambersburg PA
CBHW021940120726
47992CB00001B/78